THE WAIT

ALSO BY JOANNE DEMAIO

The Seaside Saga
Blue Jeans and Coffee Beans
The Denim Blue Sea
Beach Blues
Beach Breeze
The Beach Inn
Beach Bliss
Castaway Cottage
Night Beach
Little Beach Bungalow
Every Summer
Salt Air Secrets
Stony Point Summer
The Beachgoers
Shore Road
The Wait
The Goodbye
—And More Seaside Saga Books—

Beach Cottage Series
The Beach Cottage
Back to the Beach Cottage

Standalone Novels
True Blend
Whole Latte Life

The Winter Series
Snowflakes and Coffee Cakes
Snow Deer and Cocoa Cheer
Cardinal Cabin
First Flurries
Eighteen Winters
Winter House
—And More Winter Books—

the wait

BOOK 15

JOANNE DEMAIO

Copyright © 2022 Joanne DeMaio
All rights reserved.

ISBN: 9798408491018

Joannedemaio.com

To Point O' Woods

A special Connecticut beach—
heartfelt inspiration for
The Seaside Saga.

one

CELIA," SHANE SAYS.

She's sitting beside him on his pickup truck's open tailgate. The truck is parked in the shade of a maple tree at the local car wash. Except for one other customer vacuuming a vehicle, he and Celia are alone here. The day is hot. Roadside wildflowers wilt. The summer air is hazy. Rays of the afternoon sun drop through that nearby maple tree's leaves.

And Shane pays none of it any mind.

Instead, he sets down his empty ice-cream cup, and hers, too. Does it without saying another word—because he's not sure the last time someone's made him feel this way. It's like being on the lobster boat, working on deck, and all's good. Until the seas kick up. Agitated waves randomly toss the boat, and you don't know which way it'll pitch. Don't know which way to lean, what to grab onto.

So the whims of the sea and the watchful eyes of a

beautiful woman do the same thing to him, apparently. They leave him feeling utterly vulnerable.

Which is why all he can manage to do now is look at Celia sitting there. Her side braid is half undone, with wisps of auburn hair coming loose. And her eyes, hell, they're locked onto his. So before continuing, he takes hold of her hands, changes his mind and drops them, blows out a breath, then bites the bullet.

"Listen. I don't scare easily, but yes." He pauses, looking out on the summer afternoon. "What I'm about to tell you has me dead afraid of what you'll say."

Celia leans closer to him on the tailgate and gently turns his face to hers. She rests a hand on his jaw, searches his eyes and whispers, "*Try me.*"

$\sim$

"Okay," Shane says. "Okay. Here goes."

Then he stops. And clears his throat. And is aware of Celia's unwavering gaze. "I got a text message earlier," he finally explains. "From the captain."

"Captain?"

"Yeah. My boss, on the boat. You know I was supposed to head out first thing Tuesday morning."

"Wait." Celia squints at him. "*Was* supposed to head out?"

Shane nods. "Apparently the boat's fuel pump is busted."

"Which means?"

"It means that with today being Sunday—and tomorrow Labor Day—that boat's out of commission for the week, at least. Depending on parts' availability. Mechanics' schedules." Shane stands then. "Hang on," he says, walking to the pickup's door and grabbing his cell phone from the console. When he sits beside her on the tailgate again, he shows her the text.

Celia leans close and reads the words from his captain.

The last two lines, though, Shane says aloud. *"But keep your strength up, cuz we'll be doin' double duty when we get back out. If we ain't turning the hauler, we ain't earning the dollar."* Fidgeting with the phone, he glances from the message to Celia.

"Well, that's bad news—for the second time in days," she tells him. "First I'm out of work, with the inn closed. And now you're out of work, too."

"Right. So go with me on something."

"Okay."

"Your week's kind of up in the air."

"It is."

"And my week's wide open now. Which just about *never* happens in the summer lobster season. It's bad, definitely, for the captain. His quota will be in the red." Sitting there in the heat of the September afternoon, Shane pauses. A lone bird chirps in the tree branches above them. Traffic is light out on the street. "But for me?" he goes on. "A week's downtime *could* be a blessing—depending on what you'll say next."

"To *what?*" Celia nudges his shoulder. "Out with it already."

Sitting there on the tailgate, Shane touches her loose side braid. As he does, Celia quietly waits. Her sunglasses are perched on her head; her denim overall shorts are damp from the car wash spray.

"Come to Maine with me." There. He said it. "You and Aria."

A moment passes as Celia takes that in. "Today?" she finally asks.

Shane lightly tosses up his hands. "Right now."

⁓

Now that Celia knows what he's after, another pause comes. And Shane gets it. He threw a monkey wrench into the mix. She planned to stay in Addison. Visit her father. Get away for a few days with the baby. Try to make some sense of her life since the brakes got put on the inn opening.

Shane's asking her to dump that plan and come north with him.

To take a chance. Take one damn chance.

"What do you mean?" Celia asks him. "I'm not sure I understand."

"All right." He shifts on the tailgate. "I'm asking you *not* to stay at your father's. I'd really like you and your daughter to spend the week in Maine instead. With me. At my house on the docks. No big outings," he tells her. "Just come north. See my life."

Her eyes remain locked on his. "Why didn't you *say* anything? Before washing my car?"

"Saying it now."

Celia gives a quick laugh. A shake of her head. Neither one a sign of someone *willing* to take a chance.

"So you want me to stay at *your* place?" she asks.

"I do," he says, squeezing her hand.

"This is kind of sudden."

"I know. But hear me out, Celia."

"I'll try."

"Okay. Look. I've seen your life here."

"And I haven't seen yours?"

Shane nods. "So I want to show you. Have you in my world for a few days."

"Shane." She touches his arm, moving her fingers right up to the frayed edges of his sleeveless tee. "The baby, too? Do you know what you're asking? A baby's a lot."

"Wouldn't have it any other way."

Celia hesitates, and asks random questions. Would they take *two* vehicles, or one? Where will Aria sleep at his house? What about groceries? And clothes for her and the baby? Would what she'd already packed be okay?

Shane answers her, vaguely—the best he can, anyway.

Still, something's bothering him. Amid her asking questions and his alleviating her worries, Celia hasn't answered *his* question.

"You really want to do this?" she asks then. Instead of answering, still.

"Celia." He looks away, toward vehicles driving past the car wash. Toward the grocery store across the street. Then back at her. "When I got this news from the captain, you were the first person I thought of."

Celia slightly nods. "What would we do in Maine?" she softly asks.

"Not much. I'm not looking for that. We'd … keep it easy. Walk the docks. See the ocean. Some sights." Shane gets up from where he's sitting on the truck tailgate, takes a few steps then turns back. "Or no sights at all. We can lay low. Do as much or as little as you want."

"It'll be a new place for Aria." Celia tucks back a wisp of

her side braid. "What if she's fussy there? You don't mind?"

"No. No, I have a back deck. It's pretty big. We can sit out there with her. Breathe the salt air." He paces, glancing over at Celia. "I don't care. Get a coffee from the doughnut shop."

"And nobody would know?"

"Right. Which means we also won't have to hide from anybody. We'll be free to grab a bite out at a restaurant." When she says nothing, Shane goes on. "Or not."

Celia pulls up her knees on the tailgate and sits sideways there. "It's just that ... Well, I told Elsa I'd be in *Addison*. We're close, Elsa and I. We check in with each other. What if she puts something together?"

Shane turns up his hands, but Celia doesn't wait for his answer. She's getting to the gritty reality now.

"And ... and what about my father?" she asks.

"What about him?"

"What will I tell him? I can't lie to my father, Shane. I just can't."

"And I respect that." Shane twists the braided leather cuff on his wrist. "Guess you'd have to tell him some version of ..." he says, motioning back and forth between them. "Us."

Celia gives a little jump off the tailgate then. And crosses her arms. "Well, I have to pick up the baby. So would I just meet you up north? How would we get there?"

Suddenly, Shane's not feeling too optimistic. What he'd thought was a good thing actually has too many hoops to jump through. "Depends. If your answer—which I'm still waiting for—is yes, we'd have to make some quick decisions. But we *can* do this."

"Where are you headed now?" Celia glances back at the truck's empty bed. "I don't see any of your bags," she says while picking up their ice-cream cups and plastic spoons.

"That's because I was headed *here*. To the car wash first. Got here as fast as I could after I called you. I mean, I have bags packed at the cottage, but I … I didn't know …"

His sentence drifts off as Celia drops their garbage in a nearby trash can. Still, he notices, no answer. Instead she returns to his truck and picks up the blanket off the tailgate. She's wearing a cropped black tank top beneath those faded denim-shorts overalls. White sneakers are on her feet; her brown-tinted tortoise sunglasses, still propped on her head.

And she's silent as she neatly folds and sets the blanket in his truck bed.

Shane comes up behind her there, and loosely wraps his arms around her waist. "Both our lives are oddly paused," he says in her ear. "This chance will *never* happen again. So we use it, or lose it."

"*Chance?*" she whispers.

He nods. "Don't you think it's worth taking? This chance?" As he says the words, he feels a bead of perspiration trickle down his temple. "Maybe you don't."

Celia turns out of his hold and faces him now. "It's not that."

"Then help me out here. I'm having a tough time reading you."

"Well, I have to process this, Shane." She walks a few steps, pats her fingers to her mouth, then turns to face him again. From a distance. "You *really* want to do this? Spend several days in close quarters?"

"Come on, Celia. Don't keep me waiting."

"It's just … You don't even know me that much—to spend *that* kind of time with me."

"That's bullshit." He steps closer to her. "I know you plenty."

Celia squints at him through the dappled sunlight, but still says nothing.

"So … *what*?" Shane asks. "Are you afraid?"

"Maybe a little." Her voice drops. "Are we getting in too deep?"

He shrugs. "One way to find out."

"And if we *are* in too deep?"

"We'll deal with it then." He notices she hasn't stepped closer. Neither has he. There's this space keeping them apart. Space, hesitation, uncertainty. "But at least we'll know if it's *worth* it to get in deep together." Now, he does it. Somewhat. He takes a step toward her. "But hell, if I'm being totally honest, I'm already in."

Celia looks long at him. And checks her watch. And paces in the shade near the pickup. Her sneakered feet walk on the rough pavement. She looks north—in the vague direction of Addison, he imagines—then back to him.

Except now, when she nods? She swipes away a silent tear.

"Hey." Shane quickly goes to her and holds her arms. "Does that mean you're game?"

"I am," she says. "You threw me for a loop, but I'd *love* to."

"So you're coming to Maine." Still holding her arms, he tugs her closer. "You and Aria."

"We are."

Shane, well, he can't help it then. He just wraps Celia in

as big a hug as possible—getting him laughing and lifting her feet right off the ground for a second or two.

Slightly breathless, Celia leaves a kiss on his cheek and cups his jaw before pulling away. "But I *really* have to leave—right now. And square things with my father."

"He knows *nothing* about us?"

"Nothing."

"Will you fill him in?"

"I'll have to tell him something. What that is, I'm not sure yet."

Shane grabs his cell phone out of the truck bed and hands the phone to her. "Put your father's address in."

"Why?"

"So I know where you are."

"You're going to show up there?" Celia asks after adding the address to his *Contacts*.

"No." Shane takes the phone. "I'll wait to hear from you, okay? To see what's best. I can meet you somewhere else. Or at his house." Shane still has her keys from washing her car earlier. He pulls the keys from his jeans pocket and hands them over. "Your call, Celia."

～

A half hour later, Shane's back in Stony Point at his rented cottage—and taking the steps two at a time. A small table and couple of rocking chairs are on the front porch. On the weathered shingles beside the door, a piece of driftwood is strung with twine and hangs from a nail. The cottage name, *This Will Do*, is painted on the driftwood.

"*Ain't that the truth?*" Shane asks himself as he sits in a rocking chair to get his bearings. Yes, time in this cottage has been nothing but sweet. Changed his life, actually.

And *that* thought gets him to his feet. He unlocks the front door and hurries inside to check his luggage. It's where he left it all—stacked right at the door in the living room. In the musty space, he unzips his duffel and brushes through it, before hefting it to his pickup outside. On a return trip inside, he grabs up the couple of packed cartons and puts those in the truck, too.

Then, he waits.

Paces the cottage.

Walks through the living room; passes the glass fishing floats hanging from ropes; glances at a tin pitcher of beach grasses on a table. The slatted ceiling is rustic and unpainted. And the dank cottage scent of sea damp comes to him—now that the place is all closed up as he'd prepared to leave. He checks his cell phone for any word from Celia. Of course, it's too soon for that.

So he gives a once-over to the rooms he'd already cleaned for check-out. Looks in the bedroom. The coverlet on the bed hangs neatly. The lamp and box of dusty seashells on the dresser are in shadow now. In the kitchen, the aqua-painted cupboard is restocked with any dishes he'd used. Countertops are wiped down. He double-checks the back door lock. And sits at the kitchen table in the quiet. The silence is muffled in the closed-up cottage. He can almost hear echoes as he sits there. Echoes of voices talking. Of memories. Celia. Kyle. Even Lauren, that first week he'd arrived when he'd tried to mend fences. The day she'd dropped a handful of seaweed in his happiness jar.

Shane drums his fingers on the table. Suddenly then, he

has to stand up and suck in a breath of air. Jesus, the feeling's all too familiar. The same panic comes over him on the boat. Yep, especially after hours of calm on the Atlantic. All it takes is one fast-approaching storm, or that one rogue wave, to drop five minutes of terror onto his life.

It's happening now, too—after living years of calm while lobstering in Maine. Years of working the sea, and coming ashore to his little shingled dockside house and minding his own damn business, his own damn life. Nothing's rocked the boat in his world this past decade.

Until the past few *weeks* of sheer terror.

Until *life* surged in its own frothy rogue wave that washed right over him.

Now, just like out on the boat, panic strikes in the musty cottage. He's struggling to get a full breath. Perspiring. Feeling his heart beat. All because of these recent weeks.

Because of getting involved with Celia Gray.

Of regaining his footing with his estranged brother.

Of coming back into the tangled fold of Stony Point.

Okay, so just like he does when a rogue wave washes over the boat, Shane makes a fast decision.

This time, he pulls his cell phone from his pocket. Standing there in the middle of the shadowy kitchen, he first looks out the window to the late-afternoon sky. Then he scrolls his phone's *Contacts* for the number of the cottage owner. Because Shane knows. He needs to be able to crash here from time to time—especially when bringing Celia back later this week. So he unlocks the back door, pushes through the squeaking screen door and walks onto the open-air porch. Quickly then, he calls that number on his phone. Except for this little beach bungalow, he has nowhere to stay here at Stony Point. Because he won't impose on the few connections he's made. *And* he needs to keep his presence on a low flame.

After a few rings, the owner answers and Shane explains things.

"Need to stay on at your cottage, if possible. Will be going back and forth a bit. Is it available?" he asks, running a hand through his hair. "Let's see, it's Labor Day weekend. Can you give me a price for the rest of September?" When he hears the figure, Shane hoists himself up on the porch's half-wall and lets out a low whistle. "I know, I know. Water view. But that's a little steep, guy. Can you do better for *two* months?" He looks out to the small beach down past his yard while the owner dithers on the price. Easy waves lap at shore. Shadows are growing longer as the afternoon wanes.

When Shane hears the final rental amount, he gets off that half-wall and heads inside. "Okay," he says—with no hesitation. "I'll take it."

two

JASON BARLOW STANDS AT THE small sink in the seafood joint's restroom.

Since he couldn't shower after his beach day with Maris, the best he *can* do is clean up a little. The water is running as he scrubs his soapy hands beneath the tap. While working up a lather, he looks at his reflection in the wall-mounted mirror. Fatigue is evident on his face. Faint shadows are beneath his eyes. But there's some color there, too, from the hours he just spent on the beach. A little sunburn. So he rinses his hands, bends and scoops a handful of cold water on his face. And again, a second time. The water drips off his skin, off his hair unkempt from sea breezes and salty air. From lounging seaside with his wife. Grabbing several paper towels then, he presses them to his face, his neck. Still scrutinizes his reflection, too, while dragging a clean hand down his jaw. A raised scar shows through the whiskers there.

One thing's for certain. The faded concert tee over his swim trunks isn't helping his haggard look. Which gets him to blow out a breath. It's no secret why he's feeling tired. The day's been long. He packed up his things early this morning at the campground, grabbed a last spin in Kyle's old truck, then went back to Sea Spray for a couple of hours. Took Sal's rowboat for a paddle through the marsh at Stony Point later. Then spent the rest of Sunday afternoon in the hot sun with Maris.

And now this, dinner at The Clam Shack.

What he really needs is a good night's sleep. If life were different, he'd have a paradise morning in bed with Maris tomorrow, at their home on the bluff. Windows open. Seagulls crying. Sunlight glancing off the sea. Lazy lovemaking. And all of it would be topped off with breakfast at Dockside Diner afterward.

Tomorrow's Labor Day, after all. The last free summer day before his life amps up and the labor kicks him in the ass. Filming for *Castaway Cottage*. Renovations at the Fenwick place *and* Beach Box—now that the Hammer Law's lifted. Then there's the shotgun cottage at White Sands.

But not yet. Not even going to *think* about all that now. Instead Jason tosses one more handful of cold water on his face, dries off and walks out to the restaurant patio.

～

The Clam Shack is located at the mouth of the Connecticut River, where its waters empty into Long Island Sound. No matter where you sit, there's a view of drifting sailboats and small pleasure craft motoring past. Seagulls perch atop weathered dock posts. Round stone tables with curved stone benches are scattered across the patio area.

Right away, Jason spots Maris with Elsa at one of the tables. Maris' straw cowboy hat is pulled low against the late-afternoon sun—which still burns hot. When she'd stopped home to feed the dog, she'd changed out of her damp bathing suit, too. Now she wears a navy tank top over shredded white-denim shorts; her star pendant hangs around her neck. And she smiles and motions him over when she spots him.

As Jason nears, he hears Elsa asking Maris, "I hope you two weren't waiting long?"

"No," Maris tells her aunt. "Just a few minutes."

But what surprises Jason is seeing Cliff sitting beside Elsa. He clasps Cliff's shoulder as he approaches. "Elsa, you picked this bum up roadside, did you?"

"Jason," Cliff says with an easy laugh. "Good to see you."

"I was walking down my driveway, on my way here, when Cliff stopped by for his laundry," Elsa explains.

"Laundry?" Maris interrupts, scooting over to make room for Jason.

"No washer and dryer at my place," Cliff lets on.

"Come on, Commish." Jason sits, picks up his sunglasses from the tabletop and puts them on. "You still living in that tin-can trailer of yours? Can't get the Board of Governors to approve a washer-dryer hookup in the budget?"

"The BOG knows nothing *about* my living arrangements, Jason." Cliff leans closer. "And we're going to keep it that way, you hear?" He glances from Maris to Elsa. "And it's only temporary."

"Going on a year!" Maris adds, lifting a laminated menu from a stack on the table.

Elsa pats Cliff's arm. "Anyway, Clifton wheedled this dinner out of the laundry situation—and made me late! We had to stop at his trailer so he could change out of his uniform," she adds, brushing the fabric of the short-sleeve maroon polo shirt he wears now.

"Mrs. DeLuca." Cliff places a hand over Elsa's hand on his arm. "I drove here. I held the car door open for you. Welcomed whatever radio station you landed on, and listened to you belt out a tune or two …"

"And the wooing continues." Jason lifts a water glass to Cliff. "At least you survived another epic Stony Point holiday weekend, Commissioner."

Cliff raises his water glass back at Jason. "It's not over yet. Nick's on guard duty tonight, keeping all our fine residents in check. And wait a minute," Cliff adds, squinting at Jason and Maris. "I thought I saw you two on the sand today. It was so packed there, I couldn't be sure."

"Yes," Maris vaguely says while reading her menu. "We had a beach day."

"Which reminds me, Jason," Elsa says then. "I couldn't help but notice your new prosthesis. What are those things on it? Fins?"

"They actually are." Jason stands and walks around the table. A long, perforated one-inch fin runs down either side of the limb's structure.

"My, the things they come up with," Elsa remarks, looking at the aquatic leg.

"Yeah," Maris agrees. "He's got a whole collection of legs, depending on the use. The day."

16

"How do you like that?" Cliff gets up to check out the narrow black fins lining Jason's left calf. "So that prosthesis is special for the water?"

Jason shakes his head. "It's amphibious. Works on water *and* land, so I don't have to change right out of it. Which is really convenient."

Cliff bends and runs a hand along one of the fins. "The holes. That's what makes it good for swimming?"

"You got it. Water passes through those holes on the fins, so there's no drag. No weight pulling me down." Jason extends the prosthetic leg. "Helps keep me balanced while swimming."

"He loves it," Maris says when Jason sits beside her again. "Was in the water all afternoon."

Elsa reaches for a menu then. "Maris, what are you going to order?"

Jason and Cliff pick up a menu, too. And oh, do the deliberations begin.

> From Jason, pointing to Maris' menu: *That looks good.*
> To Maris: *We should each get something different. That way we can swap tastes.*
> Jason again: *Well, what are you getting?*
> Cliff this time: *Hmm. Crab cake sandwich?*
> Elsa's response: *Not a sandwich! Get a dinner.*
> Elsa continuing: *Maybe the baked fresh cod. Or a lobster roll.*
> Back to Jason: *Think I'll go with the fried clam platter.*

Maris nudges him. "No, you can't get that, Jason. I am. *Dibs.*"

Jason can barely take his eyes off the menu, he's that

starved. "Yeah, but you get the strips. I get the bellies," he says.

"Right. And no one will swap with you, because *nobody* likes clam bellies," Maris argues, setting down her menu.

Jason puts his menu on the stack with the others. "I beg to differ, sweetheart."

"Bellies are fine if you want the *beach* stuck in your molars," Elsa offers.

Which gets Jason to turn her way. "Just wash it down with a swig of soda."

Cliff nods. "You're not a true New Englander if you don't eat clam bellies."

"*What?*" Maris is indignant. "Do *not* say that!"

"Listen." Jason touches the brim of Maris' straw cowboy hat. "If you want to swap with me, I'll pull off a belly, and you can eat the rest. It'll be like … the best of both worlds."

"Oh, yeah." Maris swats his hand away. "That slime when you bite into a clam belly? I mean, you are eating everything that clam ate!"

Cliff leans forward. "But the frying should kill any bacteria."

"*Should?*" Elsa asks.

Jason waves them off. "You know what they call clam *strips?*"

"Bait!" Cliff answers.

Jason nods. "Whole bellies equal nirvana."

"*Sure,*" Maris says, rolling her eyes. "Until you slice one open—"

"And take a good look," Elsa finishes.

"But the *strips,* Elsa," Jason persists, "are like biting into deep-fried rubber bands!"

"Jason Barlow," Maris counters. "Biting into a clam *belly*

is biting into a ball of sand. Or … or a cotton ball! Oh, *yum*," she says, bristling at the same time.

"Maris, bellies are more a *delicacy* thing," Jason calmly informs her.

"But isn't there some clam doo-doo in those *bellies*?" Elsa asks.

"Elsa!" Cliff laughs, takes her menu and sets it aside. "Seriously, strips are just such a *tourist* thing."

Elsa squints suspiciously at Cliff beside her. "So you're *into* those squishy bellies?"

"Careful, Cliff. Could be a deal breaker," Jason warns, just as an outdoor waiter approaches to take their orders.

"Afternoon, folks. Glad to see you enjoying yourselves." He pulls an order pad from his half-apron pocket. "You dining here, or getting takeout?"

"Here." Jason motions to him. "Settle a score at our table first, would you?"

"Can certainly try." The waiter crosses his arms.

"Okay." Jason leans back and motions him closer. "Tell us. Please. What's your professional opinion on whole belly clams versus strips?"

~

And bellies versus strips be damned, the debate suddenly ends—which doesn't surprise Maris. Once the seafood's delivered, they simply dig in. In the warm air, beneath the late-afternoon sun, they sample each other's dinners. Close their eyes in pleasure. Grimace at Jason's clam bellies. There's baked cod and potato on the table. Clam strips, too. A fish-and-chips platter.

But not for long.

Appetites are hearty, and after picking and plucking, dipping coleslaw into melted butter, dragging French fries through ketchup, downing salty onion rings, dishes get shoved aside. The slightest breeze lifts off the nearby water—and it's like a tonic. Everyone sighs, leans arms on the table, and breathes deeply.

Minutes later, Jason stands and motions for Cliff to follow him. "Let's get ice cream at the take-out window."

Cliff stands, too, asking Elsa what she wants.

"Surprise me," she tells him.

As Jason and Cliff walk away, Maris calls after them. "Wait! Jason! No surprises for me. I want a sundae. Whipped cream, hot fudge. With a cherry on top!"

But what *does* surprise Maris is how Elsa right away rushes around the table and gestures for Maris to move over. Standing there in her double-layer loose white tank top over cropped jeans, Elsa means business, too, as she scoots onto the stone bench.

"*Good, good.*" Her whisper is a little breathless, a little distracted. "Now that they're gone ..." she begins while clutching Maris' arm.

Maris stops her, though. "Elsa! What's gotten into you?"

And oh, the no-nonsense look her aunt tosses her way can't be missed. "I want *answers*," Elsa says, matter-of-fact. She sits straight, adjusts the sheer fabric of her two-layer top, tugs her long gold-chain necklace, then eyes Maris. "Between the chaos of my inn announcement, the vow renewal, inn legalities and your writing, I haven't been able to pin you down. So answer me this. *Quick.*"

"Answer what?"

"You and Jason. On? Off? Back together? Quits? Waiting for legal papers?"

"Aunt Elsa!"

"Well, what the hell? I sure couldn't read you at the table. Was that all an act, that happiness?"

"No!"

"Then you should be *together*. It's so sweet seeing you two like that."

"That's because we're *really* trying." Maris glances over at Jason standing in the ice-cream line. His faded tee is loose over his swim trunks; his dark hair, disheveled from the seaside afternoon. When she turns back to Elsa, Maris drops her voice. "But things weren't sweet when Jason got a little drunk and called me yesterday on the way to camping."

"Oh, no."

Maris nods. "And it wasn't sweet after we argued super late Friday night at Ted's."

"After Kyle's vow renewal? You went out to Ted's?"

"I did. But I didn't last long there. Short visit."

Elsa takes a sharp breath. "Two steps forward, three steps back?"

"Something like that."

"Okay." Elsa looks briefly back at Jason and Cliff. "I just got my hopes up today, seeing you both so comfortable—like you used to be! Thought maybe Jason was coming home for good this weekend."

With a sad smile, Maris sets her straw cowboy hat on the bench beside her. "We're just not there yet."

"Then I'm going to say a prayer for you two tonight. And I mean that."

"I know you do. You're the best, Aunt Elsa. Love you," Maris says, giving her a side hug.

Elsa brushes aside a strand of Maris' salty hair. "It's just that nothing makes me happier than seeing my *famiglia* happy."

"Well, *this* was fun. This dinner. Just the four of us."

"Good. That's what I'd hoped for." Elsa stands then, and returns to her bench on the other side of the stone table. "And if there's anything I can do to *help* you and Jason, you just name it."

"Actually?"

Maris' one word gets Elsa to quickly look over at her.

"There is one *little* thing," Maris ventures.

"*Anything*," Elsa says as she slowly sits again.

Maris leans close over the tabletop. "Jason will be in Stony Point a lot for business now—with the Hammer Law lifting. He'll be filming at the Fenwicks'. Checking in at Beach Box construction on Ridgewood Road. And I *really* don't need him discovering my secret kitchen. So if you see him around in the next few days, keep him in your neck of the beach? Tell him … tell him I'm writing up a storm?"

"Which you *should* be," Elsa says with a serious nod.

"And …" Again Maris glances over at Jason standing in line about ready to order. "You might have to bribe him," she says to her aunt. "Give him an egg-sandwich breakfast. Or tomato-and-mozzarella lunches." Maris reaches over to clasp Elsa's hand. "*Please, Elsa? Will you do that for me?*"

Elsa squeezes Maris' hand back. "Food bribes I can *always* do."

~

22

The late afternoon is still warm, so Jason and Cliff take their time getting to the ice-cream window. They walk alongside a fence, where folks are dropping French fries and pieces of bread into the water for swans paddling below. He and Cliff stop and watch a few pleasure boats thunder past, leaving a frothy wake behind them. And all's good. Easy. Finally, he and Cliff turn and take their place in the long ice-cream line snaking from that take-out window. People in shorts and tees, summer dresses and sandals, mill about ahead of them.

"Okay," Cliff suddenly says. "Now that the ladies are out of earshot, what in *tarnation* is going on?"

"With what?"

"*With you and your lady!*" Cliff hisses between his teeth. "That there at dinner was the bona fide good old days. Don't you want that back?"

"Want *what* back?" Jason glances over at their distant table. And from the looks of Elsa leaning into Maris—she's getting grilled, too.

"Dinner banter with your wife," Cliff says, nodding to their table. "Laughs together."

"Of course I want that back. Trying like *hell* to *get* it back, Raines. You have no idea."

When a couple in front of them gives them a curious glance, Cliff nods. "Evening, folks," he politely says. But as soon as they nod, too, and turn away, Cliff is at it with Jason again. He sort of talks out of the side of his mouth. "Just saying, it was good to see the old Jason and Maris on display. Missed that lately."

"No shit. I miss it, too, Judge."

Cliff, standing there in his maroon polo shirt over cargo shorts, eyes Jason. "Elsa also mentioned that we're giving

Maris a ride home. So after being on the beach all day … you're *really* not back together yet? Unpacking your bags in that Barlow compound?"

"Want to be, but not yet. We're working on things."

"Well … What's it been already?" Cliff asks, counting on his fingers. "One, two—"

"That's right. Two weeks apart. Two long, eternal weeks." Jason glances across the parking lot to where Maris sits. She's taken off her straw hat, and her brown hair blows in the light breeze. "It's not easy, Cliff, but I have to wait," he explains as they shuffle forward in line.

"For what?"

"For Maris to say the word." Jason crosses his arms in front of him. "Guess she's not ready."

Cliff gives a sad shake of his head. "What's it going to take to get you home, do you think?"

"Wish to God I knew that answer."

"Listen, Jason. I'm sure whatever's going on between you two is personal. But if there's anything I can do, you name it."

Jason gives a small laugh. And draws a hand down his jaw while considering the question. "Okay."

"What?"

"Mow my lawn if you get a chance." And he doesn't wait for Cliff's answer. Instead, Jason pulls his key ring from his pocket and slips off the tractor key.

"I don't need that." Cliff waves him off. "I'll just bring my own mower."

"You kidding me?" Jason forces the key into his hand. "You'll be there for two days with your manual push machine. So use mine."

Cliff nods and pockets the key.

"And don't wait *too* long," Jason goes on, looking from Cliff to the ice-cream menu displayed on the small building ahead of them. "Don't need the grass getting over eight inches. I'll end up getting slapped with a *blight* ordinance."

~

"Next!" a teen calls from the take-out window.

Jason and Cliff step over and place their orders. Sundaes and banana splits and triple scoops; this topping and that sprinkle; napkins and spoons.

And when the two women catch sight of them walking closer, Maris gets up to help carry the goods. Smiles and happiness return as if no one *ever* got asked a single, pointed question in the past ten minutes.

"All right! Ice cream time," Elsa says when Cliff sets hers down on the table.

"This one's yours," Jason says to Maris as he hands her a hot fudge sundae.

"*Heaven*," she murmurs, sitting with him and leaving a kiss on his scruffy cheek. "With a *double* cherry on top, no less."

three

IF ALL ELSE FAILS, LIE.

Celia can't get that thought out of her head. Because as she's cruising down the highway, she can't seem to wrap her thoughts around one thing: How will she ever explain Shane Bradford to her father?

Oh, the dread has her open her window and let a warm summer breeze blow through the car. Problem is, being so close to Addison, it's not *salt* air now. It can't cure what ails her—worry, lots of worry. But this country air does get the seashell wind chime hanging from her rearview mirror click-clacking.

"*Good enough*," Celia whispers, inhaling a deep breath as she drives. Maybe if she *talks* out her worry. Maybe if she blends *some* truth with *some* lies, it'll balance out. So she practices what she'll tell her father.

"The inn's closed," she quietly says. Truth, all true. Keeping her eyes on the road—yet her thoughts on her skeptical father—she plots her conversation. "Lots of business paperwork to handle, so ... change of plans." Okay, a little lie there. "And I'm heading back to the beach tonight with Aria." True, because surely Shane lives near a beach in coastal Maine—where she's *actually* headed. And she *is* taking the baby.

Except, what that truth doesn't say is: *I'll be driving five hours north with a tough lobsterman you've never heard of.*

"Huh. Maybe try something else," Celia murmurs as she passes a slower car in front of her. "Okay," she continues, switching lanes again. "The weather's been beautiful, Dad. End of summer. Quiet at Stony Point now." Truth, all true. "I want to set up Aria's little beach tent. Dip her toes in the water. So I'm just going to take the baby and be on my way." More truth. Mostly. All that's missing is that she'll be on her way—*north*. "You don't mind, Dad. Do you?"

As if, Celia thinks. As if he won't see right through her bumbling phrases. The Addison turnoff is up ahead now. Every passing divided line on the highway brings it—and her father—closer.

"Hoping to talk to Eva, too, Dad," Celia pads her story. "Eva might have some cottages listed that I can stage until the inn's up and running." It's true, *and* a lie, Celia thinks as she slows for her exit. Because she *does* want to talk to Eva—truth. It just won't be this week. It won't be from a shingled dockside dwelling in Maine.

Ach. All this weaving and winding, truth and lies. It's just going to get her tripped up. Get her father's suspicions up, too.

Driving the countryside roads of Addison now, Celia passes historical colonials, and Craftsman bungalows, and simple farmhouses. Summer wreaths hang on doors. Potted flowers sit on shady front porches. Tall maple and oak trees stand sentry on green lawns.

And Celia's more confused than ever. Because what *else* can she tell her father as she bundles up his granddaughter and goes on her merry way? *This* kind of truth?

"Oh hey, Dad. Have a new boyfriend," she says while turning onto the winding lane where her father lives. "Name's Shane. Met him at the beach. But he lives five hours away. In Maine. I'm actually staying at his place this week. Bringing Aria, too. So we're going to hit the road before it gets too late. Driving up there tonight." Rounding a curve, she sees the distant red barn at the end of the road. The lush cornfield there is golden this September weekend. Celia slows the car. "You know, everybody at Stony Point hated Shane," she continues. "He's Kyle's estranged younger brother. You've met Kyle. Shane is the one who blew Kyle's first vow renewal to pieces a few weeks ago. Yeah, that's him. But they're working on things, the two brothers. Big misunderstanding between them." Celia glances at her reflection in the rearview mirror. "And, oh yeah. I'm also a new mother. One whose fiancé that everyone loved died a year ago. And now I jumped into *another* relationship. With a lobsterman."

Truth, all true.

Truth that'll never fly.

Celia keeps driving, but slows even more as she nears her destination. A crumbling stone wall reaches down the length of the shady street. And there, on the right, is her father's yellow bungalow with its white picket fence. The sight of it almost gets her to put on the brakes. Because the *rest* of the truth is yet to be said.

"Oh, Dad, this thing between me and Shane? It's *also* a big secret that nobody can know. Nobody. Especially not Elsa. Not yet. And maybe not at all. *But trust me, Dad,*" Celia whispers as she drives closer to that bungalow. "*I know what I'm doing.*"

Yeah, right. Her pounding heart and mouth that's gone dry say otherwise.

Makes no difference now. She's home.

Her father is standing in the front yard. He's holding Aria and waving her tiny hand. His head dips as he talks to the baby. As he points out Celia's arrival. He's smiling, too.

Celia turns into the driveway.

Parks the car.

Realizes that what Shane asked of her today is incredibly difficult to pull off. No denying that.

But it's time.

So she checks her side braid in the mirror, sucks in a shaky breath, opens the car door and steps outside.

And, well ... there's always her fallback plan—if all else fails, lie.

four

SHANE PUSHES A SHOPPING CART into Mega-Mart discount department store. A place like this should have everything he needs. If only he could keep up with the list his mind is compiling as he scans the store aisles. At least it's air-conditioned in here, which helps. So does his sleeveless tee. Lord knows, his nerves have him sweating. At least they did for the hour ride from the cottage to here. Here—just miles outside of Addison. He presses the back of a hand to his forehead, then soldiers on through the store. The carriage wheels shimmy every so often. Garish white lights shine from the suspended ceiling. Lime-green signs hang over the aisles. *Electronics. Toys. Kitchen Goods. Lawn and Garden.* After walking down an aisle of toasters and coffeepots, he spots the *Baby* aisle.

"Okay," Shane quietly says, heading that way. There are several big-ticket items assembled and on display in a center aisle. A few strollers are lined up; car seats; high chairs. And there, just what he's looking for: portable cribs.

Now, a problem—which to choose. There are bassinets and play-yard cribs. Folding and full size. Travel and permanent. But when he spots a portable crib with a removable changing-table top, his mind is made up. So he wheels his carriage to the indicated shelf and hefts one of the crib cartons into his cart.

But that's not all he does.

Within minutes, he adds a fitted, all cotton crib sheet.

A nightlight.

A rattle of a fuzzy lion with a felt mane.

A baby onesie—only after holding up several to gauge Aria's size.

A cotton sunbonnet.

A long-sleeve sleeper in case it gets chilly at night.

He just can't stop himself, adding a mini mobile for the crib, and a music box. Small pack of disposable diapers. Wipes. Oh, and he's not done. Quickly, he wheels his cart to the women's department and adds a new robe for Celia. He's pretty taken with a display of slipper socks, too, and drops in a pair of those. Even adds a black denim jacket— it'll ward off the sea damp if they sit on his deck at night.

Yep, he keeps tossing and the next thing he knows, his carriage is filled right up.

Shane stops then and eyes the loaded cart. Brushes through it. Hell, there's no denying what he's seeing, either. It's the life he oddly wants—all in a department store shopping cart.

At the checkout, Shane carefully places each item on the counter. Lastly, he lifts the two onesies—a short-sleeve with a ballerina bunny on it, and the long-sleeve covered with a flower print. They're both size three-to-six months, so are incredibly tiny.

"*Aww*," the cashier says as she lifts the bunny onesie. "This is so cute! Do you have a new baby?"

"Me?" Shane looks from the onesie to the cashier. "Yeah. Yeah, I do," he stammers with a nod.

The cashier scans the item's ticket. "What's her name?"

"Aria."

"That's *such* a pretty name," the cashier says, picking up the second onesie. "How old is she?"

"Three months." As he says it, Shane pulls a credit card out of his wallet.

"Well, you enjoy her." The cashier keeps chatting while bagging his items, which Shane then lifts back into his cart. "Babies are so precious," she adds, giving him his receipt now. "And the years just *fly* by."

~

The years fly by? Huh, doesn't he know it. The past fifteen years flew by in a way he didn't particularly like. They passed in a lonely way more than anything else—Shane sees that only now. Fifteen years of no family. No ties. So as he pushes his cart toward the sliding doors, maybe it isn't surprising how happy it actually made him to fill this cart.

Outside, the late-day sun shines low. He feels the close heat as he walks out of the store. People are scattered across the parking lot. A car with its radio blaring slowly passes by. Shane steps off the curb and pushes his shopping cart to his pickup truck. The cart's wheels give a few waggles on the gritty pavement. At the truck, he drops the tailgate, but gets no further. Because before he even starts unloading his bags, his cell phone suddenly rings.

~

Funny, but the sound of that ringing phone just stops Shane. He doesn't grab it from his pocket to see if it's Celia. Instead, he takes a long breath first, then fans the sticking fabric of his sleeveless tee before grabbing his phone as it rings again.

Still, he doesn't *immediately* answer the call. Because he's no fool. That call can easily be the start of something good—or it can easily put an end to his planned week. Those plans with Celia can stop squarely—right here—in the middle of a department store's grimy parking lot. Because there's no telling if things *didn't* go well with her father. Or if Celia got cold feet and changed her mind.

Only one way to find out.

"Celia," Shane finally says into the phone.

"Hey," Celia says back. "Where are you?"

Shane glances over to the busy street. Four lanes of traffic hum in the summer evening. Big-box stores and gas stations and fast-food places line the thoroughfare. "About five miles from Addison," he says.

"What?"

"I'm on the turnpike. Did a little shopping," he adds with a glance at his still-loaded cart. "Needed a few things at the store."

"Which means you could meet me soon, then? At my father's?"

"I can. Within minutes." Shane leans against the side of his truck. "So we're still on?"

"Yes. Absolutely."

Two words that get Shane's eyes to briefly drop closed. "I take it you two talked? You and your dad?"

"We did, Shane. He's out picking up some food for dinner right now."

"Okay." Another breath. "What'd you end up telling him?"

"The truth. Everything." There's a second's pause before Celia's quiet voice goes on. "I had to."

"And what does that mean?" Shane asks, his head bent into her call. "The *truth*."

"That I met someone," she explains right away. "That I didn't plan to; it just happened. Kyle's brother, actually. And there's more. I'm spending some time with him, in Maine. Taking Aria, too."

Shane begins pacing. He walks to his shopping cart at the truck's tailgate. "And how'd he take it?"

"Well, he's cautious—of course."

"I get that."

"And he wants to be sure I know what I'm doing."

"Do you?"

"I do." Another pause before Celia goes on. "And Shane?"

Shane says nothing. He just stands there in his jeans and sleeveless tee, phone to his ear, and waits. Perspires, too. A bead of sweat runs down the side of his face.

"My dad wants to meet you." Celia's voice is soft. "And

actually? I'd really like you to meet him, too."

"When?"

"Now."

Now.

Not at the end of the week. Not at some prearranged future time. Not when Shane can prep. Shower. Change into something appropriate. He glances at his jeans, scuffed boat shoes. Leather cuff. Frayed tee.

Now.

So he's in a bind. He needs to purchase *one* more item, but can't leave his bags unattended in the back of his pickup. Instead, he wheels that loaded shopping cart across the parking lot again and heads back into Mega-Mart. This time, it's the men's department he looks for.

God damn his sweaty tee. He wore it to pack up his cottage earlier at Stony Point. The tee's ragged at the shoulders from the sleeves being ripped off. He glances at his tattooed arms, too. Probably not the best look for meeting Celia's father. So he sets his cart aside and flips through a rack of long-sleeve button-downs before picking one that's decent. The olive-green plaid will do the trick. He holds it up and checks the tag. It's a poplin fabric, so should be cool, too.

"*Breathe, already*," he whispers, heading to the checkout again and still sweating. Doesn't need convincing, either, that it's not the heat getting him perspiring. It's what's waiting for him five miles away.

"Oh, one more item?" the same cashier asks, lifting the

shirt. "Hm. $19.97, but on sale for only $14.50!"

Shane hands her a twenty this time and waits for his change. "Always nice to save a few dollars," he tells her.

"Definitely!"

After lifting the shirt off the checkout counter, Shane finagles his change back into his wallet.

"Here." The cashier reaches for the button-down. "Let me put that in a bag for you."

"Not necessary." He takes the shirt off the plastic hanger and leaves the hanger on the counter. "Thanks anyway," he calls back while ripping off the sales ticket.

Shane heads outside then, while doing two things at once. He's pushing the cart *and* slipping on that new shirt— one arm first, then twisting around for the other—right over his sleeveless tee. When he gets to his pickup, he finally unloads the crib box and shopping bags straight into the truck bed before squinting west toward the late-afternoon sun.

"Okay," he says, cuffing those plaid poplin shirtsleeves halfway up his arms before driving off. "Let's do this."

five

CLIFF. *CLIFF!*" ELSA SAYS, POINTING out the windshield. "Pull in there, at Maritime Market."

"For what?" Cliff asks, slowing the car.

"What?"

"What do you need at this hour?"

"At this hour?"

Cliff turns into the grocery store parking lot. "We just had dinner. Clam strips, baked cod, you name it." He cruises closer to Maritime's entrance. "Aren't you good for food?"

"Yes. Well, no." Elsa sits back in her seat and flips down the visor. Looking at her reflection in the mirror there, she brushes back a loose strand of hair. "It's just so *hot* out. I really need some fresh fruit. Everything rots in this humidity."

Maris leans forward from where she sits in the backseat of Cliff's car. "It's true," she says. "My raspberries withered to practically prunes."

"Do you want to come in with me, Maris?" Elsa asks.

"Not really." Maris sits back. "I'm tired from being out in the sun all afternoon with Jason. Think I'll wait in the car."

"I'll stay here, too," Cliff decides. "And keep the a/c going."

"Okay, then," Elsa says while stepping outside. Right away, the heat hits her in the face. She leans back into the car. "Won't be long!" she calls out before closing the door.

Because Elsa knows. If she takes *too* long, they'll get suspicious. She has to be in and out, quick. So she hoists her black straw tote on her shoulder, crosses the parking lot and thinks. Or plots, is more like it. She needs some cool, summer dish to bring to Mitch's barbecue tomorrow. Oh, she wouldn't have to be so sneaky if Cliff never came by for his laundry and tagged along on tonight's dinner. Not that she minded. But her *plan* had been to stop here after her dinner out—*sans* Cliff. With no watchful eyes noting her every move, every purchase.

When she walks into the market, her first stop is the produce department. "*Perfect*," Elsa murmurs. Right away, an idea comes to her. She'll make a watermelon fruit bowl for the cookout. That way, a little bit of everything— blueberries, cantaloupe, honeydew melon and strawberries—can fill the hollowed-out watermelon.

The problem is—because lately it seems there's *always* a problem—Elsa feels a little criminal doing this. A little … *furtive*. As she opens plastic bags and scoops in berries and

38

melons, there's some disbelief to her stealthy plan. Her life wasn't supposed to turn into this. Mitch … Cliff … Mitch again.

The whole situation has her looking over her shoulder while tying fruit bags. And while tiptoeing around the berries—which *isn't* like her.

Well. Maybe she's making something out of nothing and all's fine, actually. She convinces herself that Mitch's Labor Day cookout tomorrow is innocent enough. He must be throwing it for Carol, and for some friends. Maybe coworkers, too.

Elsa lifts a cantaloupe and inhales its ripe aroma. And everybody loves fruit, which is so refreshing in this heat wave.

So the cookout should be good … with all those people around. And distractions. With another glance over her shoulder, Elsa heads to the checkout.

~

"Thanks for giving me a ride home," Maris tells Cliff from the air-conditioned backseat. "Jason's so busy, and was headed in the opposite direction to catch up on work at Ted's."

"Hopefully you'll both be headed in the *same* direction," Cliff says with a glance back at her. "Soon."

"*Cliff!* From you, too?"

"I care about you and Jason. Like family—which you *could* eventually be …"

Maris pulls out her cell phone then. "What are you saying?" she asks while scrolling the screen.

"Listen." Cliff squints to the store entrance before checking his wristwatch. "I need to ask you something, Maris." He turns sideways in the driver's seat and looks back at her. "And quick. I have to get this off my chest while Elsa's inside."

Maris looks up from her phone. "Cliff? Is everything okay?"

He shrugs, glances to the store again, then to Maris. "Not sure. But I'm trying to *make* things okay."

"You seem nervous." Maris tucks her phone back in her bag. "And now *I'm* getting worried."

"You and me, both." Cliff throws another glance to the store. "Which is why I really need your thoughts on something."

"On *something?*"

Cliff looks her straight on. And looks away, then back at Maris. "On my proposing to your aunt."

"*What?*" Maris lurches forward from the backseat. Her hand grips the top of the seatback. "You want to get *married?* To Elsa?"

Cliff nods. "Been thinking about it. Ever since the guys knocked some sense into me Saturday night—"

"Saturday night? *Camping?*"

"Yeah. We got to talking 'round the fire. And I think it's time."

"Oh my God! Cliff! I'm really surprised—in a *good* way." Now it's Maris who glances out her window for any sign of Elsa. "But you don't need my permission."

"Maybe not. But I'd sure love your blessing."

Maris gives a quick laugh, then shakes her head. "I'm floored! *Marriage!*"

"Well. It's about a year now that Elsa and I've been together."

"You have no idea how *happy* this makes me." Maris reaches over the top of the seat and squeezes Cliff's shoulder. "To know that someone's there for Elsa through thick and thin. That her coming to Stony Point brings so much …" A sob, or some emotion, chokes Maris up. "Brings so much good into her life." And now tears rise, too. So she swipes at them.

"Oh, boy." Cliff pulls a handkerchief from his cargo shorts pocket and hands it to her. Gives another look toward the store, too. "Hold those tears! Here comes Elsa. *Shh!* Don't say anything."

"Well." Maris has that hanky balled into her hand as she dabs at her moist eyes. "Well, do you need any help? When you propose?"

"Don't know." Cliff straightens in the front seat and watches Elsa cross the parking lot.

"But when are you going to ask her?" Maris persists.

"Wait! She's getting closer, so … so change the subject!"

"*Okay, okay.*" But first? First Maris leans over, half stands and manages a one-armed super-quick hug over the top of the seat. As she does, she whispers, "*And yes, I give you my blessing.*"

Cliff somehow pats her hugging arm, then wrangles himself out of the hug and opens his car door. "I'll go help Elsa load up the trunk."

"Do you have any of those insulated totes?" Maris hears Elsa call out as she nears. "They'll keep my fresh fruit cold."

"Yes, yes." Cliff walks around the car and pops open the trunk. "I have the ones you bought me at the dollar store.

They're right here," he says, lifting the folded totes from the trunk.

Maris spins around in the backseat and watches the two of them—Cliff and Elsa, together. Oh, and Maris is smiling, too. She can hardly contain herself. When Cliff catches her eye, his hand discreetly shoos her. She still sends a wink his way.

Does something else, too. It's *impossible* not to. Just impossible. Maris *tap-taps* at the car's rear window, smiles even wider and waves to Elsa.

six

HE'S ALMOST THERE.

Shane drives through Addison and eventually turns onto a winding country lane. The street is lined with old colonials, and rural farmhouses, and bungalows. Most have some sort of stay-awhile front porch. As he drives his pickup, he notices a crumbling stone wall reaching down the length of the street, too. The stone wall, and the street itself, lead to a red barn. Beyond, low sunlight glints off the wispy top of a lush cornfield.

"Far cry from Stony Point," Shane tells himself as he peers out the windshield.

And he knows. Celia isn't from Stony Point. *This* is actually home. *This* street. Not the sandy beach roads they've walked. Not the salty breezes lifting off Long Island Sound. No, instead home for her is more dew-covered green lawns beneath shady old maple and oak trees. Clear country air. Random Canada geese alighting on that distant cornfield.

Something catches Shane's eye, then. It's a clothesline in the side yard of a white farmhouse. He squints to be sure of what he's seeing—two wedding gowns hanging from that strung rope. Looking almost spirit-like, they're clipped at the shoulders and neckline. The white fabric—all lace and satin—glimmers in a mist of twilight. Beyond, a woman carrying a laundry basket crosses the lawn to the gowns. A young girl tags along beside her. The girl's blonde hair is flyaway this warm evening.

But it's the house next door to the gowns that gets Shane to slow his truck. He sees it—sees what Celia described to him earlier. Sees the little yellow bungalow with its white picket fence. Maybe it's not the *house* that has him slow, though. It's the approaching moment. The moment when Shane knows he'll be instantly judged, and maybe in the wrong light.

"*Try my damnedest to change that,*" he whispers when he parks at the curb. Sitting there in the truck, he brushes his hand through his closely shorn hair. Picks up his cotton newsboy cap from the passenger seat. Toys with the cap before putting it on.

Just then, the front door of that bungalow swings open. As it does, Shane gets out of the truck—right as the whole crew piles out onto the bungalow's front porch. Celia holding her baby, and Mr. Gray behind them.

⌒‿

As soon as Shane unlatches the picket-fence gate, Celia's there.

"Shane!" she says, cradling Aria while hurrying across

the lawn. Celia's hair is still in a side braid. She still wears her denim overall shorts. "You made it."

"Celia." Shane nods and turns to the baby settled in a strap-on sling. Aria wears a ruffled romper and pumps her tiny fists. He gives the infant's foot a gentle squeeze. "Hey there, little one," he says.

Celia, baby held close, stretches up to kiss Shane. He leans in, putting a hand on her shoulder and kissing her cheek right as she was going for his mouth. So they awkwardly bump, pull back and try again—this time landing the mouth kiss just right. But quick. Followed by Celia brushing his whiskered cheek. She steps back then, all smiles.

So Shane can see. She's not nervous—at all. Which leaves him feeling at a disadvantage. He clears his throat and catches sight of her father approaching. He's a tall man, tanned and in shape. His short hair is more silver than black, and he wears a heathered-gray tee loose over olive jeans and low leather sneakers.

"Shane!" Celia says again before looking back at her father. "I want you to meet someone really special to me. This is my dad."

Shane walks the few steps toward him. At the same time, he also takes off his newsboy cap and shoves it in the back pocket of his jeans. "You must be the sea glass collector," Shane says then, extending his hand.

The man nods and gives a firm handshake. "Name's Gavin."

"Good to meet you, Gavin," Shane says.

Celia stands beside Shane now. "Dad, this is Shane," she says.

"Shane Bradford," Shane finishes.

"You find the place okay?" Gavin asks, nodding to the yellow bungalow.

"No problem. Quite a street, this is. Straight out of a folk-art painting," Shane tells him.

"We like it." Gavin turns to the long, winding road ending at that distant red barn. "It's a peaceful spot."

"My friend I told you about lives over there." Celia motions to the farmhouse next door. "Amy."

"She owns the wedding shop, I'm assuming," Shane says.

Gavin looks to the now-empty clothesline. "You saw the gowns hanging on the line?"

"Sure did." Shane glances from the house, back to Celia as she leans into him.

"Listen. Dad got us some takeout. Chicken parm, salads. So we can have something to eat before we hit the road." She pats Shane's arm. "Why don't you two stay out here while I set the table inside? It'll be nice—the slider to the backyard is open to let in any breeze."

"All right," Shane tells her.

"I'll get Aria settled with a bottle, too," Celia adds. "So we'll be ready to leave after we eat."

"Sounds good." Shane turns back toward the bungalow as they all start walking across the lawn. "If you have anything to bring for the baby, I'll load it in your car," Shane calls to Celia as she climbs the front steps to the stoop. "Then you'll follow me?"

Celia nods easily before opening the screen door and stepping inside the house. When she does, Shane crosses his arms in front of him and leans against the railing at the steps.

"Really glad I'm meeting you, Shane," Gavin says then. "Before your trip north."

"Me, too."

"Must admit, though … was a little thrown by Celia's news."

Shane gives a short laugh. "If it makes you feel any better, Gavin, I was thrown by your daughter, too. Really care about Celia. She means a lot to me."

"I want to believe you, Shane." Gavin motions him ahead to the open porch and follows Shane up the few stairs. "I trust my daughter, but—"

"You have your doubts about me," Shane finishes over his shoulder.

Gavin half leans, half sits on the porch railing. He's got a blade of grass in his hand and brings it to his mouth. "Can you blame me?" he asks around the grass between his teeth now.

"Blame you for having some suspicion about a random lobsterman who came out of nowhere and has a thing for your daughter? I haven't done anything to rouse that doubt, so it feels judgmental, but—"

Gavin stops him right there. "Listen," he says. "Celia's been through a lot. First a divorce. Then her fiancé died suddenly a year ago. She uprooted her *whole* life here to be closer to his mother. To live and work with her at that inn—which I guess isn't even opening. Then, of course, Celia had the baby a few months ago."

"And then I waltzed in, huh?"

Gavin just turns up his hands. "On top of that, you've got a *helluva* commute."

"Yep. And let me tell *you* something. About trust—

which seems to be the *real* issue here. If you're a lobsterman like myself, it's all you've got. Without the trust of the crew out on the Atlantic, you've got nothing. Because there's too much just waiting to take you down. Rogue monster waves washing over the vessel, snapped towlines ricocheting like a bullet, rope entanglements that'll gladly take you to the bottom of the sea. My crewmates are the eyes on the back of my head. So I learned a long time ago how to earn trust. And *keep* it. Without my crewmates trusting me, and vice versa, I'd never have made it out of the past twenty years of lobstering alive."

Gavin twists that blade of grass in his teeth. Still leaning on the porch railing, he squints from the house's screen door, then back to Shane.

Who remains silent now. The *last* thing he'll do is try to justify his being here, or warrant his worth. Gavin can take it or leave it—Shane's silence says it all.

"Got it, the trust thing," Gavin finally says, tossing that piece of grass over the railing. "And in that case, I feel comfortable telling *you* something."

"And what's that?" Shane sits on one of two slatted-wood armchairs on the porch. He leans forward, elbows on his knees, and waits. Over beyond that crumbling rock wall, the sun is starting to sink behind the maple trees.

"While you're in Maine with Celia and the baby?" Gavin begins. "I want you to leave your truck here."

"What?" Shane looks to his pickup parked at the curb. "Here?"

Gavin nods. "Come on. I'll help you move your things into Celia's car. Then you can just pull the truck into the other bay in my garage."

"Seriously?" Shane stands then.

Gavin steps to him, briefly claps his shoulder and motions for Shane to follow him off the porch. "I can see that Celia's tired," Gavin says, glancing back. "So I'd like *you* to drive her and the baby. Better for everybody that way."

seven

ONCE CLIFF AND ELSA DROP Maris off at home, Maris bolts across the lawn. Beyond the gabled house, a thin crescent moon is just rising in the twilight sky. Shadows are long around the front porch, where black-eyed Susans grow wild. Maris' feet thud up the steps before she throws open the front door and keeps moving—straight down the dark hallway, straight to the kitchen. The whole time, Maddy is at her heels. The dog's tail is wagging; her paws dance on the floor.

"Oh, Maddy!" Maris says while dropping her purse on the old kitchen counter. She flicks on the ceiling light and squints against the stark brightness in the stripped-and-ready-for-demo room. The kitchen's really stuffy as she stands there in her shorts and navy tank top. "I have such news," she's saying while adding kibble to the dog's empty food dish, then pushing open the slider for a breeze of salt air. All around her, quartz samples are still strewn on the countertops. Design magazines are opened to kitchen spreads that caught her eye. Possible drawer and cabinet pulls are fanned out here and there.

But Maris reaches past it all for her purse and digs out her cell phone. She quickly makes a call, presses the phone to her ear and flips through a magazine—all while bouncing on her sandaled feet. "Pick up, pick up, *pick up*, Jason! Pick up, already!" When the call goes to voicemail, she disconnects and redials.

"Hey, Maris," Jason's voice finally comes to her ear.

"Oh my God, Jason," she says while closing the magazine and stacking some quartz samples.

"What's the matter?"

"What were you doing?" Maris asks. "Took forever to answer the phone."

"Lying on the couch. It's been a long day, with camping first. Then being on the beach with you. And dinner. So I'm beat. Closed my eyes for ten minutes, and shit, fell asleep for a half hour."

"Well." Maris holds the phone close. "Are you *really* up now?"

"Why? What's going on?"

"I have the *biggest* news." As she says it, she slides over some of the sample drawer pulls and moves aside the tin-can bouquet Jason bought from Carol's flower cart.

"Wait." Jason pauses. "Where are you?"

"I'm home."

"Well what are you doing? You're making a racket there."

"I am?" With that, Maris grabs up the tin-can flowers and scoots into the dining room. Maddy follows close

51

behind, nearly tripping her on the way.

"Yeah," Jason explains. "I hear scraping. Shuffling."

"Oh, that's nothing." Setting the silver flower can on her shoved-over dining room table, Maris bumps her head on the lantern-chandelier. "*Ow*," she whispers, then quickly bluffs to Jason. "I'm … I'm cleaning up the dining room," she says while switching on that chandelier before sinking into a seat. "The ladies had dinner here yesterday. And Jason, I *really* have to tell you something!"

"Okay, okay," he says, his voice tired. "So are you going to spill it?"

Maris touches the petals on a purple coneflower. "*Can you keep a secret?*"

Jason's silent for a second or two. "Maris," is all he finally says.

"Okay. But you *really* can't tell anyone."

"Tell anyone *what?*"

"I heard it from the source himself," Maris reveals while slowly spinning that can of coneflowers and daisies and zinnias. "Cliff wants to marry Elsa!"

～

"So." Cliff sets aside a folded grocery bag. "What are you going to do all week now?"

"Don't know." Elsa squints across the inn's kitchen at him. "Are you keeping tabs on me?"

"What if I am?"

"Oh!" she says, waving him off. From her marble island, she sits and watches Cliff putting away the groceries. He looks a little tired. Elsa's not sure if he even shaved at the campground this morning. Whiskers—a mix of silver and black—cover his jaw, his chin. But not enough whiskers to cover his dimple when he gives a slight smile.

"Remember the car show I told you I'm going to tomorrow?" When she nods, Cliff asks, "Want to come along? You can meet Denny."

And she'd consider it, given Cliff's easy manner, and his casual way of tending to her groceries. To her. Yes, she'd consider it if she didn't have plans for *Mitch's* cookout tomorrow. So she breezes out of the invite. "No, that's okay," she says. "Cars are *your* domain. And really, you don't have to worry about me just because my life's a little adrift." Elsa still sits there, pulling her cell phone from her black straw tote and checking the phone for messages.

"But I *do* worry about you. And what's the matter with that?" Cliff asks, maneuvering a watermelon into the refrigerator. "Don't you worry about people?"

"What?" Elsa looks up from her phone.

"You don't worry about Jason? Maris? Celia and your granddaughter?" he calls back while bent into the fridge.

"Sure I do. It's only natural to worry about them."

Cliff closes the refrigerator before lifting strawberries and a cantaloupe from a bag. "And why's this any different—me worrying about *you*?"

Elsa tips her head and starts to say something. She opens her mouth to talk, then closes it and sets down her phone.

"Elsa. I just thought you'd like to get out for a while, that's all." Cliff pulls another grocery bag closer and reaches in it. "You bought an awful lot of fruit, you know."

"Well of course I know." Elsa walks over to the two

remaining bags and lifts out a bakery-fresh loaf of Italian bread she'd also bought. "I stocked up so I don't have to stop at the store every other day."

"Okay, okay," Cliff says while rinsing a bunch of grapes in a strainer at the sink. "Anyway, the car show's at Ocean Beach," he goes on while turning again to the last bag of food. "Have you ever been? Because we could—"

"Clifton. I'm not interested in walking around in this blazing heat. Smelling the scent of exhaust. And … and *dust*." As if the car exhaust is right there in the kitchen, Elsa hurries to the sink now and opens the garden window above it. Checks her herb pots while she's there, too. "*Oh, they're dry*," she whispers before filling her mister with tap water.

"But they have food trucks at those car shows," Cliff persists with his invitation.

"Food trucks?" Elsa glances over from spritzing the little red pots.

"Sure. You can order up some cornbread topped with pulled pork. Or a barbecued-chicken burger. Grilled portabella sandwich. Cheese fries. You know. The *good* stuff."

"Oh, I can't even *have* a good time right now."

Cliff crosses his arms in front of himself. "Why not? You did at The Clam Shack."

Elsa sets down her mister and glances toward the guest cottage outside the garden window. "Because Celia's mad at me, too. On top of everything else. I just know it."

"Mad? Why?"

Elsa turns to get a fruit bowl from a cabinet. "I handled the postponed inn opening all wrong, making decisions without consulting her. And look—now she's gone and left."

Cliff looks out to the dark guest cottage, too. "She's not back from her father's yet?"

"No. She decided to spend the *week* in Addison, with her father and Aria. She's taking a breather from Stony Point, I guess."

When Elsa reaches to the sink for the grape bunch, Cliff's folding up that last grocery bag. "I'm sure Celia understands," he's saying while setting the bag on the counter. "You were just uncertain how to handle that last-minute zoning issue."

Elsa gives a sad smile. "Doesn't matter now," she tells Cliff. "Celia's gone. Aria's gone. And there's nothing I can do about it." She shakes her head. "*Oh, what a mess I've made.*" After dropping the rinsed grapes in that fruit bowl, she turns and bumps that folded grocery bag to the floor. So she bends to pick up the bag, saying, "But I'm just prattling—"

"Mrs. DeLuca," Cliff interrupts, bending to retrieve the bag, too. When they both grab hold of it, they slowly straighten—together. "I'm *here* for the prattling," he quietly says.

"Oh, Cliff." Elsa steps closer to him when he tugs on the bag they both hold.

The bag which ends up back on the floor when Cliff reaches an arm around her shoulder and enfolds her in a kiss. The way he's got her almost wrapped in his arms, well, Elsa's a little surprised at how comforting it feels. The kiss. The embrace that just about holds her up as his hand toys with her thick hair, all while the kiss goes on in the now-quiet kitchen.

"*Cliff*," she whispers, reaching to his scruffy face.

He pulls back, kisses her once again, briefly, and loosens that arm around her shoulders. "You get some rest," he tells her. "Make yourself a cup of tea, unwind, and just … take things easy."

Elsa only nods.

"Everything'll be all right. You'll work things out with Celia," Cliff says, his voice low. "Give it time." He steps away and picks up that empty bag, before pulling his keys from his pocket.

And somehow, she believes him. Whether it's his words that do it, or that kiss she never saw coming. But it's certainly one that has her watch him leave. Has her stand in the side doorway of her kitchen. Has her squint out at his departing shadow as the sun sets behind the horizon.

Even when Cliff looks back over his shoulder and casually waves, Elsa just stands there, leaning on the doorjamb, and watches until he's gone.

eight

THEY'RE QUIET AT FIRST.

As Shane drives Celia's packed car and picks up the highway north, the sun is just sinking below the horizon. Aria is strapped into her infant seat in the back. The air-conditioning is set to low, so the windows are closed—making it even quieter in the car.

"I'm glad I was honest with my father," Celia tells him across the front seat.

"Me, too."

"It made it easier, not having to lie."

Shane glances over at her. "He'd have seen right through any story. Any lies."

"You think so?"

"I do."

Celia looks out the windshield. Divided lines on the highway blur into one.

"Gavin doesn't pull any punches," Shane says a few

57

moments later. "And wouldn't let a lie slip by."

"No."

"So it's good, Celia." Shane reaches over and briefly clasps her hand. "He's all right with this."

Celia looks him straight on. "With you?"

Shane nods, and talking little now, they drive on.

⁓

Eventually, the cityscape turns rural. The highway opens up. Rolling farmland passes by. Countryside towns, too, dotted with rustic homes and quaint downtowns.

The view at twilight, and the muffled silence, has Celia think of her life. Or rather, the movie she sometimes imagines would be made from her life. The title would still be *The Nowhere Affair*, its storyline picking up with her relationship with one tenacious lobsterman. There's a new plot twist, though. Because now it feels like the nowhere affair *is* actually going somewhere. Three hundred miles north, to be exact.

Destination: Rockport, Maine.

But first? Getting there. She looks out the side window at the passing shadows of trees and countryside.

Here, the director would set the establishing shot. This time, it's from inside the car. In this dusky hour, the roadside scenery would be evocative. Soft. The highway signs indicating they're approaching Massachusetts would convey the journey. But it's when Shane's lone voice begins telling seafaring stories that the camera would turn to him. There's his newsboy cap sitting jaunty on his head. There's his serious face. The glow of the dashboard casts faint light on his features. On the scruff of his jaw. On his eyes watching the highway as he looks toward the setting sun, but tells Celia what it's like seeing that sun *rise* straight out of the Atlantic Ocean.

"Magic," his low voice says. "Just magic."

Through his careful words, the viewer would get a better sense of this man beside her. Like when he tells her how he sometimes sees wild dolphins playing in the lobster boat's wake.

"And it's funny, because they're not all that different from the boys rough-housing on deck." He's quiet, then goes on. "Social creatures, I guess. Sort of the same, somehow—dolphins and people," Shane muses.

As they drive further north, the sky darkens. The car's interior is illuminated only by the dashboard and passing streetlights. So the lighting pulses, then fades. But the director might order the camera to stay focused on only Shane. On his silhouette as his steady voice tells Celia what it's like seeing an occasional whale surfacing out at sea.

"Just one word describes it," Shane says. A few seconds pass before the camera catches that word. "Sobering."

After that, Shane reaches over. Driving with one hand on the wheel, he holds Celia's hand for several seconds. Celia imagines the camera backs off then. It pans to the entire front seat. To the two of them driving in silence now. Only the wheels hum out the miles beneath them.

⁓

When Aria stirs, Celia leans over the console and coos to the baby behind them. Still, Aria gets fussy. Little cries come from her infant seat. Her arms and legs move. It's enough that Celia asks Shane to stop at the next rest area. When he does, she walks the baby outside for a few minutes. Changes her diaper in the restroom, too, while Shane tops off their tank at the gas station there.

After parking again, Shane waits outside for Celia. A few tractor-trailers idle in a side lot. A young couple walks into a coffee shop. But the rest area is quiet in the middle of Labor Day weekend. Helps that it's late at night, too. When Celia returns with the baby, she approaches Shane.

"Would you hold Aria while I use the ladies' room?"

"Of course," Shane says, taking the infant from her.

"*Be right back,*" Celia whispers before turning away.

Shane looks from Celia departing, to the baby he's holding against his shoulder. She can't be more than twelve or so pounds, just a tiny life. When she moves, it's like holding subtle waves of motion. Her dark hair rests in lazy curls beside her face. Her cheeks are soft. And surprisingly, Aria's looking directly at him. Her brown eyes are wide open.

"Hi there, little one," he says, rubbing her back as he shifts her in his hold. He takes some slow steps near a split-rail fence. Tips up his newsboy cap and glances at Aria again. Touches a finger to her cheek. "Going to show you the harbor near my house," he quietly says. "You'll like it." He keeps walking, turning back alongside the fence. "Lots of pretty boats to look at. Some really noisy birds, too. Would you like to see them?" he asks, dipping his face close to hers.

When he turns minutes later, Celia's standing not too far behind him. Still in her denim overall shorts, her arms are crossed; her side braid is holding on; her face, smiling. "You've got her engrossed there."

"That I do." Shane walks to Celia. "Have it on good authority Aria's very excited to see the harbor boats at my place." As he says it, Celia takes the baby from him. She coos to Aria and gets her settled in her car seat. Celia's words are hushed inside the vehicle.

—————

Once they're rolling on the highway again, Celia stretches back and checks on the baby.

"*She's sleeping*," she whispers to Shane.

He looks over at Celia. "You should, too."

"Sleep?"

Shane nods while looking out at the night, right as a car passes them.

"I'm okay," Celia argues, shifting sideways on the seat to face him. "I'll keep you company."

"Come on, Celia." Shane glances at her. "You're exhausted."

She takes a long breath. "I am. You're right." She presses a hand beneath her face as she leans into the cushioned headrest. "Okay. Maybe a little nap would be nice."

Shane just keeps the driving steady. In no time, the car's quiet. And in the darkness, it's still as can be. So he knows. Celia's sound asleep.

Outside, highway markers go by.

Divided lines pass.

Hours do, too.

Traffic's light and the night's black. The further north

he drives, the thicker the forests. The fewer the towns. Sometimes the darkness is the same as out at sea, particularly on a moonless night. Right now, he can't tell the forest from the sky—the same way he sometimes can't tell the *sea* from the sky. Nighttime's interesting like that, the way it can blend two worlds.

With the car still quiet, Shane keeps his foot evenly to the pedal. The radio's off. He cracks his window to get some of that clear Maine air into the vehicle. It works the same wonders as salt air at sea—lulling sleep even deeper.

He gives another glance over at Celia, too. More than anything, he's glad she's comfortable enough with him to sleep right there.

~~

Celia feels a gentle nudge on her shoulder. It gets her to shift her position. She also opens her eyes to darkness. Though she feels the motion of the moving car, it's no longer on the highway.

Again, a soft tap on her shoulder. "Hey, Celia." Shane's quiet voice comes to her now. "We're here."

"What?"

Shane nods to the dark street outside the window. "We're here. My place is just a block away," he says, pointing ahead.

Celia sits up straight and leans forward. "Oh my God. It is!" She looks to the little shingled house there. "How long did I sleep?" she asks.

"Couple of hours, actually. It's good."

While pressing back strands of sleep-mussed hair, Celia

notices the homes outside. Some are dark; lamplight shines in others. Finally, Shane turns into his driveway. The car's tires crunch on gravel. The headlights shine on his harbor house. Its shingles are silver in the night illumination. A few faded buoys hang beside a pale blue door.

When Shane shuts off the car, he turns to her. "This is it," he says.

"I remember from when I was here last week, looking for you. Shane, it's so charming."

"Well." He nods to the house. "It's not much, but it's home." He opens his car door then. "Let's go inside."

Celia gets out and carefully lifts her sleeping baby from the car seat. It's dark, so Shane takes her arm to guide her to the front door. "Careful," he says as they approach a granite step. He goes ahead of her then, opens a screen door and unlocks the painted wood door behind it. "Come on," he tells her over his shoulder. Stepping in, he tosses his cap on a chair and flicks on a light as she follows behind him.

It takes a few minutes for them to acclimate. To get situated being here—at their destination. But it's far too late to do much more than get their things inside *and* get some serious rest. So after Shane goes out to the car and retrieves her baby totes and the portable crib he'd purchased, he asks Celia where she'd like it set up.

"*Do you have a spare bedroom?*" she whispers. Aria is still asleep on her shoulder, so she gently rubs her back and walks around the small living room.

"You bet," Shane says, heading to a nearby hallway.

Celia waits in the living room with Aria. In a few minutes, she also finds her way around the kitchen and manages to warm a bottle of formula. After feeding the baby, she ventures to the spare bedroom where Shane's finished assembling the crib. He grips a page of printed instructions in one hand; the other adjusts a plush animal mobile as he turns to her.

"It's all ready?" Celia asks.

"It is. I bought a fitted crib sheet, too." As he says it, he gently tugs the sheet's corners on the small mattress. "It's all cotton jersey. Very soft for Aria."

"Perfect. But is there somewhere that I can change her diaper? And put on her sleeper onesie?"

"Got you covered, Cee." Shane turns to a bed in the room. He lifts a changing-table insert off it and sets it in place atop the portable crib.

And Celia can't believe it. He's done—and continues to do—whatever he can to make things easy here. While she changes the baby, he plugs a nightlight into a wall outlet. And winds up a tinkling music box, then sets it on a nearby dresser. And leaves Celia there to comfort Aria in this new place.

She does, too. She hums a light tune and holds Aria close—gently rocking her on her shoulder—until the baby is heavy with sleep in her arms.

⁓

Shane knows.

He saw it the whole night. He watched it in the volume of bags and items Celia hauled here to Maine. Saw it in the fatigued sleep she stole in the car. Glimpsed it in the relief on her face once the portable crib was all assembled.

Damn straight, Shane knows. Celia chose the hard option, coming here. There's no denying it.

Now he brings in her luggage and sets it in his bedroom. Folds down the coverlet on the bed. Grabs the black denim jacket he bought for her earlier, too. When he looks into the dimly lit spare bedroom across the hall, Celia's just putting Aria in the crib. It's been a long, long day. Still, Celia fusses—clattering a seashell wind chime she's rigged from the curtain rod. Then she waits there in the shadows while watching Aria settle into sleep again.

Quietly, Shane takes Celia's denim jacket to the kitchen. He opens the back door to the deck, swipes his happiness jar off the counter and heads outside. When he's just lighting a dry piece of spaghetti and lowering it to the candlewick in the jar, Celia joins him there.

The flickering candlelight glimmers on pieces of sea glass in the happiness jar. That candle is the only illumination at this late hour. Celia, sitting on a deck chair beside him, lets out a sigh. She does more, too. Shane hears her when he reaches over and drapes that black jacket over her shoulders. She breathes in a long breath of the pungent salt air lifting off the Atlantic.

"Cures what ails you," Shane mentions.

"Neil's old saying, right?"

"Right. So … *is* something ailing you?"

Celia shakes her head.

"Come on. Tell me." He reaches over again and takes her hand. "Salt air brings out the truth, too."

"*Oh*, that air. And sensing the Atlantic Ocean at your doorstep. It's beautiful. But—"

"But what?"

She shrugs. "Sometimes it just feels wrong, or sad—or both—that I had to lose *Sal* to find *you*."

Shane pulls back and eyes her. "It's not really like that."

"Isn't it, though? You'd never be in my life otherwise. Lauren *never* would've sent you that invitation if it wasn't for Sal."

Shane says nothing. In the distance, water sloshes in the harbor. Small waves lap at the dock piers, splash against the boat hulls. But here on his deck, it's just the two of them. Celia and himself, and their words in the darkness on a late summer night.

"I see things so differently now," Celia's quiet voice goes on.

"Like what?"

"Like … you let me in. You *tell* me what you're thinking or feeling … or missing. Like your friendship with Neil. Then there are those boat stories you told on the drive here. Interesting little things. But Sal? He didn't do that. He actually *kept* things from me. So now I second-guess that relationship sometimes. I wonder if we would've even worked out the way I'd thought."

"Hey, Celia. It's okay."

She gives a regretful laugh. "Sal's my beautiful daughter's father. He was my fiancé. We were going to get married, and I don't even know if we were really right for each other?"

"Listen." Shane sits forward, hands on his knees, and looks over at her. "You don't have to compare Sal to me. I don't *want* you to."

Celia stands then. She pulls that denim jacket tighter and looks out at the distant harbor where scattered lights shine. Dock lights, boat lights—all are reflected on the black night water.

"Celia," Shane says, coming up behind her. "Look at me." When she silently turns, he goes on. "Sal was briefly in your life, and you loved him. You still do. How *we* are with each other shouldn't change that."

A distant foghorn wails then—low and muffled in the damp air.

Celia steps closer, takes Shane's hands and gives him a light kiss. Her words are whispered now. "*I guess I'm just tired, that's all. Are you coming in?*"

"Not yet." Shane tugs her toward the back door. "You go on in first, get to sleep. I'll sit out here for a while."

Celia nods. "Okay," she says as he holds that door open for her.

"I turned down the bed," Shane tells her when she walks past him. "In the room across the hall from Aria."

From where he sits on the deck then, Shane has a view inside, too. He sees Celia walk into the spare bedroom to check on Aria first, then cross the hall to his bedroom. The most he can do is hope she sleeps well there.

But still, he stays outside. The day's been as long as they come.

nine

At DAWN, ALL CELIA SENSES is the sea. Maybe that's why she'd slept so deep. All night, salt air drifted in the open windows. And just now, the gurgling of diesel engines stirred her awake. That sound comes from the nearby harbor as fishing boats there start up. Even on Labor Day, they are getting to it. So in the very faint morning light, she opens her eyes and looks around.

The sea is everywhere.

It's in the deep sage-green painted headboard. Wide stripes lining the bed's coverlet are the same deep sage. Celia imagines that shade of green is familiar to Shane. It's some color of the Atlantic beneath the changing light of sun and clouds and hour of day. She looks to the windows. Jute rope loops around the long curtains. Loose sailors' knots in those ropy tiebacks hold aside the draped fabric. And on the nightstand, there's a tarnished brass crab beside a distressed clay lamp glazed a pale sandy brown.

The sea. It's so much of who he is. Celia sees it here. She lies in bed and listens to the boat engines. Shane is lying still beside her. In a moment, she strokes his arm. Traces his tattoos.

"*You up?*" she whispers.

"I am."

"*Me, too.*"

Shane kisses the top of her head. "Want me to get some breakfast ready?" he says into the kiss.

Celia's fingers trace the inked words of a psalm on his upper arm first, then trace across his chest, along his belly. "*No,*" she whispers. "*Not yet.*"

So Shane reaches a hand beneath her chin and tips her face to his. They kiss then, to the scent of the sea. To the misty light edging the blinds. While they kiss, Shane's hands reach lower. They slip beneath her silky nightshirt and glide over the curve of her hips. Her breasts.

"Celia," he says, nuzzling her neck.

But she lets him say no more. Instead she pulls back and presses a finger to his mouth. "*Shh,*" she whispers before sliding off his boxers.

They're quiet then as Shane lifts off her nightshirt before moving over her—*quiet, quiet*. They're simply a part of it all here, the rhythm, the pulse of that vast sea right outside.

Later, Shane *does* get that breakfast put together—Maine style. Celia watches as she sits in the kitchen. Wearing a new robe Shane bought for her, she's also giving Aria her bottle.

Coffee's percolating. Orange juice is poured. Shane's standing at the counter and buttering thick slices of whole-grain toast.

"Love this raw Maine wildflower honey." He spreads a dollop on the buttered toast and brings the plate to where Celia's sitting. "Have a taste," he says, lifting the toast to her mouth.

Celia, still feeding Aria, leans over and takes a bite of the sweet delicacy. Her eyes drop closed with the flavor. "Oh my God," she manages around the food. Her tongue feels the bread's grains, and flecks of sea salt Shane dashed on—all blending with the natural honey and melted butter. "I've never had anything like it."

"Eat up." Shane touches her shoulder before leaving the plate there on the table. "Lots of natural pollens in that honey. Good for your immune system."

After they eat, and sip coffee, Celia sets Aria's empty bottle aside. She stands with the baby then, and walks to the door to the deck—all while gently rubbing Aria's back. As she stands there at the open door, Aria gives a healthy burp from Celia's shoulder.

"Whoa, sailor," Shane calls from where he's digging in to another honey-slathered piece of toast.

Celia smiles and explores some, moving toward the living room. On the way there, she passes a wall of striking paintings. Some of their heavy frames are gilded gold; others are wood distressed with age. The paintings' subjects vary, from dark landscapes to portraits of Victorian-era women. Most seem to be oil on canvas—and look quite valuable. Celia says little phrases to Aria about them, then turns back toward Shane still sitting in the kitchen.

"You're an art collector, then?" she calls out.

In a second, he calls back, "More an art *thief.*"

So Celia makes her way back to the kitchen. One of the hallway walls is covered floor-to-ceiling with these framed paintings—some tiny, some massive. They seem to be museum-quality pieces of art. "What?" she asks in the kitchen doorway. "Did you say you're an art *thief?*"

"I did."

"You mean …" She looks from the paintings to Shane. "Those are all *stolen?*"

Shane nods. "From places right here in Maine. Up in the country. On the coast."

Celia looks at a framed canvas right there near the doorway. The oil painting is breathtaking; its wooded landscape draws her right in. "So how'd they end up here?"

"*I* stole them." Shane joins her and Aria in the hallway then. He stands there in his jeans and a loose tee while looking at that landscape painting. "Used to do some exploring here, back in the day. Found all these in some pretty incredible abandoned properties. A church. Houses. Well, mansions …"

"Abandoned?"

"Yep. Deserted. But filled with furniture and appliances and personal things left behind—including paintings. As if the people just walked away from their lives. So occasionally I'd go through the places, room by room. Brought Neil a couple of times, too. And I took these."

"Just … *took* them? Lifted them off the walls and drove away?"

"I did. Like to think I did the artwork a favor by saving it. It all would've rotted away left in those empty, dank buildings."

Shane walks the hallway with Celia. He points out different paintings, and mentions the crumbling homes in which he'd found them. Some paintings were left hanging on the walls. Some wrapped in blankets and shoved behind dressers, or under beds.

"And I rescued them. Got some of them cleaned up. Framed properly," he says, nodding to an oil portrait of a woman from centuries ago. Her dark hair is pinned up; a ruff collar surrounds her neck. "Mind you, this was after my father died, *and* after I lost Maris, *and* when the rift happened with my brother." He looks at Celia while quietly explaining. "After losing all that, I was just going to take whatever I wanted."

ten

GRAINS OF SAND FALL FROM the top bulb of Maris' pewter hourglass. Monday morning, she can't get the words out fast enough. The writing feels so urgent, she brought her breakfast and coffee to Neil's old shack so she could hurry up and get started. Brought the dog, too. Lying near the open door, Maddy's chewing on a large dog biscuit there.

Maris pauses her typing now and lifts an English muffin spread with peach jam. Outside, the sun rises higher in the eastern sky. Warm salt air drifts into the briny shingled shack. After taking a bite of that muffin, she brushes away crumbs, then lowers her hands to the keyboard again. Her typing fingers can barely keep up with this latest DRIFTLINE passage.

The night is black as can be. What makes it even blacker is the calm. But they both know—something's behind the calm. Some roiling, churning storm is about to rear its head again. So their minutes out here on the quiet beach are dwindling. Every now and then, a short gust of wind kicks up. Or more like—cautions. Get moving, that wind says as it skims across the sea and rustles the salt water.

"Come on," he tells her, running ahead, but turning and walking backward then. Watching her.

She shakes her head and veers closer to the water. A wave—fed by that windy gust—breaks at her bare feet. The water splashes onto her black bell-bottoms. For a minute, she plays a game of cat and mouse with the sea. She steps close, then hurries backward as another wave reaches for her like some outstretched paw. He joins her, and they stand side by side. When they squint into the darkness at the rising black sea, he feels her hand slip into his. The next wave is bigger. And this time, the wind gust is more a warning gale. The water lashes at their legs and he pulls her back onto the beach.

"Let's go!" he shouts, still holding her hand. He hitches his head to the cottage-on-stilts behind them. The cottage is dark, too. With its windows boarded, they can't even make out the candlelight inside. So that last cottage on the beach blends right in with the night.

When another wave splashes too close, and too violently now, she only squeezes his hand. There's something wild and free about the storm's stealth as it inches closer. It gets her dark hair blowing; his shirt whips in that wind.

"Let's stay," she says.

～

Maris stops then, but only to scold the dog. The German shepherd's done chewing her mega biscuit and has moved on to a wooden duck decoy she lifted off a low shelf.

"Maddy!" Maris says as she bolts up from her seat. "You're *not* being a good girl for me." After brushing off the salvaged decoy, Maris steps out into the yard and finds a stick fallen from the big maple tree there. "Now settle down with this," she says, giving the dog the stick. And as Maris sits again at her laptop, as her fingers lift the English muffin for another bite, and as she types another paragraph in her manuscript, Maddy clutches the stick beneath her front paws and gnaws away.

⌒‿

As the sun is rising, so is Cliff—rising out of a lunge.

Heck, after taking Matt up on the strength-training offer he made while camping, Matt doesn't let up. Now he's leading Cliff through a lunge-walk across the boardwalk. When they drop down beneath the warm sunshine, Matt tells him, "Knee at a ninety-degree angle, Judge. Then straighten and the other leg takes the next step, keeping the knee over the *ankle* as you drop into the lunge."

Cliff lunges, his spine long, knee over ankle. He wears a loose gray tee over navy workout shorts and sneakers. As he lunges, he keeps that sneakered foot flat on the boardwalk planks.

"Lunge, step," Matt's saying, walking in sync with Cliff. "Good for the quads. Hamstrings and glute muscles, too."

Doesn't Cliff know it. He feels the ache already once he's back at his trailer. Even so, his muscles unkink as he's eating his toasted bagel and sipping his fresh-squeezed orange juice. Sitting at his bistro table with his breakfast and the local newspaper, *The Day*, he settles in. Scans the town news. Flips to the police blotter. Ponders the opinion page—bagel in hand.

But when he turns to another page, he sits up straight and slaps the table. Lo and behold, look what's staring him right in the face—in full-color, half-page glory.

"Wait a second," he says, biting into his bagel and leaning closer to the newspaper. He skims the words once, then again. What he reads gets him to sit back and down a mouthful of OJ, too—all while eyeing that page. This can't be ... Or *can* it?

With that, Cliff reaches for his cell phone on the counter, scrolls through his *Contacts* and does the only reasonable thing—calls for backup.

⌒

Elsa's been up far too long already, and the sun's only just rising. Her eyes opened way before the seagulls cried out over the rocks. Before the sea breeze wafted in her open windows.

She's been up all right—chopping and balling melons and strawberries for the Fenwicks' Labor Day cookout.

Wearing her turquoise caftan, she's sitting at her marble island. More evidence of how long she's been awake is before her: The watermelon is all carved out and nicely edged like scalloped waves. Now she's only got kiwis left to slice. So she gets one from the fridge and peels off the fuzzy skin. Cuts two thick slices.

And pauses—well aware that if she doesn't watch it, her eyes will have dark circles from lack of sleep.

So Elsa puts the two cold slices on a small plate that she carries to the living room. There, she lies on the sofa and gently sets a kiwi slice over each closed eye. Oh, the cool sensation feels *so* good.

Until one thought gets her bolting upright. It's that she's actually on the couch that *started* all her distress. Sure, a tender sliver-removal here, and a spontaneous shagging-dance there—it's all nothing, really.

Spoonfuls of chocolate icing.

Innocent laughs.

Easy, flirtatious talk.

All excusable. All those didn't leave her with under-eye circles needing kiwis.

This nautical-striped *sofa* did—when she landed on it with Mitch Fenwick a few nights ago.

So she gets up, tosses out the kiwi slices, cuts fresh ones and finishes filling her fruit bowl. Thinks, too. *Damn that man's laid-back vibes getting under my skin.*

"Oh, we got under each other, all right." As she murmurs it, she puts a cool kiwi slice to her chest. "Damn Cliff Raines' kiss last night, too." It was just like their first kiss at Foley's a year ago, in the back room there, as a tree limb was being sawed outside the window. "*Enough,*" Elsa says to herself. "*Time to cool it.*"

Cool the watermelon fruit bowl, too. So she hefts that into the fridge.

Now all that's left is to cool Mitch.

And Cliff.

The only way to do that is to keep it cool, *real* cool, herself.

"Focus, Elsa," she says on her way to the bedroom

closet. "Get a grip," she warns herself while choosing an outfit to wear to the cookout later today. "Just cool it," she insists. And breathes. And shakes out some knots in her shoulder muscles.

Cool, yes. That's what she thinks as she lifts a cropped royal-blue V-neck tank top and sets it on her bed. She looks at it, tips her head, then snaps her fingers as she spins around and steps quickly back to the closet. "Yes!" she says, lifting out a khaki wraparound skirt with a utility-patch pocket at the hip. It's just the right look—cool ... and keeping things loose.

"Easy does it," Elsa tells her reflection as she heads to the shower. "Easy does it."

All right, all right. Blame it on the burrito. It's the one thing making Jason's stay at Sullivan's place worth it. Sort of. Sitting outside beneath the umbrella at the teak patio table, he slides over his take-out breakfast. The food truck stationed near the Sea Spray Beach entrance has the best eats around—and he just swung by there to fuel up.

Now he's lifting that breakfast burrito. It's filled with scrambled egg, sliced avocado and cilantro leaves. Not to mention melted cheddar cheese with sour cream and hot sauce.

"Let the day begin," he says before biting into the burrito. He opens a sketchpad, too, and picks up a black marker while eating. The owners at Beach Box are waiting for a kitchen revision. They want the tiny room to at least *appear* bigger, and Jason's got just the trick. After another bite of burrito and a few sips of hot coffee, he begins sketching. Vaulting the ceiling will work wonders. As he thinks out the details, his hand is busy rough-sketching the room. A white beadboard ceiling will keep the charm while the vaulting adds space.

Halfway through sketching, though, he's interrupted by his cell phone.

"Eva," he says around a mouthful of burrito while reading her incoming text. "You're finally after me." He scrolls the message, which goes on. And on.

Making batches of chicken cutlets this morning. You at Sea Spray tonight? Can bring you a platter for the week.

Then, nothing. Oh, but Jason knows. Waiting for his answer, Eva's probably drumming her fingers on some countertop. Tapping a foot, too. He rereads her lines. Bring him a platter, like hell. Because what else will be on that plate? Judgment at his leaving home for two weeks now? Annoyance? Bossiness?

Problem is, there's no arguing with his sister-in-law. She's *always* got Maris' back. So there'll probably be an ass-whupping on that platter, too. Along with those cutlets he could definitely live on.

Okay, Eva wins. With a reluctant breath, Jason types back, *Yeah, I'll be here*, then gives the address.

And gets back to work. In the client's preliminary sketch, he adds a few design details. Crisscrossed oars hang over the doorway. Gooseneck lamps shine from a high wall shelf. When his cell phone actually rings then, he picks it up without looking at it.

"Eva," Jason begins.

"No," a man's voice clarifies. "Not Eva. *Cliff*, Jason."

"Cliff." Jason sets his marker down and leans back in the deck chair. The day's going to be a hot one; the sun's burning off a haze over the beach beyond the dunes. Already, umbrellas and chairs are staked out on the sand there for the Labor Day crowd. "What's up, guy?"

"You busy this morning?"

Jason looks at his sketches, his wristwatch. "Catching up on revising a client's prints."

"Today?"

"Yeah. Backlogged here."

"Have the newspaper handy?"

"*The Day?* Got it right in front of me." Jason pulls it out from beneath his take-out bag.

Cliff wastes no time, then. He's already directing Jason—before Jason even clears away his food wrappings. "Open it to page nine," Cliff orders. "It's in the second section."

Jason lays the newspaper out flat on the patio table and turns the pages. He passes the national news, opinion page, and is in the town news section. "*Page nine*," he says, turning one more page. And there it is; he can't miss it. Surely this half-page, full-color spread is what Cliff is all worked up about. "Whoa, Raines. Are you saying what I *think* you're saying?" Jason asks into the phone.

eleven

CLIFF HURRIES DOWN THE METAL steps of the Stony Point Beach Association trailer and heads straight for his car. This is a surprise turn in his day, that's for sure. Now he has to meet Jason—right away—and can't keep him waiting. So Cliff peels out of the gravel parking lot, his car tires spitting stones behind him as he books it down the beach road.

But first? Some business. He parks curbside near the guard shack. The train trestle's just beyond it, and Nick's on duty over there. A beach umbrella is staked into the mulch at Nick's post. A walkie-talkie and water bottle sit atop the rock wall beside it. Nick sees Cliff and crosses the street—clipboard in hand.

"Yo, boss!" Nick calls out as he trots to the guard shack.

Cliff's half bent into his car trunk and lifts out a megaphone and an extra *Commissioner* hat. "Want to earn a holiday bonus today?"

81

"For Labor Day? Sure. I have to be here anyway, might as well make some extra dough."

Cliff shoves the megaphone and hat into Nick's arms. Then Cliff fishes around for the keys to the trailer and supply shed, as well as his *Commissioner* badge. "You're in charge," he says, dropping the things on top of Nick's now-tottering armload of official commissioner accoutrements.

"What?"

"You're in charge. Anything goes haywire," Cliff informs him as he slams shut his trunk, "it's all on you."

"Why?" Nick shifts the items in his arms. "What's happening?"

"I have some important business to take care of this morning, then I'm off to a car show."

"*Wait!* Wait, wait, wait. Folks get wacky here on the holidays, you know. Pushing the limits. Moving the speed barriers. Practically hauling their refrigerators on the beach—in *hidden* coolers—when there's no food allowed. And all that does is bring the yellow jackets. Heck, ordinances are broken with no regard now that summer's coming to a close."

"Oh, I *know*. And you've been well trained in how to handle rule breakers, Nicholas."

Nick sets the megaphone just inside the guard shack. "What if I need assistance?" he asks, pinning the *Commissioner* badge on his shirt now.

"I'm out of reach." Cliff squints through the sunlight to Nick standing there in his guard uniform. "You work with the other guards. Jim's patrolling the beach. He can lend a hand, if necessary. But *you're* the boss, Nicholas," Cliff says while hurrying to his car. Once he settles in behind the wheel and takes off, he calls through the open window, "I'm counting on you!"

Nick half trots behind his car as Cliff heads toward the stone trestle. When he pulls into the shady tunnel beneath it, he hears Nick's voice echo behind him. *"I'll do you proud, boss!"*

Saluting out the window, Cliff turns his car onto Shore Road and gives it the gas.

~

Blue Heron Jewelers is located in a pale silver cottage. Expansive display windows have replaced the cottage's original windows. The jewelry store's entrance door is beneath a dusty-blue awning. There's a short staircase leading to that entrance—which is where Jason stands later that morning.

And waits.

With his arms crossed, he leans against the handrail of that staircase. And checks his watch. And looks for Cliff's approaching car. The street is busy—no surprise. This block of run-down coastal cottages has been renovated into a retail mecca filled with boutiques and small shops. Tourists and locals alike frequent the stores here: a knitting cottage; a gift shop shanty; a lamp-and-clock bungalow; clothing boutiques in shingled shacks; a tiny hut of miniature seafaring vessels and schooners crafted of the finest woods; the jewelers.

But no Cliff in sight.

So Jason checks his watch again—it's just before ten. While waiting, he also pulls a ripped-out newspaper ad from his pocket and reads it closely.

Summer ends, but love doesn't have to.
Continue your season of love with an engagement ring.
Labor Day Only!
Blue Heron Jewelers Diamond Ring Blowout Sale.
Buy today, take home today.

In the ad, fine scrollwork frames the name and address of the jewelry store. Above it all, there's a precious gemstone image. The photo is of a casual cluster of rings topped with glimmering diamonds. All of it must've spoken to Cliff. He surely pictured one of those diamond rings in a black velvet box—a box that Elsa would one day open.

At the sound of a car horn, Jason looks up to see Cliff getting out of his parked car. He's wearing layered tees: a dark short-sleeve over a white long-sleeve—those sleeves requisitely shoved up. All of it over gray jeans and suede navy slip-on sneakers. Cliff's hair looks damp from a shower; his face is unshaved.

"Jason!" Cliff calls out as he approaches from the curb. "Glad you could make it."

Jason steps onto the sidewalk and shakes Cliff's hand. "Big day for you?"

"Could be. Sorry I'm late," Cliff tells him. "Had to take a quick shower after my morning workout with Matt. You waiting long?"

"Few minutes." Jason glances at the newspaper clipping he still holds. "And I have to tell you, this all seems pretty sudden," he says. "You *sure* about this?"

"Now hang on a second. Let's not forget who told me to get Elsa a gemstone last *fall*." Cliff points a finger at Jason.

"Yeah, but from my end now? It looks like once you got word that Fenwick's romancing DeLuca ..."

Cliff crosses his arms in front of him. "You going to finish that sentence?"

Jason blows out a breath. "Just saying. You *really* sure about this?" he asks, holding up the diamond ring ad.

"No, I'm not. That's why I need your help."

"To be honest, I wasn't *that* surprised to hear from you today. Because Maris called me last night and told me about your parking lot conversation."

Cliff shakes his head. "I should've known."

When Jason motions him to follow, they turn and climb the stairs to the jewelry store. "So what's gotten into you?" Jason asks over his shoulder. "The guys were just razzin' you at the campsite Saturday. You know, telling you to put a ring on it. To lock it down with Elsa. But they were just having some fun. You don't *have* to do this."

"Maybe I do, though." Cliff stops at the store's entrance. "Maybe this Labor Day sale is the push I needed." He opens the store door then. "Let's go in," he says.

⌒⌒

They get a little caught off guard inside the store. A jeweler approaches and asks Jason if he's ring shopping for a special lady. When Jason hesitates, the jeweler looks to Cliff and mentions how nice it is for the father of the groom to assist.

"No, no," Jason explains. He motions to Cliff beside him. "No relation. And it's *this* sly fox who's doing the shopping today."

85

Together then, they browse the selection of engagement rings. Tray after velvet tray is pulled out from the display cases. Something happens, though, as they scrutinize the rings. Jason can't miss it. Cliff starts out all pumped, but fades fast. He hesitates. Says the diamonds are too small. Or too flashy. Or not what he had in mind for Elsa's hand.

And he's right.

When Cliff looks to Jason about one, or another, Jason gives a slight shake of his head. Just enough for Cliff to see the particular ring's *not* a DeLuca diamond. The more rings they consider—oval, round and square—the more Cliff wavers.

After a half hour of looking, Jason pulls him aside. "Listen, Cliff. This is big, buying a ring. And these things take time."

"I've got the time today."

"Well maybe you're just *window*-shopping today. Because if you're not feeling it, you're not feeling it."

"But I *am* feeling it, Jason. Just not feeling anything I've seen." Cliff glances to the jeweler waiting at the counter. "Let's try one more tray."

"Okay," Jason agrees as they return to the diamond counter. "I've got an idea, too. It might help."

"An idea? Like what?" Cliff asks.

"Watch."

When the jeweler reaches down for another black-velvet tray of rings, Jason stops him. "Go up a tier," he quietly says.

And when the jeweler looks to Cliff, Cliff nods.

Which is all it takes.

Because there, on the upgraded tray set on the glass

counter, is the ring. Oh, Jason sees it. Sees Cliff reach for it, too. Yes, it's *thee* one—no doubt about it.

"That's a classic three-stone, emerald-cut ring," the jeweler says.

"And Elsa is a classic," Cliff muses as he lifts the substantial, yet understated ring.

"It's a timeless design." The jeweler points out the diamonds. "The emerald-cut stone, in the center, is flanked by a diamond baguette on each side. All set in eighteen-karat yellow gold."

Cliff holds the ring at arm's length. Gradually, he brings the ring closer. And turns it. Squints at it. And finally looks at Jason beside him. "What do you think?" he asks, his voice low.

Jason takes the ring and eyes it closely before giving it back to Cliff. "I think you couldn't do any finer, Commissioner."

Just like that, something comes over Cliff. Jason can't miss it. Cliff's actually happy. And relieved. His face lights up as the jeweler explains the diamond quality, and shows him the accompanying gold wedding band. It glimmers beside the engagement ring.

Jason lets out a low whistle at the sight of it. Shakes Cliff's hand, too. "Those are legit, guy. You're doing right by Elsa. Top shelf," Jason says, nodding to the rings. "I'll treat you to lunch to celebrate."

Cliff steps up to the plate, then. He seals the *Buy today, take home today* deal as they wait for the rings to be polished, prepped and set in a velvet box. Cliff did what he set out to do. He's committing to Elsa and means business. It shows in his swagger now. He's satisfied with the ring choice, but there's a seriousness in him, too.

Yes, Jason sees it—Cliff's *not* taking this lightly. Not one bit.

Which inspires Jason. He'd done some browsing himself the past hour as Cliff deliberated diamonds. So when Cliff is being rung out; and asked about a gemstone protection plan; and given a coupon for a future purchase, Jason wanders to another counter. He hears the jeweler telling Cliff that they'll email all the receipts, too, and put him on a mailing list for upcoming sales.

While all this is going down—and Cliff is giving out his email address and tallying his receipts—Jason motions to another salesperson off to the side. Her silver hair is cut in a severe bob; a light jacket covers her fitted sheath. "Can you come over here?" Jason asks.

The woman gives a single, decisive nod and approaches the glass case where Jason's standing. "What can I do for you, sir?"

Jason points to a pair of earrings beneath the glass. When he saw them earlier, he knew he couldn't leave here without them. "I'll take those," he says.

"They're beautiful." The saleswoman sets the earrings on a velvet tray. "For someone special?"

Jason touches the earrings and thinks of Maris. Thinks of how much more than special she is. "Yeah. She's pretty special," he says, pulling out his wallet. "Can you wrap those for me?"

twelve

IN THE LIGHT OF DAY, Rockport's a different world.

Or at least, Shane's home is, Celia thinks. Holding Aria in her arms later that morning, she waits outside on the deck. It gives a clear view of the harbor, and the docks—where there are stacks and stacks of lobster traps. Lobster boats are out on the water, too. Seagulls swoop and cry. Their guttural calls suit the wildness of the ragged coast. And there's the air. She can't stop inhaling its sharp saltiness.

"Look, Aria," Celia says, pointing to the harbor. The blue water sparkles beneath the morning sun. "*Ocean stars,*" she whispers.

Just then, Shane wheels Aria's stroller out through the slider. "Ready?" he asks, lifting the stroller off the deck to a narrow walkway beside his shingled home.

"I am." Celia follows behind him. As they walk, she hears music. A neighbor has a radio tuned to some Labor Day weekend countdown of the top rock songs. But Celia doesn't see anyone as she carries the baby to the front yard.

Which is when a voice calls out, "There you are, Shane!"

Celia looks and sees the neighbor she'd talked to last week—when she was here with only Aria. Dressed in a tee and jeans, and a baseball cap over dark hair, the man's painting a picket fence in his side yard.

"Bruno," Shane calls back, veering in his direction.

"Watered your window boxes, just the way you like," Bruno tells him, paintbrush in hand. "And hey," he adds, turning down the nearby boom-box radio. "You found her!"

"That I did." Shane turns to Celia still holding the baby behind him. "Guess you two met last time, right?"

Celia nods, walking closer. "Good to see you again, Bruno."

"Ayuh." Bruno reaches over and clasps one of Aria's tiny hands. "And hello again, sweetheart," he tells the baby.

Right away, Celia notices something she'd never have known if not for this visit. As Shane and Bruno catch up, and laugh and shake hands, she glimpses Shane's other life. His life at home. With his neighbors. A life that's casual and easy. He's got good people around him. Looking out for him. Caring.

"We're headed up the road apiece, for a walk on the docks," Shane's telling Bruno. "Showing Celia and the little one around."

Bruno looks at the blue sky. "Great day for it." He eyes Celia and Shane then. "Hey. Want a photo?"

"What?" Shane asks.

"A picture. You guys look nice. I'll take a picture near your house."

"Oh, that's okay," Celia says, shifting Aria in her arms.

"We don't want to trouble you."

"Get outta here." Bruno just waves them off. "I gotta record this for posterity."

"Record what?" Shane asks.

Cuffing his shoulder, Bruno tells him, "The happiness on your mug."

To which Shane shakes his head. "Cee," he says then, pulling his cell phone from his pocket. "Let's do it."

～

Easier said than done.

After Shane gives Bruno the phone, they move in front of Shane's gray-shingled house. Celia adjusts her off-the-shoulder peasant blouse, and lifts her brown-tinted tortoise sunglasses to the top of her head. A sea breeze blows wisps of her hair. With Aria in her arms, Celia turns sideways so the baby's somewhat facing the camera, too. Aria coos and wraps her fingers around the thick gold necklace Celia wears.

Meanwhile, Shane stands beside Celia. He straightens the pocket tee over his cuffed-canvas shorts, first. Next he puts an arm around her waist and holds her close. Celia's still fussing, though. She shifts her stance, then adjusts Shane's newsboy cap—tipping it back somewhat. And clears her throat. And lifts Aria a little higher.

"Celia." Shane bends close to her ear. "*All you have to do is smile*," he says into a slight kiss to the side of her head.

When Celia leans into him and gives a knowing laugh then, Bruno gets the shot.

～

The harbor docks spark a memory for Celia.

As she walks them with Shane now, wood planks creaking beneath their feet, she can't believe she was here just a week ago doing the same thing. That she'd driven to Maine on a whim—which is so unlike her. It was the day of Neil's Memorial Mass and she didn't want to sit in church all morning. She'd end up thinking of Sal—and his funeral in that very church—and feeling sad.

No, she couldn't do it. Instead, she hit the highway. Shane, after all, had told her that if Stony Point ever got to be too much, come to Maine.

So she did.

And she missed seeing him by mere minutes. Oh, she *saw* him—but was too late. With Aria strapped close in her baby sling, Celia stood on the docks and watched Shane off in the distance. Watched him board the lobster boat and head out to sea. That day? She thought it was the end for them. Shane tossing his duffel aboard ship was a sign. He went his way and she went hers as she turned away, walked with Aria off the dock and drove back to Connecticut.

She accepted that whatever they'd started up was over.

She even persisted in that thought once a note arrived from Shane days later, a note saying he *saw* her on the docks. Oh, she'd answered that note quickly, writing that it was better this way—making a clean break. That there was too much salt air between them. Miles and hours of it.

Now? Now there are *no* miles between them.

Now? Walking the harbor docks *with* Shane is the moment she'd sought a week ago. The day is as beautiful as a dream. She and Shane walk side by side. She pushes Aria's stroller and can see the baby's feet pumping, and her head turning. Aria's invigorated by the scents and sights here. Celia reaches down and adjusts the baby's sunbonnet, then keeps walking with Shane.

"Look." He turns and points beyond the docks. "There's my house. Over there. It's the last thing I look for when the boat leaves the harbor. Always say a little prayer, too, that I'll see that house again."

"Your home means a lot to you."

"It does."

"And what's that?" Celia asks, pointing to a shed right *on* the docks. The shed's shingles are painted green. Weathered lobster buoys are strung from salty rope on a side wall. An overhang in the front creates a porch-like area. There are roped fishing globes dangling from rafters there; fishing net drapes along that front wall. Beneath the overhang, a couple of old wooden lobster pots are stacked near the doorway.

"That there is a little coffee shop for the fishermen, lobster crews. Wait here, I'll go grab us some java."

While she waits, Celia wheels the stroller past a few boats in their slips. The pull of the tide has the vessels creak against the pilings. A seagull sits atop a dock post and ruffles its wings when she passes. And the sky? It's as blue as the sea, with more gulls soaring overhead. In the distance, a bell buoy clangs. Celia stops and closes her eyes. Feels the sun on her face. Is so glad she's here.

In a moment, she crouches down beside the stroller. She strokes Aria's silky brown hair. "*Smell the salt air, sweetie?*"

One of his crewmates sits on a stool near the coffee shed's front door.

"Shiloh," Shane says. "What's happening?"

"Killing time, bub," Shiloh tells him. He's wearing some faded *Halibut* tee over jeans and has a booted foot propped on an old lobster trap. "Sittin' high and dry with that busted engine."

"No shit. How long we off the water, do you think?"

Shiloh gives a shrug. "Hard tellin' not knowin'. Boy, you missed a doozy when the fuel pump quit. Captain was in a wicked bad mood."

"I'll bet," Shane says, leaning on a rickety railing between the shed and the water.

"What about you?" Shiloh stands and nods off to the distance. "I *knew* it, man. A few weeks away and you're in love."

Shane looks over his shoulder toward Celia, then gives Shiloh a shove. "What do you know about love, punk?" he asks, then brushes past him into the shed. After pouring two hot coffees and leaving a few bucks in the tin kitty, Shane grabs the cardboard cups and shoulders open the shed door. "If you see the captain around," he tells Shiloh, "ask him to give me some notice before we head out."

Shiloh looks back from where he's leaning on the railing overlooking the harbor. "Will do, Bradford. Take care of yourself."

～

Shane continues on toward Celia. He sees her talking to the baby. The morning sunlight glints off Celia's auburn hair. And she looks really rested today—like nothing's on her mind but the summer morning.

"Here you go," he says, handing her a cup of hot coffee. Shane pushes the stroller now as they walk a stretch of dock reaching out over the harbor water. They stop at a bend in the dock, where there's a little lookout spot. A few dinghies are moored nearby. Piles of coiled fishing rope are scattered about.

"This is so nice, having coffee out here," Celia tells him.

"Well. It's lobsterman coffee. So it's pretty strong."

She nods, lifts her cup and takes a swallow—which gets her sputtering. And trying to hide her wince.

Shane laughs, raising his cup in a toast. "It's an acquired taste," he assures her.

"Got it. I'll take small sips."

"You know, that coffee shed is like a communal café on the docks." As he talks, Shane leans on the weathered railing. The scent of the sea permeates the air. "Whoever gets here first in the morning starts a fresh pot before boarding a boat. As more of the crews come in, someone makes a new pot when the coffee runs down."

"You've got it down to a science," Celia remarks.

"We do. Some guys bring in doughnuts. Or a box of muffins, maybe, from the local grocer. Sometimes there'll be extra wrapped sandwiches in the fridge for anyone needing a lunch." Shane sips his coffee and looks over toward the green shed. "Don't kid yourself. Lobstering gets pretty cutthroat. Territorial and all that. It's a rowdy biz, for sure." He turns then, tips up his cap and faces Celia. "But at the same time? We look out for each other."

He can tell, too, that Celia likes what she hears. And sees. And even sips. There's no sadness in her eyes. No fatigue. The trip's good for her.

Minutes later, Shiloh approaches on his way off the docks. Shane introduces him to Celia and Aria. They talk some, have a few laughs, before Shiloh moves on. Shane and Celia finish their coffee then, before continuing along the dock. When they near a pile of coiled rope set against a pier post, Shane stops. He leans over and picks up the end of the rope. Beside them, the harbor water laps easy. A breath of salty breeze lifts off it. Celia stands close. Aria's tucked in the stroller beside her. Shane glances to Celia before unwinding more of the rope from the coil. He wraps that rope loosely around her shoulders and around himself, too.

"Got you in the bight," he says.

"Bight?"

Shane nods, and gives the rope a shake. "It's a loop of rope ... a slack part of the line. Now, *entanglement*," he goes on, tugging her closer, "is a really dangerous risk of lobstering. Get *caught* in the bight as the pot goes in? Get tripped up in that uncoiling rope? It'll take you to the bottom of the sea right with the pot." He touches the tip of the rope to Celia's exposed shoulder. "Scary stuff."

Celia watches him silently. Her sunglasses, propped on top of her head, hold back wisps of hair blowing in the breeze. But it's her eyes that get to him. They tear up as she strokes Shane's jaw. He can't miss it, some sudden emotion on her face, in her tender touch.

"*We're caught in a bight, too,*" she whispers, taking the end of the rope from his hand and tugging him closer.

"Yep." Shane lightly kisses her, and presses back a strand of her auburn hair. His low voice turns serious then. "All tangled up."

thirteen

AFTER RING SHOPPING AND LUNCH with Cliff, Jason takes a detour.

The first thing he notices when parking in front of his gabled house at Stony Point is that the grass is getting high.

Hell, who's he kidding. The *first* thing he notices is that he actually *misses* his house. As the sun rises in the noontime sky, he takes in the sight of the dark silvery shingles. And the shrubs lining the side yard. Vines of wild roses wind through the bushes. Beyond the house, the bluff faces a distant Long Island Sound.

Oh yeah, he misses being home.

So he gets out of his SUV and crosses the overgrown front lawn. He knows he shouldn't. It's Labor Day, and he *should* be getting ready for work tomorrow. *Should* be one hundred percent on top of his piled-up papers for the busy week ahead. Yet all he's managed so far today is some sketching on the Beach Box project during his burrito breakfast.

Then Cliff called.

So now? Jason *should* be back at Sullivan's place.

Should be answering his pending emails.

Should be getting his prints together.

Should be getting his wardrobe in order for *Castaway Cottage* filming tomorrow.

Should be checking off that work itinerary.

But he isn't.

Instead, on the way back from lunch with Cliff, Jason swung in here and is walking up the steps of his own front porch. And is knocking on the wooden door.

And waits there, knowing he'll just have to burn the midnight oil tonight.

～

Jason hears the approaching growl on the other side of the door. Oh, if Maddy only knew it was him. Moments later, Maris shushes the dog and opens the door.

"Jason?" She stands there, half behind the door, and squints at him. "What are you doing here?"

"Have to ask you something." As he says it, Jason clearly sees that she doesn't sweep that door open. Doesn't ask him inside. Instead, she only shifts—still half behind the door—and glances at the impatient dog at her feet. Then Maris looks back down the dark hallway when the microwave timer beeps inside.

"Wait right there. Right *there*, Jason," she warns him. "That's my lunch beeping."

"Maris, come on," he says as the dog presses against the screen door now.

"We had a deal," Maris reminds him. "You can't come inside until you're *living* here again." She unlatches the screen door and lets the dog out. "Talk to Maddy instead."

As if Jason has a choice. First, Maris closes the heavy wood door behind her. And second, Maddy is so happy circling around his legs, and wagging her tail, and licking at his hands, that she gets Jason laughing. He bends low and slaps her flanks. "You miss me, Maddy?" he asks. "*Glad someone does.*"

The German shepherd gives his face a sloppy lick. Which is when Jason notices something.

"What's this?" he asks, pulling back and touching her collar. But before he can inspect it, Maris distracts him. Managing two plates and a bottled water, she steps out onto the porch.

"Tomato-and-cheese sandwiches on whole-grain bread," she says, handing Jason a plate. She sits herself down on one of two cushioned chairs, sets the water on a small table between them and digs into her lunch. "The tomatoes are from Elsa's garden," she says around the food. "She dropped off a basket earlier."

Jason sits in the other chair, sets his plate beside the begonia plant on that table and lifts half his warm sandwich.

"Figured I better make you one, too. Otherwise you'd be eating half of mine," Maris says, still eating. "I put lots of mayo on it."

"And I'm not about to pass this up," Jason tells her, biting into the gooey sandwich. "Even though I just had lunch with Cliff."

"Cliff?"

Jason nods and fills her in on how he met up with Cliff at

the jewelry store. "He wanted help buying Elsa a diamond ring."

"Wait. He went ring shopping—*today?* That was fast! He only told me last night he was thinking of proposing."

"He's really serious about it."

"Did he actually *buy* a ring?"

"A stunner. Here," Jason says, pulling his cell phone from his cargo shorts pocket. "I took a picture."

Maris leans over and pulls his arm closer. "Oh, my word! Now *that's* a diamond!"

"Might've broke the bank for him."

"And he roped you into going with him?"

"First thing this morning. Think he needed moral support." Jason returns his phone to his pocket, then presses the rest of that sandwich half into his mouth. "Big Labor Day sale at Blue Heron Jewelers. But you can *not* tell anyone." As he says it, Jason lifts the other half of his sandwich and motions it between them. "I promised Cliff this is where it ends."

With her mouth full, Maris nods and crosses her heart. "So what'd you want to ask me?"

"I'm getting to it." Mid-chew, Jason points to Maddy gnawing on a squeak bone on the porch floor. "But first. What's that on her neck?"

"It's a light-up collar, Jason."

"For what?"

"For safety."

"Safety? On the … beach?"

"Yes. It gives her visibility at night. And it's USB rechargeable."

"So I have to charge a dog collar now?"

"Doesn't it seem like a good idea? I mean," Maris says, unscrewing her bottled water and taking a swig, "we have that big charging station in the kitchen. And a light-up collar will keep Maddy visible in the dark."

"But if I'm walking her, it's like the collar's shining on me. And I like to keep a low profile, Maris." Jason reaches for the water bottle she set down. "I can't believe you bought a megawatt collar."

Maris turns up her hands. "That's what happens when you leave. Decisions get made solo."

"Fine. And you have another one to make now." Jason takes a swallow of the water and wipes the back of his hand to his mouth. "You free this afternoon?"

"For what?"

"A date. A little Labor Day date."

"Hm." Maris glances back toward the door. "I have like one page left in the chapter I'm writing."

"I hear you. Got a pile of work stuff waiting for me, too." Jason stands and pulls his keys from his pocket. "But I'd rather ditch all that for an hour or so and go on a date."

"Me, too. You know something?" Maris asks with a slow shake of her head. "We see each other more now than we did living together." Standing then, she picks up the two crumb-covered dishes. "Do I have to change?"

"No." Jason steps back and eyes her. She's wearing her olive V-neck tank top over a faded denim skirt and flat leather sandals. Her hair is pulled back in a low twist; her gold star pendant glimmers on her neck. "No, you look perfect." He reaches over and touches her jaw. "Beautiful, actually."

They end up a few beach towns over. The main drag is lined with tiny cottages stacked one after the other. Seasonal shops sell tubes and towels and cheap sunglasses. There's an ice-cream hut down the block, and a place called The Beach Shanty serves fried dough dusted with powdered sugar or covered in cheese and tomato sauce.

But Jason bypasses all that for the arcade.

"I thought this place closed up last summer," Maris says after they park.

"It did. New owners managed to revive it. Got it open by the Fourth of July this year."

Maris looks at the families and teens milling about this hot end-of-summer day. People are dressed in tees and shorts; flip-flops and sundresses. The arcade apparently is the place to be. Buzzers buzz; bells ding; whistles blow.

Their spontaneous date is jam-packed, too. It's an hour of Skee-Ball and electronic darts. At the mini bowling lane, Jason wins her a plastic pen. "You know, to pen your masterpiece," he tells her. They race each other in padded bumper cars and finally end up at a vintage fortune-telling machine. When Jason deposits coins in the cabinet's money slot, a mechanical gypsy behind the glass turns her head toward them. Her glittery silver earrings shine; her eyes slowly blink; her hands wave over a crystal ball. After that, she nods and lifts their fortune cards. Jason takes those cards when the gypsy drops them down a narrow chute. He folds Maris' card and gives it to her, telling her to put it in her purse.

"Don't you want to know what the gypsy predicts?" she asks.

"I do." He takes Maris' hand and heads to the door. "Over a drink on the way back."

～

The Sand Bar is custom-made for a day like this. While the early afternoon sun pulses outside, the bar inside is dark and cool. Maris picks some slow summertime bluesy number on the jukebox. Jason shoots the shit with Patrick at the bar.

"Where've you been hiding yourself, my friend?" the bartender asks while drawing a draft beer. "Haven't seen you around."

"Eh, you know." Jason glances at Maris approaching the bar now. "Here and there."

Problem is, Jason knows, he's been mostly *there*.

Mostly away from *here* as he's been living the past two weeks at Ted Sullivan's. And it's taking a toll.

"Keepin' your guy in line, I hope?" Patrick asks Maris.

"Doing my best," she tells him before she and Jason take their drinks to a booth in the shadowy bar. Jason shoves open the sticking window there, and sits back in their booth. They linger and talk a little. "Let's read our fortunes," Maris says, digging hers out of her purse and sliding it across the wood table. "You read mine to me, and I'll read yours."

Jason takes her fortune ticket and unfolds it. "Remember to bring an umbrella. When it rains, it pours."

"Oh, great." Maris lifts her wineglass for a sip.

"What?"

"Don't you get it? The message means that something

bad's going to happen. When it rains, it pours is *never* a good thing."

"Maris—"

"No, Jason. So what's it saying? That I won't finish the book? Or … or some pipe will burst at home, and it'll rain all over the ceilings and make a big mess?"

"You're overthinking it." Jason lifts the ticket and reads it again. "Just bring your umbrella when you go out."

"Fine. Let me read yours now."

Jason pulls his ticket from his pocket and hands it to her. He leans back as she unfolds it.

"*Huh*," Maris says. "Interesting."

"What's it say?"

"Keep waiting. Good things come to those who wait."

"*Son of a bitch*," Jason barely utters under his breath. It's as if that mechanical gypsy knew, didn't she? Jason looks away, then at Maris across the table. A strand of her brown hair has come loose from its twist. Her brown eyes watch his.

"What?" she asks.

"Nothing," he says. That's not what he *thinks*, though. Because damn it, that gypsy-behind-glass was right. Lately, all he's been doing is waiting—to come back home, to be living with his beautiful wife. He just doesn't know how the hell to get Maris to say the word. To tell him it's time. To end the wait.

"That's so vague—good things come to those who wait. It could work for anyone." Maris sets down the slip of paper. "Silly fortunes, huh?"

"Yeah." Jason sips from his glass of beer, then lifts his fortune and reads it himself.

"Listen." Maris reaches across the table and lightly touches his face, beneath his eyes. "You look tired."

Jason wraps his fingers around her hand and presses them to his lips. "Little bit, I am."

"*We should probably go then*," she whispers.

"In a few minutes."

"Just a few," she says, squinting at him. "Because I know you're backlogged with work. Don't you lie to me, Jason Barlow," she adds when he leans back, wincing. "You really need to take care of it *and* get some rest tonight. You'll be filming tomorrow at the Fenwicks'."

But Jason knows. It's not the workload tiring him. It's that wait. It's seeing Maris for only snatches of time, like today, then wasting the rest of his day without her.

It's wanting something you once had—and not knowing if you can get it back.

～

When they drive beneath the trestle later, Nick's standing guard.

"Hey, hey, it's the Barlows," he says when he approaches Maris' passenger-side window.

Jason leans over the front seat toward him. "I hear the commish left you in charge today."

"Sure did. Guess he had some business to take care of, then he's off to a car show with his son."

"Writing many tickets?" Maris asks.

"Oh, man." Nick adjusts the *Commissioner* cap he's wearing. "Folks are pressing their luck. Food on the beach. Speeding golf carts. Skateboards on the boardwalk. Got

105

enough fines to keep the budget in the black," he says, tapping the top of the SUV when a car pulls in behind Jason.

So they wave him off and Jason drives the narrow roads. They pass some teens trekking to the beach; inflated tubes are hooked over their shoulders. For the few sandy blocks, Jason doesn't say much. Finally, he parks at the curb in front of his house and idles there as Maris unbuckles her seatbelt.

"Thanks, babe," she says, turning to him. "I had fun."

Jason watches her for a long second. "Me, too." He leans across the seat and lightly kisses her. Afterward, she tips her head, smiles and touches his jaw, then gets out. He says no more. When she glances back at him before closing her door, he just lifts a hand and casually waves.

～

Maris walks across the lawn toward the front porch. The sun beats hot; the salt air is still. It's early enough, almost three, that she can get that chapter done. But she turns around when she hears Jason.

"Wait! Maris! I almost forgot," he calls out through the open passenger window. He's leaning across the front seat and waving her back. "I got you something," he tells her when she nears.

"What?" She bends down and looks inside the SUV. "When?"

"This morning. When I was out with Cliff." He hands her a wrapped box.

"Jason!" She looks from him to the box.

"Open it."

Again she looks at Jason. He's leaning forward now. An arm is looped over the steering wheel as he watches her. So standing at the curb, Maris peels off the blue wrapping paper to a velvet box. When she opens it, she slightly gasps. "*Jason! They're beautiful,*" she whispers, gently touching a pair of earrings. The stones are blue topaz mounted in white-gold stud baskets.

"They reminded me of our beach day yesterday," Jason says. "Of that blue sky we sat under."

Now? Now Maris looks through the open window and across the seat at him. Is she mistaken, or did she hear something in his voice. Longing? Regret? Regardless, some emotion was there. So she's glad for her dark sunglasses, and the way they cover her suddenly tear-filled eyes.

fourteen

"Am I early?" Elsa calls up to Mitch while climbing his deck stairs that afternoon. She's carrying her watermelon fruit bowl and a few garden-fresh tomatoes in an insulated tote. A leopard-print crossbody cell-phone purse is strapped over her shoulder.

Mitch turns from where he's watering potted marigolds. He's wearing a loose button-down over linen pants. Leather two-strap sandals are on his feet; his hair is pulled back in a short ponytail. "You are right on time, actually," he says, setting down the dripping watering can.

"But nobody's here." Elsa lifts off her cell-phone purse and glances around the empty deck.

"Except you." As he says it, Mitch reaches for her tote. "Shall I bring this inside?"

"No. I made up a fruit bowl, so we can have some now." Again, Elsa glances around while slowly sitting at the deck table. "A cool hors d'oeuvre before dinner?"

Mitch agrees. He brings out plates and napkins while Elsa removes her watermelon fruit bowl from the tote. Before sitting, Mitch also cranks up the patio umbrella.

"That's better," he says, sitting across from Elsa now.

Elsa nods and pulls her chair in closer. Tin-can wildflower bouquets are scattered atop the deck railing behind Mitch. And a cluster of tall rope-wrapped jars hold unlit candles on the table. She looks from it all, to Mitch. "Is Carol around?" she asks.

"No," he begins while scooping a spoonful of fruit chunks from the watermelon. "She's working. Stationed with her flower cart over in New London."

Elsa gives a quick finger-snap. "That's right. She mentioned that the other day at Maris'."

"Yes, well … Carol's a big hit in these beach towns."

"I can see why. Her flowers are so charming. I mean, tin-can bouquets? And the glass bottle arrangements?" Elsa touches one bowed with a burlap strip and filled with sprigs of lavender. "So she won't be joining us at all?"

"Not today," Mitch says, spearing a melon chunk.

Which means, for now? It's just the two of them. Elsa spoons fruit onto her plate and nibbles on berries and melon pieces. She and Mitch make small talk. But it's a little strained— Elsa's mention of the nice weather, and Mitch's compliments on the fruit bowl. The ruckus all around them on the beach only amplifies their awkwardness. Voices are easily chatting and laughing; children are splashing and making sandcastles; couples walk right past the Fenwick cottage as they stroll the beach. Waves lap onshore and seagulls soar overhead.

Yet up on the deck of this elevated cottage? Muted quiet.

"So … your renovation moves into full swing this week," Elsa says, glancing at the imposing Fenwick cottage.

"It surely does." Mitch lifts a sandaled foot to his knee. "We'll be filming tomorrow with Jason. Some demo kicks in and away we go."

"Well." Elsa clears her throat. "Before you fire up the grill, can I help you get *ready* for tomorrow?" She lifts her cat-eye sunglasses to the top of her head, then glances to the cottage slider. "You must have things to pack before the crews arrive."

"Now that's mighty nice of you, Elsa. But today's a holiday, meant for relaxing."

"And we *will* relax. Once the cookout commences. In the meantime, many hands make light work …"

"Now that you mention it, I *do* have some items on the porch that oughta come off the wall. Hate to have them shatter with swinging sledgehammers and such," Mitch says, then nods to her blue cropped tank top and wraparound skirt. "But you're not dressed for—"

Before he's even finished with his thought, Elsa's standing—ready to help. Ready to be busy instead of uneasily waiting. Ready to do *anything* until the other guests arrive. So Mitch carries her insulated tote and watermelon fruit bowl inside to the kitchen.

"Now what in heavens is *that* sweet creation?" Elsa asks when she opens the refrigerator door. She touches a ceramic baking dish filled with some sinful dessert of banana chunks and golden custard and vanilla wafers and crumb-topped swirls of whipped cream.

"That there," Mitch explains, "is roasted banana pudding. I made it earlier today."

THE WAIT

"Did you now?" Elsa asks, looking from the pudding to Mitch.

He nods. "Just waiting for those wafer cookies to soften. Hopefully they will by dessert time." He squeezes the watermelon onto a lower shelf, closes the fridge and motions for Elsa to follow him to the enclosed porch. "This won't take us long," Mitch says as he lifts a pitted-tin pitcher there and tapes bubble wrap around it. "Few minutes, tops."

Elsa scans a couple of framed pictures hanging on the wall. She lifts the photograph of an angry storm wave during Hurricane Carol. The monster wave crashes over cottages on Stony Point Beach. "It's such a striking image," she says of it. "Really don't want to damage this one." She looks longer at the picture before picking up some of the bubble wrap, too. "Hurricane season *is* upon us again, isn't it?" she remarks while wrapping the framed photo.

"And anything can happen when those storms blow up the coast." Mitch sets the wrapped pitcher on an end table. "Especially if they catch us off guard, the way they sometimes barrel right at us."

"Indeed they do," Elsa quietly says while wrapping the storm photo. But she's not looking at it. She's looking at Mitch across the porch. "Indeed they do."

Mitch glances over his shoulder at her standing there. He turns and steps closer. "We talking in metaphors now, Elsa?"

Elsa gives a slight shrug. She walks to him, too, and hands him the framed storm picture. But passing the kitchen doorway then, she notices something odd. There's food on the butcher-block countertop—hamburger rolls

111

and corn on the cob all peeled and prepped. A platter of cheese and crackers. *But*, she thinks, *not enough to feed a crowd.* So she steps into the kitchen and takes a better look around. She scans the shabby white cabinets and peers into the dining room. A white chandelier hangs over a white table there—a table with no other cookout food on it. So Elsa turns back to Mitch on the porch.

"Mitch." She takes a step his way. "We're *not* waiting on anyone, are we?"

"What do you mean?" Mitch asks, setting down that wrapped photo.

"I mean, no one else is coming to your cookout. No more guests are due to arrive, are they?"

Mitch turns up his hands and starts for the kitchen. "Well, now. Don't believe I ever said they were."

"But … But you invited me to a Labor Day *cookout.*"

"I certainly did," he says from the kitchen counter.

Elsa crosses the gray-painted, wide-planked floor. As she does, Mitch lifts the plate of cheese and crackers off that butcher-block countertop before heading for the slider.

Following him outside to the deck, Elsa persists. "Well I had an expectation that *Carol* might be here," she says. "And neighbors. And … I don't know." Elsa pauses and looks past him to the crowded beach. "Maybe your coworkers would be invited. Or, or some of Jason's crew." She takes Mitch's arm and turns him around.

"And distractions, maybe?" he asks.

"Well. I just—"

"Just what?"

Elsa smiles, and lowers her sunglasses to her face again.

"When I heard … Come to a Labor Day cookout at your big cottage on the beach—"

Mitch turns and walks over to the patio table now. He sets the cheese platter down there, then pulls out Elsa's chair. "You never thought it'd be a cookout for two?"

⁓

From a bench, Cliff spots Denny arriving at the Ocean Beach car show. His son's driving the old Nova SS coupe they'd restored together. The car's marina-blue color catches Cliff's eye. Thing is, it's not only the color that gets his attention. The rumble of the engine does, too. Denny gives it a healthy rev once Cliff crosses the parking lot to meet him.

And when Denny parks and gets out, Cliff stands there, watching. He hasn't seen his son in about a month and misses his easy way, his wide smile. Today, that smile's beneath a full light beard, the whiskers covering his face, his jaw. He's dressed casual, in a loose tee and khaki cargo shorts. A thin cord of leather is wrapped around his wrist, too. Cliff gives his son a hug, slapping his back, then tousling Denny's shaggy brown hair.

Right away, they get the good times rolling. The steamy September weather is just right for walking around, checking out the restored muscle cars, hanging out together. The sun beats hot on their backs. Music is broadcast from a local radio station's van. People mill about. Vintage Mustangs and Camaros and GTOs gleam in the afternoon light. Cliff and Denny look under hoods, inspect dashboards, listen to engines start up.

They do more, too. They grab cold drinks and trays of nachos, and sit on a bench overlooking the crowded beach. At one point, when Cliff hears someone call out his name, he and Denny walk over to greet Carol Fenwick. Her flower cart's set up near the entrance of a wide boardwalk. Carol's sitting in the shade of the cart umbrella and chats with them. Cliff introduces his son. Carol explains her summer flower gigs. Denny tells her a little about his Nova here.

"It's a classic, restored it with my dad. I'll swing by later and take you for a spin," Denny says. "If Pop can keep an eye on your flowers for a few."

They wander off then, Cliff and Denny. Cliff tells him that whoever loses a game of mini golf buys dinner. Cliff does something else, too. He flips his domino for luck, then pockets the talisman. And of course, when his son *loses*— taking four putts just to get his golf ball beneath the windmill paddles—dinner's on Denny.

But not before Denny manages that ride with Carol. When he gives her a cruise around town in his Nova, Cliff mans the flower cart. Calls Nick, too, to catch up on the beach scoop.

The whole afternoon passes that way. Hours blend into each other. The sun sinks lower in the sky. Denny picks up the food-truck dinner tab—a Philly cheesesteak sandwich and a lobster roll, shoestring fries and coleslaw and a side of fried mac and cheese. They eat at a picnic table. Music plays from that local radio station's satellite van. The sea air lifts off the Sound.

"I want to show you something," Cliff tells Denny as they finish up their dinner. He pulls out his cell phone then.

"Thinking of proposing to Elsa," he says while flipping through his *Photos* tab and landing on the diamond ring he bought this morning. He flashes the picture to his son.

"Seriously?" Denny leans across the picnic table, takes the phone and lets out a long, low whistle. "Hot diggity, Pop. That's quite a ring."

"It is. And Elsa's quite the lady. So you know, I wanted to ask what you think. Of me getting married—if she'll have me." Quickly, Cliff reaches for his cell phone again. "Look. Here's a few pictures of Elsa. Don't believe you've ever seen her before."

"No. Usually you just talk my ear off about her." Denny pushes aside his food basket and takes back Cliff's phone. He scrolls through the photos there, pausing at the picture Cliff took last fall of Elsa kite-flying on the beach. She wears a belted sweater over her leggings. A thick scarf is wrapped around her neck. And her honey-highlighted brown hair blows as she tips her head up, laughing into the wind.

"Dad." Denny looks across the table at Cliff. "She's beautiful."

"She is."

"So what are you asking me for? I'm thirty-two years old just last weekend. You live your life, I live mine. You don't need my permission."

"I disagree, son," Cliff says, taking the phone back. "I think I do. Because for all these years with your mother gone, it's just been you and me."

Denny, sitting there in his loose tee over cargo shorts, eyes Cliff. "Well. I don't know all that much *about* Elsa."

Cliff nods. "Let me tell you some, then."

"Lay it on me, Pop."

Cliff looks out toward the beach, takes a long breath, and does it. *Everything* he loves about Elsa spills out. How she bought the old Foley's place and turned it into a grand beach inn—not yet opened. And he talks about her wildly abundant Sea Garden. The Italian phrases she tosses into conversation. How she bops around and sings with *no* shame in the car. Oldies, classics, new tunes—she knows all the words. And oh, how she really tries to whistle, too. Then there's her Sunday dinners for the gang. Her *inn*-spiration walkway. And the way she *really* listens to people's stories.

"You stop by to tell her something, and she'll sit you down for coffee and biscotti," Cliff explains, then pauses. "And you realize later that those were the best ten minutes of the whole damn day."

"Wow," Denny says then. His smile is wide, and there's some awe, maybe, in the way he shakes his head.

"Wow, what?" Cliff asks.

"You just light right up when you talk about her."

fifteen

SHANE STANDS CLOSE BY AS Celia leans into the backseat and lifts out Aria. The car is parked at the curb a block away from the Red Boat Tavern. The sidewalk crowds have thinned; Labor Day afternoon wanes. Beneath the slant of sunlight, the harbor across the street is dotted with sailboats. Lobster traps are stacked on the docks. Wild white roses climb among rocky ledges along the water.

"I loved that driving tour," Celia says, turning to Shane on the sidewalk. "So many amazing sights."

"Got a favorite?" he asks while closing up the car.

Celia shifts Aria in her arms. "Oh, I don't know. The opera house, maybe? Or the lighthouse? Then there's that outdoor chapel, with its gardens and stone walls." She looks out at the harbor. The salt air is pungent. It has her breathing deeply before turning to him again. "But maybe it's the *water*. No matter where we went, it's just blue, blue, blue. I've never seen a more pure blue."

Shane says nothing. He just reaches forward, tips up Celia's straw fedora and gives her a kiss. Her smile beneath it is palpable, and he's glad for that. She's happy here. Aria is, too. The baby's been cooing and gurgling in her mother's arms during their afternoon sojourn.

They stand there in the sunshine for a few minutes more and watch the harbor. Seagulls swoop. The bell buoy clangs. A light breeze blows Celia's auburn hair beneath that fedora. Shane's not sure he's ever seen her more at ease. Her loose white peasant blouse over faded denim shorts suits her. Small tassels hang from the delicate string tie at the blouse's collar. Tortoiseshell sunglasses are on her face, and Aria's fingers touch her thick gold necklace. It's apparent the trip here has freed them all to relax. There are no prying eyes in Rockport; no one to hide from; no lies to be crafted.

"I'm so hungry!" Celia says then, leaning into him. "I can't wait to try the food here."

"Finest kind, Cee. Red Boat Tavern's got the best club sandwiches this side of the Atlantic." He lifts that fedora again and kisses the side of her head, then her mouth when she turns to him—still smiling. "Let's go in and order."

Celia glances to the tavern's patio. "You go," she says. "I'll wait outside with the baby, okay?"

"Of course. What do you want to eat?"

Another smile. Another touch of Celia's fingers to his jaw. "Get me one of your favorites. I'll eat *anything*, I'm so famished!"

"Yeah. Me, too. I'll grab something good and we'll have it back at the house, on the deck."

"Sounds perfect."

Shane taps Aria's fingers. "I'll bring her little carrier outside, too."

"She'll like that," Celia says. They walk to the patio beneath a pergola strung with white lights and fishing rope. Rays of sunshine dapple the area. "Me and Aria will wait at a table here. She's just *loving* the fresh air."

Shane pulls out a chair for them and gives Celia one more kiss before crossing the patio to head inside.

"Well, lookie here," a voice calls from the tavern's side door. A man of about fifty, with a shaved head and manicured close beard, walks out. "Our boy Shane finally went and did it," he says.

"Landon, hey!" Clapping his shoulder, Shane asks, "Did what, my friend?"

Wearing a full maroon apron over his short-sleeve button-down and slacks, Landon nods to Celia at the table. Throws a wink Shane's way, too. "Went and caught yourself a mermaid."

"That I did." Shane looks over at Celia sitting beneath the pergola. Her auburn hair is down beneath that straw fedora as she tips her head low and whispers something to Aria. "Caught two, actually," Shane adds.

Landon, standing there with his arms crossed, looks to Shane. "I didn't know you had a kid."

"No, no. That's not how it is." Shane hitches his head for Landon to follow him. "Celia," Shane calls out as he nears the patio table. "Want you to meet Landon. He owns this salty shack. And serves up the best eats around."

"Celia!" Landon motions her to stay seated as he takes her hand in a light shake.

Does something else, too. Shane can't miss it. Landon

goes to mush—yep, mush—as he gives Aria's sandaled foot a waggle. "And *cootchie-coo* to you," he babbles on. "Who are *you*, little darlin'?"

"This is my daughter. Aria," Celia says, turning the baby propped in her lap.

Aria's mouthing teething beads clutched in her hands. She's smiling, too—a smile as wide as everyone's gathered around her.

Landon bends even lower and softens his voice. "*Isn't she special?*" he asks, brushing her cheek. "You are a beautiful baby if I *ever* saw one, cutie-pie."

"Okay." Shane drops a hand on Landon's back. "She is. *And* we're all famished, guy. Let's go in," he says as Landon straightens. "Need to order some takeout."

"Sure thing," Landon tells him. But he also gives a finger-wave to Celia as he walks away. "You take care now, ladies," he calls with another wink.

Shane's standing in the propped-open doorway now. "Come on, Landon."

"Ayuh." Landon catches up to him and throws an arm around his shoulder as they walk into the dark tavern. "Now what's the story with this friend of yours?" he asks.

"For starters," Shane tells him as they cross the tavern's wooden floor, "Celia's a *hell* of a lot more than a friend."

⌣

Celia turns her seat toward the distant harbor. The late-afternoon sunlight is golden; the air, warm. A salty breeze touches her skin, and Aria's too. Celia toys with wisps of the baby's dark hair. She bends and kisses the top of her head, then whispers, "*You're being such a good girl, Aria.*"

Aria, clutching her teething beads, waves her hand and gurgles a smile up at Celia. As she shifts the baby on her lap, Celia notices a pretty waitress nearby. She's wearing a fitted red V-neck tank top with a black denim skirt. Several fine chains hang around her neck; a half-apron is slung around her hips. She's sponging off a few tabletops and straightening a chair or two.

"Hi there," the waitress says when she looks over and catches Celia's eye. She walks a little closer, too. "I take it you're from away?"

"I am," Celia tells her. "Just visiting for a few days."

"Perfect weather you're having. You lucked out." The waitress swipes clean another table. As she does, her thick blonde braid falls forward. "Sometimes it gets really damp and foggy here on the harbor."

Celia looks from the waitress to that harbor. "Not today! It's gorgeous."

The waitress tucks her cleaning rag in an apron pocket and approaches Celia's table. "So … you visiting Shane?"

Celia turns quickly to her. "Oh, you know him?"

"Sure, sure. Shane gets around in these parts." She holds out a hand. "I'm Mandy."

"Mandy." Celia manages a handshake around the baby. "Nice to meet you. I'm Celia."

Mandy gives Aria's hand a tiny shake, too. "And this is your *daughter*, I hear. She's so young!"

Celia shifts the baby on her lap. "Aria's just over three months."

"She's *beautiful*," Mandy says, then takes that damp rag and lightly wipes off a table next to Celia's. "Aria's daddy visiting here, too?"

"Her father?" Celia looks over at Mandy. "No."

"Oh. Okay. Must be working?" Mandy asks, pocketing that table rag again. "Couldn't make the trip?"

Celia looks around to where Mandy *had* been, several tables over, and wonders if she hadn't seen her and Shane's stolen kisses here and there. She looks to Mandy again, then. Maybe she didn't—if she was busy tidying up. "Well, you'd have no way of knowing. Aria's father actually died very suddenly last year."

"Oh my God! I'm really sorry," Mandy says as she pulls out a chair and sits at Celia's table. "That has to be *so* hard for you."

"It is, sometimes," Celia says with a small smile. "But I have the help of friends, family. And recently, Shane."

"Now *that's* good to hear." As she says it, Mandy gives Celia's arm a quick squeeze. "Friends get us through so much."

Celia nods. "Don't know where I'd be without them."

"So what do you do, back in …"

"Connecticut. Stony Point, actually. I was going to be an assistant innkeeper at a seaside inn."

"Was?" Mandy sits back and tips her head. "Did something happen?"

"Legalities, red tape," Celia says with a wave of her hand. "So the inn didn't open when the brakes got put on everything, last minute." She glances to the harbor, then back to Mandy. "Last minute, as in this past Friday."

"Oh, I'm sorry to hear *that*, too." Mandy's voice is soft; her smile, sad. "Jeez, misfortunes never come alone, huh? That's an awful lot of bad news for someone nice as you."

"Thanks. It was, but that's how life is sometimes." Celia

gently rocks Aria in her lap. "Everything changes—just like the tides, right? Every six hours, twelve minutes, I hear?"

Still sitting back, Mandy gives a slight laugh. "Ah, Shane must've told you that. *6h 12m*. His first tat?"

"Yes! I'd never heard that before—how often the tide changes."

"*Right*," Mandy says with a knowing nod. "That's a good story of his for the ladies." She glances back at the tavern door, then leans close to Celia and lowers her voice. "Often gets told between the sheets, no?" she asks, giving Celia's shoulder a light pat.

"I beg your pardon?" Celia tips up her fedora and eyes this waitress.

"*6h 12m*. The changing tides," Mandy quietly repeats with a shake of her head this time. "Guess it sounds better than the truth."

"The truth?"

"Hm. I probably shouldn't say anything. But, well, it might be better for you to know. The truth is that Shane was passed out *drunk* for 6h 12m—six hours and twelve minutes. His crew reminded him with the ink."

"What?" Now Celia looks to the tavern door, then shifts Aria in her lap.

"Tale's a little saltier than you realized?" Mandy asks through a squint.

Celia starts to talk, then stops. Her mouth's gone instantly dry. So she lifts Aria to her shoulder and rubs the baby's back, all while managing another glance to the tavern door. Of course, there's no sign of Shane. A seagull swoops low just then, *caw-cawing* as it does. And Celia gives a little jolt when she feels Mandy's hand on her arm again.

She's leaning close. Her blonde braid hangs over her shoulder. Her eyes are caring, and concerned.

"*You just be careful, honey,*" Mandy whispers. "*You and that precious baby.*"

"Careful? What do you mean?"

Mandy looks to the tavern door, then stands and pulls that rag from her apron pocket. Her smile is sympathetic before she talks. "Sounds like you've been through the wringer, and maybe haven't known Shane that long." She tosses another glance to the door. "If I can save you some heartache, well, I'd be glad to. Because I'd hate to see someone sweet as you get tangled up in Shane's kind of trouble."

"Trouble?" Celia sits up straighter, holding Aria close. "That's not the Shane I know."

When the tavern door opens then, Mandy starts wiping off the table. As her arm swipes, she bends low to Celia, whispering, "*Trust me. Some things take time.*"

Celia keeps her eyes locked on Mandy.

"See you around, Landon," Shane's calling back through the open tavern door.

But Celia doesn't look over at Shane. It's Mandy who has her attention.

"You and your mermaids take care now!" Landon's voice echoes out onto the patio.

Mandy straightens, but Celia still watches her for *something*. A nod, or an affirmation. A reason to doubt her, even. She gets none.

"Hey, Mandy," Shane says as he approaches the table. His arms are full of take-out bags. "Good to see you."

"Likewise, *pirate*," Mandy says with a wink.

And Celia knows. She's an outsider here—unsure how to navigate Shane's seaside life of salty bar owners and flirting waitresses. Of tough lobstermen and rough seas. When Shane comes up beside her and sets a hand on her shoulder, it's all she can do not to flinch.

"You met Celia?" he asks Mandy.

"I did!" Mandy brushes a wisp of escaped blonde hair off her face. "We had a nice chat."

Celia pushes back her chair and quickly stands. Still holding Aria against her shoulder, she reaches to the table for her tote, then turns to Shane and Mandy.

"You all enjoy your dinner now," Mandy's saying as she pats Aria's head. But when she meets Celia's eye, Mandy raises a discreet eyebrow. Slips her a knowing look, too.

"Can't wait to dig in." Shane shifts the food bags and turns to Celia. "Ready?"

From beneath her straw fedora, Celia looks at him and only nods.

sixteen

CELIA GLANCES AT SHANE AS he drives back to his house. What was it he said this morning? That he was an art thief? And took whatever he wanted? *What, like me?* she thinks now. Has an unexpected week off with nothing going on, so might as well use her for a good time? Parade her around Rockport? Hell, she's only known him for a few weeks. *Weeks.* Maybe her father was right. His caution was justified.

By the time they get to Shane's house, and bring in all the food bags, and Aria, and baby totes and her own purse—some awful doubt latches onto Celia like a shadow.

"Let's just have dinner inside," she says while filling a bottle with Aria's formula. The baby's starting to cry in her infant seat on the table, all while Shane's pulling their food from the take-out bags.

"Inside?" Shane glances over at Celia. "But it's a beautiful night."

Without looking at him, Celia tells him she really wants to keep things easy. "And I have to feed Aria first," she says while standing the bottle in a pot of warm water.

"It's no trouble setting up outside, Celia." Shane puts a container of sides on the gray-and-black quartz counter. "I was going to move Aria's things to the deck. That chair she likes. A little cover-up if it gets damp. She can hear the water in the harbor. Breathe the salt air."

Celia bends over and fusses with Aria at the kitchen table, but throws Shane a slight smile. "It's been a long day," she says over the baby's growing cries.

Now? Now Shane walks closer and turns Celia to him. "Been a *great* day."

Celia just brushes past him. She gets the bottle from the pot, tests a few drops of formula on her wrist, then lifts the crying baby into her arms. "And maybe I overdid it," she says while sitting in an old wooden chair.

Shane doesn't let up. He walks to the table, grips a nearby chair top and leans close. "Even with the nap you took after lunch?"

Celia only shrugs then.

"Okay," he says. "Whatever you want."

He stands paused there, hands on top of that chair while he watches her. Though Celia won't look at him. Instead, she nudges the bottle nipple into Aria's mouth and gets her suckling.

After a few quiet moments, Shane turns to open a window, then opens the kitchen door to the deck. Digging in a drawer next, he pulls out two placemats and sets them on the kitchen table. "You sure you don't want—"

"I'm sure." Celia adjusts Aria's bottle as she says it.

More quiet, before Shane asks, "You want wine?"

"Maybe." She glances at Shane standing there. His wrinkled tee is loose over his cuffed-canvas shorts. "Okay."

Shane tips his head. Starts to say something—what, Celia's not sure—then stops. A second later, he crosses the kitchen to the hallway. "Going to wash up first," he says. "Change my shirt, too."

Again, Celia says nothing. She just busies herself with feeding the baby—in this tiny kitchen, in this small shingled dockside house three hundred miles from home.

⌒

When Shane returns to the kitchen, he's still wearing his cuffed army-green shorts, but is slipping on a short-sleeve button-down over a fresh tee. Celia's done feeding the baby, he sees that, and she's walking her around on the deck. She holds Aria to her shoulder while rubbing a hand in easy circles on the baby's back.

"You want me to get our food ready?" Shane asks through the screen door. But the way Celia turns, and is quiet for a long moment before answering, clues Shane in. Something's off.

"Yeah," Celia tells him, heading to the door. "We're coming in."

So he first slides Aria's infant carrier across the table, closer to Celia's place setting. That done, he sets a warmed triple-decker turkey club with pickle spears on the table. Then he heats his own meatloaf club covered with melted cheddar and fried onions. There's a plate of baked potato wedges, too, and fried zucchini chips. When he picks up the wine from the counter, Celia's settling Aria in that baby carrier. "It's Borsao," Shane tells Celia as he fills a glass. "A Spanish wine. You'll like it," he says before pulling out her chair.

"Thanks," she replies, sitting there and sliding her dish closer.

They eat, then. Just eat. The baby moves in her seat. The sun outside is sinking lower in the sky. Salt air drifts in through the screen door. Forks and knives click on their plates. Celia sips her wine.

Shane does, too, then holds the glass in front of him. "Below deck, on the boat? It's a real comfort zone," he says. "No matter what happened working on deck that day, no gripes are brought to the table. We all just eat and connect. There's always a cook among us in the crew, someone who gets a hearty meal ready. And we just sit there. At the table." After another swallow of wine, he sets the glass down and drags a baked potato wedge through a puddle of ketchup on his plate. "Have some good eats with the boys, you know?" he asks while putting that potato in his mouth. "I like it."

Celia nods before nibbling at a piece of her turkey club. "What do you talk about?"

"Everything." Shane pauses. "Nothing."

There's more quiet between them now. Their voices seem hollow in the strain of it all. Celia tastes a pickle spear, then lifts her sandwich again and takes another bite.

"*This* table?" Shane says, leaning back in his chair. "My father actually made it out of reclaimed wood."

"Really?"

Shane nods. "One of my crewmates? His family was

dismantling an old barn on their property. Me and Dad took a ride and helped ourselves to some of the lumber." Shane runs a hand along the planked-and-notched tabletop. "It was one of the last things we got the chance to do together before he died."

Celia sets down her sandwich and brushes her fingers across the wooden table. "Must mean a lot to you."

Shane takes another bite of his meatloaf sandwich and wipes his mouth with his napkin. "Hey," he says, nodding to her plate. "You're not eating."

"I am." Celia looks from her turkey club to him. "Little bit."

"Something wrong with the food?" Shane asks, noticing her practically untouched meal.

"What?" Celia slightly turns her plate. "No. No."

"I can get you something else, no problem."

"No, it's fine. Really!"

Shane reaches for her dish. "Let me have a taste." When Celia nudges the plate across the table, he lifts a piece of that turkey club. Looks at the triple layers of sliced turkey, bacon, spinach leaves, tomato, avocado, mayonnaise. And digs in. "Oh my God," he says around the food. "So good! You don't like?" he asks, sliding her dish back.

"It's a little heavy, maybe. I don't know."

"All right. Have some of mine, then." Shane cuts a slab of his meatloaf club and puts it on her plate.

Celia adjusts the neck of her peasant top. And reaches over to brush a finger across Aria's cheek. And finally takes a small bite of that meatloaf sandwich. And forks a fried zucchini chip. "It's getting late, Shane. For the baby," she says.

That's it. Nothing else. No leaning close. No laughs. No

touches across the table—wiping a crumb from his jaw, or tracing a tat on his arm. No debating whose dinner is better. Just some awkward small talk at the rustic table.

"I have to get Aria ready for sleep soon," Celia goes on.

Yep. Close quarters hit. When Celia stands suddenly to bring her plate to the counter, Shane leans back in his chair and stops her. Actually stretches an arm out and blocks her. "I'll clean up, Celia," he says, annoyed now. Annoyed at that awkwardness in the room. Annoyed at the change that came over her. "Why don't you call your dad and check in? You can take a walk with Aria to the docks—it's still light enough. Call him from there."

Celia looks long at him. "Maybe that's a good idea." Still holding that nearly untouched dish, she turns, looks to the sink then back to the table.

So Shane abruptly stands and takes the dish from her. "Go. Get some air with Aria."

Celia backs up a step and nods—then reaches for Aria and lifts her out of the baby seat. And doesn't look back. Just grabs her tote from the counter before pushing through the kitchen door to the deck. There, she settles Aria in her stroller and quickly wheels her off.

Shane doesn't watch them. He only hears the noises after he sits again and sets down Celia's dish. Pulls his chair back in close to the table, too. Once Celia's walked away and everything is still outside, he lifts his meatloaf club and manages a few more bites. He lost his appetite, though. So he wraps what's left of dinner—his *and* Celia's—and puts it all in the fridge.

~

The docks are a favorite spot for Aria. Maybe it's the stroller tires *thunking* over the wood planks that does it. Aria coos, and looks up at the soaring seagulls, the pastel horizon.

Celia keeps wheeling the stroller. "*What am I doing?*" she whispers while walking past the little coffee shed and a stack of lobster traps. She nods to a couple of guys fresh off a boat and coming ashore. They look tired—weather-beaten and sunburnt from a day fishing on the water. Once they're behind her and the dock's empty, she stops and crouches beside the stroller. "*What am I doing?*" she whispers again, this time to the baby as she brushes a wisp of her silky hair.

Should she be here with Shane? Or was Mandy doing her a favor by warning her? Maybe saving her from a huge mistake. Celia stands and glances back to Shane's house off in the distance, then pulls her cell phone out of her shorts pocket.

"Dad?" she says a moment later. "Hi. It's me."

"Celia! How's your trip?" he asks.

With the phone pressed to an ear, she slowly shimmies the stroller with her other hand. "Oh, it's great," she answers. "I'm at the harbor now. In Rockport. Here, I'll send you a photo. Hang on." Switching her phone to camera mode, she snaps the scenic sunset. Wooden rowboats and skiffs are tethered to the dock; lobster boats are moored further out. Sailboats, too. And the lavender sky is reflected right back on the glass surface of the seawater.

Quickly, she texts the image to her father. "Did you get it?" Celia asks then.

"Not yet," he says. "How's Shane? He there with you?"

"No, Dad. He's good, but we just had dinner. He's cleaning up while I take Aria for a bedtime walk."

"Okay. And yeah, there it is," her father's voice goes on. "Got the picture. How about that sky?"

"Isn't it something?" Celia looks out at the horizon while talking. "It's really warm here, but there's a breeze lifting off the Atlantic." She asks about his day, then, and what he's up to this week. "*Okay, take care, Dad*," she quietly says when her father thanks her for calling.

After disconnecting, Celia pockets her phone and turns to look at Shane's house again. It's so charming, with its weathered shingles and paned windows. But it's hard to start wheeling Aria there. She does, though, and on the way, briefly closes her eyes against stinging tears.

"*Breathe*," Celia tells herself.

When she and Aria near the parking lot, Celia spots an empty picnic table off to the side. The wood is dried out and splintery, but it's a place to sit. And breathe some more. And get her thoughts—and Mandy's words—straight in her mind before heading back.

seventeen

"THIS REALLY WORKS, ELSA?"

Mitch stands beside her at the gas grill on the Fenwick cottage deck. He's got on his safari hat against the hot afternoon sun. Several uncooked hamburger patties are on a platter. A bowl of small ice cubes sits beside it.

"Like a charm," Elsa says as Mitch slides a spatula beneath the patties and sets them on the grill. "Got it from the cooking guru himself, Mr. Bradford."

"Kyle? I *like* Kyle."

Elsa nods. But from behind her cat-eye sunglasses, she's noticing things. Noticing that Mitch's hair is getting longer as the summer goes on. His fading blond ponytail isn't as tiny as it used to be. And his goatee is quite full. As always, it all suits that laid-back vibe of his.

But she says none of that. No. "Ice cubes are one of Kyle's tricks at his diner's outdoor grilling station," she says instead, leaning closer to check out those sizzling patties.

"He swears by it. Keeps the hamburgers moist and juicy, the way that ice cube melts right into the meat."

So Mitch lifts a cube from the bowl and sets it atop a raw patty. His thumb presses the melting cube right into the hamburger. As he's doing this, Elsa discreetly snags a cube from the bowl, too. But *she* presses the ice to her throat, her chest, before tossing it right over the deck railing.

And quickly looking around to be sure it wasn't noticed.

⌒‿

While Mitch mans the grill, Elsa brings out mustard and ketchup, and potato salad, and a strainer of steaming corn on the cob. By the time she's got the patio table set with plates and glasses, the burgers are done. The cheese on them has melted. Mitch sets the platter on the table before sitting there in the shade with her.

"Now," he says, setting his safari hat on the railing, then reaching for a glass pitcher dripping with condensation. "Some good old-fashioned iced lemonade."

"Perfect."

"It is." Mitch lifts that pitcher and begins pouring. Ice cubes clink into the glasses with the drink. "Something cool to sip on this hot day."

"Oh, yes. While the burgers rest." Elsa leans back in her chair. Behind her, waves lap onshore.

"Rest?" Mitch asks while filling her glass to the brim.

Elsa nods. "Kyle says the meat has to sit for five minutes, at least. Helps those ice-cube juices stay inside."

She *thinks* something else, though. Those five minutes

135

can have *them* rest, too. Have them take a breath. Relax. Sip their cool drinks and unwind. Let any early awkwardness between them evaporate. Physical tensions seem to drift off on gentle sea breezes now. It shows in the way they slow right down in this five-minute burger rest.

⁓

Ten minutes later, the burgers have rested and are dressed with lettuce, tomato and ketchup.

"Well, I do declare," Mitch admits after biting into his burger. "I think I've died and gone to heaven. That there is the juiciest cheeseburger I've *ever* had in all my livelong days."

Once she bites in, too, Elsa right away dabs her mouth—patting the juices that drip there. "*Helluva burger, indeed,*" she murmurs as she does.

⁓

Now that the cookout is truly upon them, time passes unnoticed.

Potato salad gets scooped. Corn on the cob gets buttered. Lemonade gets sipped. Slabs of fresh tomato get slathered with mayonnaise and sprinkled with sea salt. They laugh and talk easily now. Elsa tells Mitch about her mountain of inn paperwork needing completion for Stony Point zoning. He mentions his scaled-back teaching schedule at the college.

"Just two classes a week in the fall semester," he says, "to accommodate *Castaway Cottage* filming."

At his mention of filming, she reminds him of some on-camera tactics. "Remember. No sunglasses when taping outside. Viewers want to see your eyes. And … and *hydrate*. To keep your voice clear."

What happens then is this. There suddenly isn't enough time for all they *want* to say. Mitch talks some about his son on the West Coast. Elsa tells Mitch how her granddaughter's been trying to roll over. And holding up her head more.

When the sun sinks lower in the late-afternoon sky, they move from lemonade at the patio table to wine on deck lounge chairs.

And they don't *stop* talking. Instead, they try to squeeze in everything—stories, interests, funny remarks, what have you.

Mitch, in the lounge chair beside Elsa, reaches a hand to her arm. "I just remembered the banana pudding," he says, standing up. "Let me go in and check if those vanilla wafers are soft enough yet. You wait right there."

Elsa stays behind all right. Watches him go inside, too. And oh, is she conflicted. Damn it, she was *so* ready to put out the fire earlier—when she arrived here. Now? She leans over to catch a glimpse of Mitch inside at the kitchen counter. Now she's not so sure if maybe she wants to *fan* the flames.

"Not ready," Mitch announces when he returns to the deck with her watermelon fruit bowl and two dishes. He sets them on a table near their lounge chairs, then sits beside her again. "Those wafers should just about melt in your mouth," he explains. "And not be crunchy. We're not there yet."

So they wait.

And nibble on pieces of chilled fruit.

And sip wine.

And watch the shadows grow longer as the sun sinks even lower.

"I heard something I liked on a podcast the other day," Mitch eventually says, dragging a hand along his goatee.

"And what's that?"

"That it's important to just ... *pause*."

"Pause?"

Mitch nods, then spears a chunk of watermelon on his plate. "Pause your thoughts. Your words. Your actions," he says, eating that fruit piece. He looks at her beside him. "To be *mindful* of your surroundings. Of the colors you're seeing," he says, motioning to the violet horizon above the water.

"And the sounds you're hearing?" Elsa asks when a wave splashes on the sand below the deck.

"Exactly! We're bombarded with so *much* every day, we often miss what's right in front of us. Like how refreshing this fruit is," he says around a piece of cantaloupe now.

"It is." Elsa reaches for a strawberry from her plate. She slowly, and silently, eats it.

They both are quiet now—in this late-summer moment as the sun sinks into the sea. A seagull flies low over the water. A young couple strolls past the cottage deck. The salt air is luxuriously warm.

"Mitch," Elsa finally says, reaching over and letting her fingers drift across a stack of beaded bracelets he wears. "About the other morning ..."

Mitch looks at her from his chair beside hers, but says nothing.

"You know," Elsa goes on, clasping his arm now. "After you spent the night, and then Cliff—"

"*Uh-uh-uh*," Mitch interrupts while shaking his head. "Taking us right out of the moment. Please, I'm asking you." Mitch squeezes her hand on his arm. "What's between you and Cliff, you'll have to work out privately. But when you're with me?" He gently presses back a wisp of her hair, then brushes his hand across her cheek. "You're *just* with me."

eighteen

AND JASON'S DAY MARCHES ON.

The first thing he does after his arcade date with Maris is drive back to Ted Sullivan's cottage and change into something cooler. His stone-color sweat shorts with a sleeveless tee do the trick. Loose, casual. Normally he'd kick back and swap out his prosthesis for his forearm crutches. But Eva's coming by later, so no-go.

Then he gets to that toppling work pile. He sets up out on the deck, where there's at least a breeze lifting off the water. By the time a few hours pass and Eva's pretty much late, he's transferred sketched ideas for the Beach Box project to his design tablet. Now he checks his watch. Tinkers with the semantics of Beach Box's vaulted ceiling, and looks over to the deck stairs—right as Eva's finally climbing them.

In the evening light, Jason actually does a double take. Eva's resemblance to Maris is uncanny. No one ever saw the similarities *before* knowing they were sisters. But since learning that truth a few years ago, Jason can't miss it. Especially in the eyes.

Eyes that are cautiously watching him.

"Eva, what the hell?" Jason says as he pushes off his chair. Eva's bumbling up the stairs with a large cooler in her hands. "What'd you bring, the whole fridge?"

"Maybe," she says, shifting that cooler. "Now listen, I'm really not here to badger you. Just to talk."

"And feed an army, apparently." Jason hurries across the deck. "How was the drive? Okay?"

"It was fine. Except for a deer that spooked me. It was grazing too close to the road." She shifts that cooler in her grip. "Saw it at the last minute."

"Have to be careful for that. Kyle says where there's one, there's always another." Jason reaches for the deck gate. "Here. Let me unlatch that."

As soon as he does, Eva sets the cooler on the deck floor and manages a hug. "Did you eat yet?" she asks.

"No. When you texted me earlier, I hoped to wrangle a meal out of your chicken cutlets."

"I figured." Eva leans against the railing and takes a look around. She's got on a gold linen tank top over high-waisted denim shorts. As she stands there, her fingers toy with a seashell choker. "I was making a batch of cutlets for Tay and Matt because I'm going away later this week."

"Why? What's up?" Jason asks while lifting that cooler.

"Real estate conference," she explains, following him inside the cottage. "I made extra cutlets for you, too. A platter for the fridge, and a platter for now. With some other goodies to keep you healthy."

As is typical then, once Jason gets the cooler inside Ted's kitchen, Hurricane Eva takes over. She gets plates, brings them outside. Lifts tomatoes, foil tins of cutlets and a bagged salad from that cooler.

"Just tell me where everything is," she says while grabbing two bowls from a cabinet. "Elsa came by and dropped off the tomatoes. So I'll cut some into the salad."

Jason passes her a plate, and her hands slice and chop then. And open cutlery drawers. All while she gives a low whistle as she takes in the kitchen's gray-swirled marble island; cream-colored cabinets; stainless-steel farm sink; planked, hardwood ceiling.

"Nice place," she murmurs, squinting over at Jason.

"Yeah. Designed by one of the best, I hear."

Eva just shakes her head. "Listen," she says, "there's a few bags of rosemary-and-olive-oil potato chips in the cooler, too. Why don't you bring them out to the deck?"

Jason doesn't argue. Doesn't resist. He just lifts the bags and heads to the slider. "Did *you* eat yet?" he asks on the way.

Eva's back is to him as she slices tomatoes at the counter. "No. Thought I'd have a long overdue dinner with my brother-in-law." She stops mid-slice and looks over her shoulder. Her blunt auburn hair is blonde-streaked—and she manages a crushing glare beneath those sideswept bangs. "We're still *family*, right?"

She doesn't move, either. Not until Jason nods, telling her, "As far as I know," before bringing the chips and napkins out to the patio table.

～

Outside, Jason lights a few lanterns set on the wide deck railings. He switches on the white lights strung around the patio umbrella spokes. Clears his work papers off the teak table and resets the big white conch shell centerpiece there. Brings out the salads and drinks.

And all the while, he waits. It's imminent. He feels it. This is the calm before Hurricane Eva kicks in again. She makes up a platter of chicken-cutlet sandwiches on toasted bread slathered with mayonnaise and tomato slices and melted cheese. She admires the red geraniums spilling from Ted's whiskey-barrel planters. She sits down and they dig into the food.

"So good," Jason says now around a mouthful of sandwich.

Eva nods while dropping a handful of potato chips on her plate.

They lift forkfuls of salad, sip soda from glasses, drag chips through the sandwich dressings.

"You *are* the best sister-in-law," Jason says, lifting a second sandwich half for a bite.

"And I want to keep it that way," Eva tells him, then pauses. "Which brings me to Maris."

～

"Figured that was coming."

"Jason." Eva pulls her chair in closer. The umbrella's tiny white lights glow on their dinner plates. "I'll get right to the point."

JOANNE DEMAIO

"The point?"

"Yes. Which is that I *never* realized how heated some of the situations were with you and Maris this summer. But she filled me in."

"I'm not surprised," Jason says around a mouthful of chicken sandwich. "I'm well aware it was a package deal when I married your sister. So you know stuff."

"Which is why I'm really concerned about you guys. So … okay." Eva motions to the plate of cutlets, and bowl of chips, and hefty salads covering the patio table. "Okay! That's why my cooking went overboard. I had to process things with you and Maris."

"*Process?* What the hell'd she say to you?"

Eva sips her soda. "It's not *what* she said. It's that she's upset—but tries to hide it. I mean, you've been apart for two weeks already. Not two days. Two *weeks*. Next thing, Jason? It'll be two months!"

"Eva, it's not like that."

"Could be."

Jason shakes his head, then stabs his fork at his salad. "I'd be back home in a heartbeat, and Maris *knows* that. We *have* been talking," he says, lifting his lettuce-laden fork to his mouth.

"And *she* told me everything. I know about the shack, and Shane. And how you walked in on the two of them that night. It wasn't good, I get it." Eva tucks back a wide strand of her blonde-streaked hair. "*Nothing* happened, though. Maris would never lie to me about that."

Jason looks at Eva across the table, then stands. He leans against the deck railing and considers his sister-in-law. "Maris shouldn't have even *been* tempted, Eva. So what does that say about the state of a marriage?"

"But Jason—"

"Regardless." Jason raises a hand from where he still leans against the railing. "We *really* have gotten past that. And understand it. I *don't* hold it against them."

"Honestly?"

"It's just not a sticking point anymore." Jason sits again at the table. "Hell, Shane and I worked it out. Bygones are bygones. Fences mended and all that shit. Shane's our old friend and it's good he's back in the fold."

"So what is it, then, with you and Maris?" Eva asks. "What's the problem?"

"I'll tell you." Jason drags a sandwich piece through some mayo drippings. "It's the God damn distance that my leaving created." He stuffs the food into his mouth, chews, then goes on. "A distance I'm trying like *hell* to bridge."

"How?"

"Dating. Finding our way back to each other. One date at a time." He looks out toward Sea Spray Beach beyond the dune grasses. Takes a deep breath of salt air. "One hour at a time."

After a moment, Eva's quiet voice gets him to look at her again. "Is it working?"

"Tough call." Jason sits back in his chair and drags his knuckles along his jaw. "Maybe. The dates are great. Beach walks. Picnic dinner at the New London docks. Coffee at an Italian bakery." He clasps his hands together on the table now. "I … Well, I think I fall in love with her a little more with each date."

"Jason! That's so sweet."

"Yeah. But, you know. Afterward? I just come back here

alone. And that takes something out of me."

"Oh, I hate to hear that." Eva reaches across the table and squeezes his hand. "So what are you going to do about it?"

"Wait."

"What?"

"Wait. It's all I *can* do. That's been made *very* clear to me. I made the choice to leave. Maris gets to make the call on when, or *if*, I come back."

"Okay. Okay, Jason." Eva stares at him, then looks away, stands up and paces. Toying with her shell necklace, she circles around in the evening light. Her tense sandaled feet cross the deck as she throws him furtive glances. "I know something, all right?"

"Like what?"

Now it's Eva who leans against that deck railing. The lantern light glimmers around her. The distant horizon beyond, over the sea, is dark violet. "I *know* why Maris is keeping you away," she finally admits. "And I'm *not* supposed to say anything. But it might be the *only* reason she's keeping you away. I just don't know."

Jason sits back and crosses his arms over his chest. And doesn't take his eyes off Eva. "Spill it," he orders her.

"*Ooh*, I'm on the fence with this." Again she paces, circling around one of those whiskey-barrel planters and snapping off a geranium blossom as she does. She fidgets with the flower, plucking off some of its petals. "You *can't* let on that I told you."

Jason doesn't move from his crossed-arm position. "What is it," he says, his voice low.

"*Fine.*" In a huff, Eva takes a deep breath as she twirls

that wilting geranium blossom. "Maris is actually doing a secret kitchen renovation because she wanted to surprise you with something *good*, and now that the Hammer Law's lifting, she's *trying* to make a lot of progress. But between Neil's book, and kitchen design decisions—which she got all the ladies' input on …"

Jason just listens to Eva's rapid-fire ramble about countertops and the granite yard and hardwood floors. She barely takes a breath as she gets out *all* of Maris' secret—in long, run-on sentences that he can barely follow. But he gets the gist.

"And I feel really guilty telling my sister's secret because if Maris finds out, she won't trust me anymore."

"Eva Gallagher." Jason clasps his hands behind his head and leans further back in his seat as he eyes his overprotective sister-in-law. "Aren't you forgetting something?"

"What?"

"The Stony Point doctrine," Jason says, reaching for the soda bottle and topping off his glass. "There are no secrets at that beach."

"Wait …" Eva takes a step closer. "You knew?"

He only nods, then takes a swallow of soda.

Another step closer from Eva. Her voice drops, too. "*Who told you?*"

"Cody." Jason nudges out Eva's seat so she can sit again. "He suddenly became unavailable for my jobs—and Cody's my *top* contractor. Not to mention, I drove by the house one day and saw his truck parked there. So I wheeled it out of him."

Eva slowly sinks into her seat. "But he promised Maris—"

"He didn't want to rat her out," Jason interrupts. "But he got caught by the boss. Me. And I told him I didn't care. If Maris wants a new kitchen, give her the best." Jason leans an arm on the table. "Maris can have anything she wants."

"*Ooh*, Jason Barlow, you make me *so* mad!" Eva says, throwing a balled-up napkin at him. "You *knew!*"

"I did." Jason laughs and swats at the napkin. "But I also know that a secret kitchen isn't all that's holding Maris back."

Eva leans forward in her chair and eyes him through those sideswept bangs of hers. "I can't *believe* you knew!"

"Don't tell Maris," Jason says then.

"I won't. Really." Eva crosses her heart. "But I *still* can't believe it."

"Come on." Jason stands and hitches his head to the sunset sky. "You can mull it over on the beach. Take a little walk before it's too dark?"

"Fine." Eva gives him another sidelong glare. She stands, too. "Just hold on a sec. I have to do something."

"What—" But before he even gets the word out, Eva pops him one in the arm. Hard. "Hey!" he says. "What the hell's that for?"

"For walking out on my sister. I've wanted to do that for two weeks now. It's been festering."

"Jesus, Eva." Jason runs a hand along his upper arm.

"Okay, got that out of my system. So I feel better."

"Well I'm glad *you* do. Now are we walking, or what?"

"I'll wash the dishes first?" Eva offers.

"Nah. I'll get them later. There's only a few." He motions her to follow him off the deck to the sand.

"Jason!" Eva calls behind him.

"What?" he yells back. "Want to clobber my other arm, too?"

But when he stops, she hurries over, turns serious and gives him a hug. Whispers, too. *"Don't worry."*

And he knows. She *sees* his worry, still.

nineteen

"YOU ARE WITHIN WALKING DISTANCE to the water. Remarkable." Elsa leans on the deck railing of the Fenwicks' cottage-on-stilts. The sunset horizon is violet-red far out over Long Island Sound. Waves lap at shore just beyond the beachfront cottage. To the left is a long stretch of sand. To the right is the bank of boulders where the guys like to fish. Elsa holds a glass of wine and looks at Mitch leaning on the railing beside her. "How many steps to the sea is this place?" she asks.

Mitch sips his wine. "What do you mean?"

Again, Elsa turns toward that water. Right here, the air is thick with salt; two seagulls fly low, crying as they skim the sea. "I mean, how many steps would it take to get from the bottom of your deck stairs to the water?"

"Well, now," Mitch muses, drawing a hand down his goatee. "I guess it depends on the tides. During high tide, the water is closer. Low tide, farther away."

Elsa squints out at the water. It's steel blue and calm during this twilight hour. A few pleasure boats are moored there, too.

"Want to make a bet?" Mitch asks, raising his wineglass with his dare.

"I do." Elsa looks at Mitch. There's a twinkle in his eye as he watches her back. A double strand of rawhide loops around his neck beneath the collar of his loose button-down. "I *will* bet you," Elsa says, then sips her wine and turns again to the salt water. In a moment, she walks to the stairs leading to the sand and guesses the distance. "Nineteen?" she asks with a glance to Mitch. "Nineteen steps, maybe."

"Nineteen steps to the sea? Hmm. I believe I can get to the water in … fourteen steps."

"*What?* Under fifteen?"

"Come on." Mitch walks to the stairs and motions for her to go down ahead of him. "After you."

Elsa sets her wineglass on the patio table and scoops up her cell-phone purse off a chair.

"You can leave that here," Mitch says. "We won't be long."

"No," she says, tucking her sunglasses into a purse pocket, then looping the thin strap over her shoulder. "I always keep my phone with me. In case Celia needs to call. Or if there's a question about my granddaughter, Aria. But it's okay," Elsa adds, holding up the leopard-print crossbody purse. "The phone's all protected behind clear plastic. Sea spray can't reach it."

They head down the deck stairs, take off their sandals and leave them in the sand.

But Elsa pauses then. Standing there in her wraparound skirt and cropped tank top, she turns back to Mitch. "Now this is a *bet*. So ... what are we actually wagering?" she asks.

"If you lose?" Mitch squints from her, up to the cottage. "That you come back for dessert."

"For that sweet banana pudding you've been checking on all day?"

"That's right. We're still waiting on those wafers to soften. So if you lose—you'll have dessert with me."

"Of course I will!" Elsa says. "And if *you* lose?"

"Oh." Mitch turns to the water and lines himself up directly beside Elsa for the competition. "I'm *not* going to lose."

"Very well, Mitch Fenwick. You're on." Elsa extends a hand to shake.

Mitch shakes that hand, and nods to Elsa, too. "Ladies first."

So Elsa turns right there at the bottom deck step. She sets her bare feet firmly in the sand, takes a deep breath *and* her first step. "One," she says, and keeps going. While counting out each step closer, she gauges the distance to the lapping waves and adjusts the length of her stride.

But—she miscalculates. "Eighteen," she finally says, breathless. "Nineteen. And ... *ach*! *Twenty* steps to the sea," she announces, spinning back to Mitch. "*Ooh!* Just missed."

Mitch gives an easy shrug. "My turn," he says. But first, he sets his hands on his knees and squints out to the water as though calculating the distance. Finally straightening, he begins *his* trek to the sea. Each step is counted aloud—and with conviction. "One … five … nine … eleven." At this point, he adjusts his remaining steps to *very* long strides.

"Wait a minute!" Elsa calls out from the shallows so that he stops suddenly. "Who walks like that, practically making a split with each step?"

"Well, now. We set no parameters on *how* we'd walk to the water," Mitch says, resuming his *very* lengthy steps. "Thirteen. And … fourteen!" he declares with a firm splash into the lapping waves. "How about that? Fourteen steps to the sea."

Smiling, Elsa shakes her head and turns back toward the cottage. "Looks like I'm having dessert."

"That you are." Mitch takes her hand then. "But first, let's slosh."

"Slosh?" Elsa looks back at him. "You mean, walk the beach?"

"No, no. *Slosh.*" He tugs her closer to the water. "Means you can't walk on any dry sand for the entire length of the beach." He lets go of her hand and bends to roll up the cuffs of his linen pants. "Your bare feet *must* stay in the water. The *whole* time," he says, while stepping into the shallows and giving a kicking swish. "It's *very* relaxing."

"Okay." Elsa gathers up some of her skirt hem to keep it dry. She steps into the small lapping waves, too, and gives it a go.

⌒〜

Which Elsa finds herself doing more and more with Mitch Fenwick—giving things a go. Counting the steps to the sea. Learning how to shag on the dance floor. Cruising around in his open-air safari-style vehicle.

And now this—sloshing through the shallows.

To her left, lights illuminate the boardwalk. A few stragglers walk there now. To her right, a crescent moon hangs low over the water. The raft floating out near the big rock is empty. No one's swimming at this hour.

Only sloshing.

She and Mitch slosh all the way to the far end of the beach, stopping near the footbridge crossing the channel. Beyond, the cottages up on the hill are all lit up. It's the last hurrah of summer, Labor Day night. So people linger on lantern-lit decks. Grills are smoking for late dinners. Voices rise in the dusky light. There's love and gladness in the sounds. No cottage is dark; no one is alone.

"I sometimes enjoy an evening slosh," Mitch is saying as they turn back now. "Sleep so soundly afterward."

"I'll bet," Elsa agrees. She's quit holding up the hem of her skirt and gives herself over to the easy slosh. Water splashes on her calves, her knees. It licks at the skirt fabric—and it all feels good.

Still. She can't help remembering what a plan she had earlier today. She was going to cool it all off with Mitch—yes, she was. Cool down *everything*.

Oh, you're cooling off all right, she thinks as the lapping waves swirl around her bare ankles. *Just not in the way you'd figured.*

Even the sound of the sloshing comforts her—the rhythmic *splish … splash* of the sea lapping at her legs. She feels every nerve unbunch. Every muscle relax. It gets her to slow her pace as Mitch sloshes beside her. His pant cuffs are wet now, too; his voice soothing as that low moon shines over the misty sea.

"Well," he says as they near his cottage-on-stilts. "I'll walk you to your path, through the beach grasses. Get you safely home."

"Mitch, it's only eight o'clock. I'll be fine walking alone."

"No, no. I insist."

"But what about the banana pudding?" Elsa asks when they emerge from the water and onto the sand.

"That pudding has to set. I checked it right before we sloshed, and it's still not ready. So, Elsa. You must come back tomorrow morning." He picks up her sandals from the sand and gives them to her. "A wager's a wager, after all."

"But ... Are you serious?" She loops her sandal straps over her fingers. "*Tomorrow?*"

"Yes, I'm serious. Those wafers are just not soft enough yet." Mitch takes her free hand and they cross the beach to the secret path. "And it's best the *flavors* mingle overnight, anyway. So it'll be a banana pudding breakfast in the morning."

As they walk the sandy path through whispering beach grasses, Elsa turns back to Mitch. "What about *Castaway Cottage* filming? I've *been* through that ordeal—it'll be a big day for you."

"It will. But first there's some morning meeting happening at CT-TV's studios in Hartford."

Elsa walks further along the path. "Are you going, too?"

"No. It's for production crew only, with filming afterward. Which won't be until after lunch. So you come by early."

"How early?" Elsa asks when they emerge from the sandy path onto the cool lawn of the inn. She bends and slips on her sandals then.

155

"When the seagulls wake. How about sunrise?" Mitch takes one of her hands in his. "We'll have sunrise banana pudding. Because I *want* you to enjoy this Southern delicacy that I made special." He tips his head and squints at her through the evening shadows. "And we *did* wager." After he says it, he raises Elsa's hand and leaves a kiss on it.

Elsa goes quiet with that kiss. She looks from Mitch, to her distant inn. The paper lanterns she left hanging out on the deck for the rest of September glimmer in the summer night. When she looks at Mitch again, she backs up a step and smiles. "*We did wager,*" she whispers. "So I really don't have a choice, do I?" she asks, turning to cross the lawn. She looks over her shoulder, though, as she walks away. "I lost the bet, Mitch. And I'll see you at sunrise."

twenty

Shane's waiting Celia out.

He's pacing the kitchen while turning over the *Chance* rock he bought from Carol's flower cart two days ago. Over and over, he slips that smooth rock this way, that way, in the palm of his hand.

It doesn't help, though—fidgeting. Because ever since Celia returned from calling her father down on the docks, Shane feels *every* damn minute passing by. Can almost hear the seconds ticking. Celia came inside, breezed past him with a few obligatory words, and went straight to the spare bedroom with the baby. Got Aria changed into her sleep onesie. Wound up her music box. Gently shook her plush lion rattle.

Now, not a sound out of Celia. So the passing seconds practically *tick-tick-tick* in Shane's mind.

Well, he'll make his own noise, then. Drown out those ticking seconds by putting down that rock and picking up the broom. By *swish-swishing* the broom bristles over each board on the deck outside. When that's done, he goes back into the kitchen and puts some dried dinner dishes away—*clattering* them as he stacks them in a cabinet. He stops in the spare bedroom doorway and sees Celia bent over the crib as Aria starts crying. Asks if he can do anything to help. Throws in a load of laundry when she tells him no.

Yes, he's waiting. Waiting for Celia to come out with whatever the hell's troubling her.

Waiting while closing the window blinds in the living room. While turning on some lamps.

Funny how Aria's fussy now, too. She wasn't before. She'd been a delight all day—nothing but gurgles and smiles and coos. Wide-eyed and interested in the coastal sights and harbor sounds around her. Turning her head toward the bell buoy. Smiling when a salty breeze lifted her wispy hair. Sleeping soundly at naptime. Eating easily.

Now? Now she's picking right up on her mother's distress.

Shane brings a box fan into the baby's room. He tells Celia maybe the whirring sound will help, like some kind of white noise. When it doesn't, Celia carries Aria to the window and lightly clatters that seashell wind chime she'd hung from the curtain rod. The shells click and clack, but there's no calming the baby. Instead, she starts up with short, crying gasps, so Celia brings her to the kitchen. She tries to give her more of a bottle, but Aria turns her head away. So Celia walks her around outside on the deck again. She doesn't talk, though—Shane notices that. Not even to Aria. Celia's gentle and loving with her touch. But silent.

Still, Shane waits her out.

Celia's not sure she minds Aria's fussing tonight. It gives her an escape. Gives her time to think. As she walks the baby out on the deck now, a crescent moon hangs low in the sky over the harbor. The salt air is heavy, too, at dusk. The atmosphere is misty—like you're actually *seeing* the salt.

Celia takes it all in while holding Aria to her shoulder. When the baby squirms and cries a little, she rubs her back and whispers near her fine, dark hair. Leaves a kiss on Aria's head, too.

And uses this time outside to gauge the Shane she'd come to know versus the Shane she heard about today from that waitress.

What's true? What isn't?

Shane stops at the screen door. When he asks from inside if everything's okay, Celia says she's just settling down the baby.

And she is. Truth.

But she leaves out more of the truth—that she's still scrutinizing Shane's character. Just this morning, he explained his stint as an art thief fifteen years ago. Since their car ride from the restaurant, she's been thinking of his words justifying it all. *I was just going to take whatever I wanted.*

And she can't shake one nagging question … Is that what he's doing now to fill his sudden week off? He's just *taking whatever he wants* from her? She glances into the dimly lit kitchen. Shane's at the counter. His back is to her as he wipes things down there. She turns away then, shifts Aria and holds her close. Cradles the back of her head against her shoulder and hums as the baby gets heavy with sleep.

Still, Celia stays outside in the salt air—where seawater sloshes in the distant harbor. The evening is getting darker;

the sliver of moon, rising higher. It's the only time she can grab to look at some truths she'd conveniently ignored thus far.

Truths like this. She's only known Shane for three *weeks* now. Truth, truth.

And during those weeks, how many hours has she actually *spent* with the man? She blows out a regretful breath with the answer to that one: not that many as he wrangled his own life with his brother, his beach friends. As he backtracked to Maine for his work.

Some things take time, Mandy said outside the Red Boat Tavern.

Like getting to really know someone? Okay, Celia never expected Shane to be a saint. But she never expected the story Mandy laid out today, either.

Aria is asleep in her arms now, so Celia quietly steps inside. She puts a finger to her lips when Shane turns at the counter. But she keeps walking. She goes straight to the spare bedroom and sets Aria in the crib there. A soft breeze blows from the box fan Shane left in the room. Celia glances at it, then brushes Aria's flushed cheek with her fingers. Bends and kisses her forehead.

Finally, she straightens in the room lit only by a nightlight. And she turns. Shane is still in the kitchen. He's putting some dishes away now. So Celia leaves the bedroom and lightly closes the door—but stops in the dark hallway. She adjusts tassels hanging from the collar of her peasant blouse. Takes a quick breath, too, before walking to the kitchen.

Shane closes a cabinet right as Celia walks into the kitchen. He crosses his arms and leans against the counter. "Aria asleep?"

"She is." As she says it, Celia gives him a slight smile. She kind of stops at the table, too, but doesn't sit. She just stands there with a hand on the top of a chair.

"Then … can I get you something?" Shane asks, not moving. "Some leftovers?"

"No." Celia looks at him before walking to the screen door to the deck. "I told you before, I'm not really hungry," she says over her shoulder.

Silence for a moment, with Shane only watching her. "But you said you were starving at the restaurant. *Famished* is how you put it, no?"

She just nods with a quick glance back.

"So what happened?" he asks.

"Maybe I'm just really tired, okay? Why don't you believe me?"

"What?"

"The way you keep at me about dinner. Maybe the trip here was too much, after all." Still looking outside, she runs her hands back through her hair. "Or … I don't know. It's just late now and I don't feel much like eating. Don't make a big thing out of it."

"I'm not. Just asking." He takes off his short-sleeve button-down and hangs it over a chairback. Spins that chair around, then, and sits on it with his hands crossed over the top. And watches Celia. "Was it something your father said?" he asks her.

Celia turns toward him. "Was *what* something my father said?"

161

Shane tosses up his hands over that chairback. "This change I'm seeing in you. You shut right down, Celia."

"Oh, for God's sake. No, my father didn't say anything. And I'm *not* changed. I'm *tired*. Clearly you haven't lived with people much and don't see that's all it is."

"Maybe not."

Maybe Celia's right. Lord knows, he hasn't been in close quarters with anyone he's *serious* about for years. And living below deck with the crew on lobster boats *isn't* what she's saying. So all right, maybe he's rusty when it comes to a *legit* relationship. Shane looks through the shadows at Celia, beautiful Celia.

And knows all that's bullshit.

The change in her is too sudden. And bothers him something fierce.

"Listen, what's going on?" he presses her. "Because I *know* you."

"*Do you?*" she whispers. "And do I know *you?*"

"Wait, wait." Shane still sits, but shifts on his chair. "Wait just a goddamn minute. This has nothing to do with being tired."

"What are you talking about?" Celia leans against the wall at the screen door. She won't come near him.

So Shane stands, spins his chair back around and lifts his button-down off of it. "Just cut the shit, Celia, and get to the point," he says while putting his arms into the shirt. "Say what's on your mind, for God's sake."

"No." She actually points at him, then. "*You* cut the shit. Parading me around town like you did today."

"*What?*"

"Meet your neighbor, Bruno. This person. That friend.

Landon. Your shipmate, Shiloh. As if Aria and I are on display for *everyone* you know."

"That's just how it is here." Shane looks long at Celia. "You bump into people around town. So where's this coming from?" He steps closer to her and lowers his voice. "We were having a great day."

Celia watches him from the screen door still. "Or maybe I just went along with the charade."

"Charade?" He throws his hands up.

Celia only nods.

And Shane only watches her.

But his heart's beating. And a panic's simmering. Because for some godforsaken reason, she's spooked. Got a foot out the door. What happened, he doesn't know. But it's not good. He and Celia toss phrases back and forth now. Quietly. In harsh whispers. Words fly like sharp daggers. At least to him, that's what they feel like. Celia's nonsense about fatigue, and not knowing each other. It's bullshit. With each exchange, he steps closer because Lord knows, she's not making a move toward him.

Not reaching out.

Not touching him.

Not letting down some *incredible* new wall around her.

"Maybe it's *you*," Shane tells her, really quietly. "Maybe it's *you* who doesn't know how to be in close quarters with someone. Because I'm just not getting your—"

"It's not me," she cuts him off and crosses her arms now. "It's something I heard today, all right?"

"Heard?"

She nods.

"Like what?"

163

Nothing, just a quick shake of Celia's head.

"Celia. It's not a question. Like what."

~

When Celia comes out with it, Shane glances at the tattoo on his left forearm: *6h 12m*. The tide turns every six hours, twelve minutes. It's the first tattoo he'd ever gotten—his initiation into lobstering.

"The way *I* heard it was that you were actually passed out *drunk* for six hours, twelve minutes. *That*," Celia says, nodding to his arm, "was your crewmates' way of reminding you."

"Are you kidding me?"

"No. And I was informed that the salty truth of *your* version—*6h 12m* being the *tides'* cycle—is that it's a tall tale to impress the ladies." Celia looks out onto the deck. "Often told between the sheets."

Shane walks to that door and stands there, too. Stands right next to her. "Who told you that?" he asks.

"Doesn't matter. What matters is that the person was very convincing." Celia walks to the kitchen table and sits there now. "And Shane? If your version *isn't* true, then that calls into question everything I know about you."

Leaning against the doorjamb, Shane gives a short laugh. How can he fight this one? He looks at Celia sitting at the table. She's tired, no doubt. But she's also visibly upset. It's in the way her face is just drawn.

"Who told you that story, Celia?"

"I *said*, it doesn't matter."

"It *does*, though," he says back.

A minute passes with no answer. The kitchen is dim. The only light on is over the sink. Salt air drifts in through the screen door. And Shane calculates the day. He thinks of everywhere they went; everyone they talked to. Did someone pull her aside when he went for coffee on the docks? Was it a neighbor? He looks outside at the dark night. In a moment, he walks to her again. Drags out a chair right beside Celia and sits there.

And waits for her to look at him.

"Mandy." He pulls back, eyeing Celia. "It was Mandy, wasn't it?"

Celia shrugs. "We got to talking at the restaurant. She told me some things about you. Said she wanted to save me a lot of heartache. And her take could absolutely be true."

"Which would paint me differently then, wouldn't it?"

"Very much so."

Their talk gets heated; their voices drop—with the baby asleep in the other room.

"Sometimes I don't know what the hell your intentions are with me," Celia admits. "Because the insinuated word around here is that *you* just like a good time. These few days with me fit the bill, huh?"

"Is that what you think? That you and Aria don't mean all that much to me? I'm just killing some time here? Fooling around, whatever. Shit, Celia. You got it backwards, darling— it's *you* who doesn't know jack about me."

"I don't know *what* to think."

He just gives a slow nod.

"On top of that ..." Celia goes on. "I have to wonder if you have a drinking problem? Hitting the tavern every time you get off the boat?"

"*Jesus Christ.*"

"Well, Mandy mentioned some kind of trouble—oh, forget it."

Still, Shane only watches her.

"Why won't you *say* anything?" Celia asks. "I mean, I'm a new mother—and have to be careful with who I trust."

"You trust someone who cornered you for five damn minutes? Trash-talked me behind my back?"

Nothing from Celia. Not a word.

"Listen to me, Celia. I'm *not* going to try to convince you. I'm only going to tell you once—*once*—that Mandy's story is not true. None of it." Shane abruptly stands and pushes in his chair. When Celia looks up at him, he reaches for his harmonica on the counter and heads to the deck. "You can take my word or not," he tells her from where he's holding the screen door open. "Your call."

twenty-one

CELIA WATCHES SHANE GO.

He closes the screen door behind him and walks out onto the deck. Darkness just about swallows him up. She can only make out the shape of him—a shadow beneath the faint light of a crescent moon. The deck is large; clear bulb lights are strung around it. But the lights are off. So from where she sits in the dimly lit kitchen, she squints to keep Shane in her sights. He walks to the far railing and faces the harbor. Leans on that railing, too, as he looks toward the sea.

Standing and turning away, Celia feels so completely alone. She heads down the hallway and goes into the bathroom. At the sink, her own reflection in the mirror stops her. So she turns on the faucet and cups warm water beneath her hands. Tosses it on her face. Keeps her fingers pressed there for a long moment. When she lifts the hand towel, she pats her face with it. But each pat stays pressed a little longer, and longer still, as she blocks her reflection.

Blocks the sadness, the hurt. Squeezes her eyes tight against burning tears behind that damp towel. Finally, she rehangs the towel, straightens it, brushes her hair and turns to the bedroom.

She has to make one of two decisions. Right now.

There's no use in putting it off. Shane won't stand for it—that much she knows. She can either believe him and stay, or she can believe Mandy and go. End this trip first thing in the morning and get out while the getting's good.

She switches on a dresser lamp and takes off her thick gold chain necklace. Her earrings, too. Her wristwatch. Lays it all out across the dresser top, where the lamplight is soft. She turns, then, and walks to the window where jute rope ties back the long curtains. Her fingers skim over the rope's coarse fibers. It's a feeling that speaks of the sea, and of lobstering. Of Shane's world.

From the window, she looks over her shoulder back toward the kitchen.

But Celia doesn't go there. Instead, she walks straight to her duffel on the bedside chair. Unzipping the bag, she pulls out a folded sweatshirt. Something stops her, though—a quiet strain of harmonica. It's a soft sound— bluesy, of course. It winds through the darkness like a wisp of sea fog. Slight, touching her. Getting her to rub her hands up and down her bare arms. She hears Shane's breath in the song. Here and there. Speaking to her. After a few moments, Celia looks toward the kitchen again before slipping that sweatshirt on over her peasant top and pulling it close around her shoulders.

There's a white-planked bench built right into the deck railings. Shane custom-made it years ago. He removed a section of the corner railings and built the full bench, plank by plank, in its place. The seat gives a good view of the distant harbor waters.

Shane sits on that bench now. He's got a foot propped on an old, wooden lobster trap as he leans into his harmonica and lets a lonely riff wail into the night. Might as well be his heart, for what he knows is surely coming. So he plays more of the blues.

And stops. Stops, sits back on the bench and watches Celia walk out through the kitchen door. She's got a sweatshirt on over her shorts and peasant top. Halfway to him, she wraps her arms around herself and stops, too—right there in the middle of the deck. In the middle of the night.

"Shane." She gives a small shake of her head. "I'm sorry."

"Sorry?" He sets his harmonica on the railing, but doesn't stand. "You're leaving, aren't you?"

Celia looks long at him. Tips her head and squints through the shadows before she takes a step. And another. And keeps going until she actually sits on the bench with him. "*No*," she whispers, turning to face him. "I'm sorry I didn't *believe* you."

Shane drops his head while blowing out a quick breath. When he looks up, Celia's still there. It wasn't his imagination. It wasn't a dream. Her face is inches away from his. "You're staying?" he asks.

"I am." She gives his hand a squeeze. "Mandy. Shane, she was so ... *convincing*. And she really threw me there. Undermined my thinking, you know?"

Shane nods. "I get it. Some people are like that. Have an evil bent in them."

"But I do believe you, Shane," Celia says, touching his jaw now. "And I see Mandy for what she is."

"And what's that?"

"Someone who doesn't like seeing you happy." Lightly, then, Celia leans close and kisses him. "And who certainly doesn't want me in the picture."

"*Jesus*, Celia. I feel awful. Never thought she'd have an agenda like that."

"Oh, she did. And I was so preoccupied with the baby, I was caught off guard with *how* Mandy steered that talk." Celia stands then and walks to the railing. She leans on it and looks out at the distant harbor. "It's really frightening how manipulative a person can be."

Shane goes to her at the railing. "Celia," he says, his voice low.

Celia looks at him with a sad smile. "I'm especially sorry that I ruined this beautiful day."

When she closes her eyes then, Shane can see. It's against some stinging tears. About the day. About Mandy. About her own vulnerability here.

"Hey, Celia," he says, stepping closer. "Look at me."

She does, opening her eyes and looking away, then right at him.

"You didn't ruin anything." He tucks a finger beneath her chin. "You didn't."

"Shane."

"Wait. You hold that thought—whatever it is—and wait right here, okay?" When she says nothing, he asks again, "Okay?"

She only nods, which is all he needs to see. "Sit," he tells her, walking her to the patio table near the door. "I'll be back in a minute. Two, tops."

⁓

Celia waits.

Watches, too. There's enough light in the kitchen for her to see Shane moving around. She's not sure what he's up to as he crosses the room, and opens the refrigerator, and reaches into the cabinet. A short while later, he's back on the deck. This time, he's carrying two plates. One is her reheated triple-decker turkey club with pickle spears; the other is his meatloaf club—barely touched earlier. He brings out the baked potato wedges and fried zucchini chips, too. And that Borsao wine they never got to enjoy before.

"Oh, one more thing," he says after filling their wineglasses. He gets up, reaches inside through the screen door and hits a switch so that the clear bulbs strung around the deck light up the dark night.

"How do you do it?" Celia asks.

"Do what?"

Celia glances from those glimmering bulbs, to Shane standing there. "Make everything better."

He just squeezes her shoulder and kisses the top of her head.

She can't even help it, the way her eyes drop closed with relief. The air is salty and damp. The crescent moon shines high above.

And Shane sits in the chair across from hers. Sits and

171

lifts his meatloaf club oozing with melted cheddar and fried onions. He holds up a sandwich half as if making a toast.

So Celia lifts a pickle spear and digs in. Lifts her toasted turkey club, too, and takes a hefty bite. Actually? She can barely contain herself as she tastes the warm sandwich and all its drippings.

"So *good*," she manages around the mouthful of food that she just can't stop eating now.

～

Later that night, Shane opens his eyes in bed. The room is pitch black. The window is open to salt air drifting in. He's lying on his side and feels Celia behind him. She's tracing a tattoo on his arm.

"*You up?*" she whispers.

"I am." He says the words, but doesn't move. He just relishes the sensation of her fingertips on his skin.

Celia presses closer behind him—the silk of her nightshirt cool against his back now. She drops an arm over his belly. Kisses his shoulder.

When she stills on the bed, quiet minutes pass like that. Finally, Shane rolls onto his back. He puts an arm around her and pulls her close. Kisses her head, too, in the dark of night. "*It's okay, Celia,*" he whispers. "*It's okay.*"

twenty-two

TUESDAY MORNING, JASON'S LEANING AGAINST the doorway to the Dockside Diner's kitchen. In one hand, he holds a mug of hot coffee; the other hand holds a cinnamon cruller. Kyle's standing across the room at the big stove. He's wearing his standard chef fare—black tee, black pants, white apron over it all. The diner's not open yet as Kyle lines up tongs and turners, whisks and weights at his cooking station. He seems tired, though.

"Lookin' a little beat around the eyes," Jason remarks. "You sleeping okay?"

"No, I'm not." Kyle glances over from his stove. "Lauren and I were talking about you last night."

"About me?"

"Shit, yeah. And then I couldn't sleep, wondering if you're *ever* moving back home with your wife."

"I hear you. Same damn question keeps me up at night, too." Jason takes a double bite of that cruller. "And what about you?"

Kyle sets a stack of plates on a shelf over his stove. "Me and my old lady are good."

"No, no. I mean, when're you picking up your new *wheels*?" Jason asks around the food.

"Later this week. Can't wait," Kyle says, moving over to a tub of macaroni salad he's also preparing for the day. "Finally unloading that hunk of metal."

"You're getting a sweet truck, man."

"Sure am. Thanks to the Bradford-Barlow negotiation skills. We clinched a good deal."

"That we did."

Kyle's stirring the drained macaroni now. "Hey, surprised to see you here at the crack of dawn. The seagulls aren't even up yet."

"Yeah, well do you know what day it is?"

Kyle glances at a wall calendar behind him. "Tuesday."

"It is." Jason dunks that cruller, then takes a bite. "But it's also the day the Hammer Law lifts at Stony Point."

"*Right*. Nothing like the sound of lapping waves and power saws now," Kyle remarks while stirring that macaroni. "*Ah*, serenity."

"Even better? Work's about to go into overdrive, too. Starting with a meeting at the studio in Hartford this morning. Reviewing production details for the Fenwick job." Jason sips his coffee. "Fueling up my tank here, first."

Kyle looks over at him leaning on the doorjamb. "Well sit down, then." He kicks over a beat-up stool. "Food actually tastes better when you're sitting."

"That right?" Jason moseys over to the stool and takes a seat. Dunks that cruller in his hot coffee again, too.

"It's a known fact," Kyle says while spooning mayonnaise into the cooked macaroni. "Standing puts physical stress on the body, and that stress hampers the ability to taste. So if you're standing, that cruller you're chowing down is less satisfying."

Jason nods and presses the last of that coffee-soaked cinnamon-coated dough into his mouth—right as his cell phone rings. So now he juggles his coffee mug and his cell phone at once. Listens to his producer, too, talk about running late.

"Change of plans," Jason tells Kyle after the call. "Trent's been tied up at the Cape with car trouble. Few more hours before he's back, so our meeting's cancelled."

"All *right*, dude. You got some downtime," Kyle says while mixing the macaroni and mayonnaise.

"Not exactly." Jason stands and pockets his phone. "Have to meet Zach at the Fenwick cottage to grab some pre-demo footage instead."

"Hell, that's way less of a commute than Hartford." Kyle hefts up that tub of macaroni salad. "So I'll get this in the fridge and meet you out in the diner. Have a coffee with you before the day unrolls."

Jason checks his watch as Kyle heads to the big refrigerator. "Whip me up one of those egg sandwiches? On a soft roll," he calls to Kyle. "Extra cheese, too."

⌒

Elsa thinks that everything about the morning's been *sublime*. Wearing her sleeveless black paisley-print maxi dress, she walked along the sand to the Fenwick cottage right as the sun rose. A sea breeze skimmed off the water and fluttered her silky dress—getting the light fabric moving like ripples of waves. Then there's the sea view from the patio table she's sitting at on Mitch's deck. Ocean stars glimmer beneath rays of that rising sun. And of course, there's the banana pudding—its wafers softened to perfection. Elsa's eyes drop closed with that first delectable taste.

Then, there's Mitch. He's sitting beside her so that they both face the sparkling blue water of Long Island Sound. Mitch has on a loose tan tee over faded cuffed jeans and his two-strap leather sandals. His gray-blond hair is brushed back; he wears a short braided-leather necklace.

"Where's Carol this morning?" Elsa asks, holding aloft a spoonful of that *sublime* banana pudding. "Back from her flower-cart gig?"

"Carol? Yep, packed up from her rental and got home from New London at the crack of dawn. She's knee-deep in the community garden now. Likes to tend her flowers there early, before the sun gets too hot." Mitch draws a hand along his silver-flecked goatee. "Have you ever seen the community garden here?"

"I haven't, actually," Elsa manages around her mouthful of pudding. "I'm so busy in my own. You can usually find me on a floral kneepad myself—in my Sea Garden behind the inn."

Mitch nods and plucks a maraschino cherry from his drink on the table. "Well," he says while eating that red cherry, "I think you'd appreciate Carol's garden plot. My goodness," he muses, leaning back in his chair while swirling that cool drink, "it's a work of art. You oughta visit sometime. Carol'd like that."

As the dawn's red horizon lightens far out over Long Island Sound, Elsa and Mitch sip, and chat, and eat that divine pudding. Elsa asks about the reno about to start for *Castaway Cottage*, too.

"I've been meaning to tell you something about that," Mitch says.

"Really?"

Mitch sips his drink. "I've got this vintage lantern. It's a masthead light."

"From a ship?"

"That's right. And its brass-and-copper casing is aged to a *beautiful* patina."

"I'd love to see this lantern, Mitch."

"And you will. It's out at a restoration shop right now. We're having it converted to an electrical fixture. But," he says, hitching his head to the cupola atop his cottage, "the lantern will eventually hang there. In the third-story ... well, wait a minute."

Elsa looks from the cupola to Mitch.

"There's a word for that room up there, and I reckon you might appreciate it. Jason told me about it. It's an *Italian* word."

"Really? Do tell." As she says it, Elsa spoons out the last of her pudding.

"*Belvedere.*"

Elsa stops her spoon-scraping and looks at Mitch beside her.

"It's Italian for beautiful view," he explains.

"Yes, of course."

He tips his head and squints at her then, too. "Huh, you know something?"

"What's that?" Elsa asks, spoon held aloft.

"I'm actually looking at a beautiful view right now—your beautiful smile."

Before she can say anything, Mitch leans over and gives her a light kiss right there at the patio table, beneath the morning's sunrise, as small waves lap on the beach below them. "And now," he says, standing and reaching for their empty glass bowls, "I've got a hankering for seconds of this banana pudding. You, too?"

 ⁓

Jason parks at the very end of Champion Road. The Fenwick cottage is close by—the only cottage right on the sand. There's no sign of the CT-TV van, so his cameraman, Zach, isn't here yet. While he waits, Jason decides to scope out the lighting and the cottage angles they might want to film. So he heads to a split-rail fence leading to Mitch's property. There's some scrubby dune grass there, which Jason walks through to get to the cottage-on-stilts. The three-level cottage is boxy in shape—its angles designed to deflect storm winds. Sliding windows look out to the west at the rocks where the guys fish. To the east is a clear view of the entire Stony Point Beach. And to the south, a vista of the sea.

Jason catches sight of something else, too. Or, *someone* else.

It's Elsa—which stops him right there on the sand. She's sitting up on the deck, but hasn't noticed him approaching. Not only is she here, but she's wearing some long black paisley-print dress. Or is it a night-robe type of ensemble? Hell, did she actually *spend* the night here? Why else would she be on the deck in that … that … *silky number* at this early hour?

"*Son of a bitch*," he whispers, giving another look to Elsa. He could leave. Just turn around and she'd never know the difference. He glances toward the road where his SUV is parked.

Or he could call her on this situation. Feel her out. So he makes some noise—tapping at the outside wall of the cottage as if inspecting it—just to give Elsa some warning of his presence. Maybe she has to pull herself together. But he doesn't wait to find out. Instead, he just climbs the deck stairs. And notices her shocked expression when she sees him there.

"*Busted*," he calls in a hushed voice from the top of the stairs. "Elsa! What are you *doing* here?"

Elsa sits up straight in her seat at the patio table. "What?" She looks out in the direction of her inn, then back to Jason. "Well, what are *you* doing here?"

"I asked you first," Jason says as he crosses the deck.

"Jason." Elsa takes a breath. And shifts in her seat so that when she crosses her legs, a lengthy slit is exposed in that slinky dress of hers. "It's … complicated."

Through the slider, Jason spies Mitch in the kitchen. So Jason grips the top of a chair, leans over that patio table and drops his voice. "You're coming to Ted's for dinner tonight. Five o'clock. I'll text you the address. We have to talk."

"But—"

"No is not an option." Jason glares to Mitch's kitchen, then back to Elsa. "You. Be. There."

"Hey, Jason!" Mitch calls through the slider screen. He's stepping outside and holding two breakfast-loaded dishes. "Wait a second … Don't you have a production meeting this morning?" Mitch asks.

Jason tosses up his hands. "Trent's held up at the Cape with car trouble, so the meeting got canned. I was sent here to grab some pre-demo footage with Zach. Didn't Trent okay it with you?"

"Damn. My phone's upstairs—been a little preoccupied this morning."

"I'll bet," Jason quietly says, all while catching Elsa discreetly fist a hand at him.

Mitch glances up at the cottage windows, then walks to that patio table. "I'll have to go in and check. In the meantime," he says with a nod to Jason, "sit yourself down! And how about some banana pudding while you're here? It's a specialty of mine. Think you'd really dig it."

"As a matter of fact," Jason says, looking from Elsa to Mitch, "I'd love some." Jason eyes the pudding in those loaded glass bowls. It looks like banana chunks are in there. And some sort of cookies, and whipped cream, all sprinkled with a crumble topping. Sitting in the chair *across* from Elsa, he nods to her glass of juice that's topped with a maraschino cherry *and* a sliced orange wheel. "Some of that orange juice, too, Mitch."

"Now that there's not just any ol' OJ. It's a Southern Sunrise, my friend. Got a shot of tequila in it. Splash of grenadine, too. A bit of the South on this New England beach," Mitch says, squinting out at the sun rising higher in the sky now. "I got a pitcher inside. You good with that?"

"Sure am." Jason leans his elbows on the table beneath

the shade of the patio umbrella. He throws a glance at a noticeably quiet Elsa, too. "Thanks, Mitch."

"I'll check my phone for Trent's message, then grab you some of this banana pudding. It's just about done to sheer *perfection* this morning." He sets a bowl of that pudding in front of Elsa, and sets one at his own seat too, before heading back inside. "All those flavors nicely mingled overnight," Mitch calls over his shoulder from the slider.

Jason looks at Elsa—sitting there with her honey-highlighted brown hair all pulled back in a big clip. Sitting there in that summer dress with the leg slit and wide black-straw belt. Wooden bangles are stacked on her wrist.

With his eyes locked on hers then, Jason drops his voice. "I'm suspecting that's not *all* that mingled overnight."

twenty-three

SHANE'S HOUSE IS QUIET EARLY Tuesday morning. Wearing a robe after her shower, Celia walks with Aria to the kitchen—but no Shane there. She peeks out on the deck. Nothing. Turning then, with Aria in her arms, she spots a piece of paper on the kitchen table. There's a rock anchoring it in place, a rock with the word *Chance* beautifully painted across it. So she picks up that rock and shows the baby.

"Look at that," she quietly tells Aria. "*Chance*. Take a chance. Hm." Putting it down, she picks up the note and reads Shane's slanted handwriting.

Bringing back breakfast—a Maine delicacy!

Oh, Celia can only imagine what that might be. Something natural and fruity and farm fresh, maybe—but she'll have to wait and see. So after setting Aria in her baby seat on the table, Celia preps a bottle of formula and heats it in a pot of warm water. When it's ready, she takes Aria to the living room and gets cozy on a sofa there. All the while, Celia lightly hums. And touches Aria's hair. Gives her a little kiss. Settles Aria in the crook of her arm.

While the baby drinks, Celia looks around the room. There's a brick fireplace on the far wall, a wall painted ocean blue. The built-in bookcases on either side of the fireplace each have a narrow floor-to-ceiling shelf in which Shane evenly stacked logs of split firewood. Books and ceramic jugs fill the other shelves. There's a brass armillary stand there, too. A beautifully framed seascape oil painting—surely a stolen one—hangs above the mantel. And leaning against the corner of the painting is the red sailboat Shane found at that little blue cottage at Stony Point. A large leather ottoman with a knitted throw tossed across it sits beside the hearth. All of it comfort; all of it, Shane.

A salty breeze drifts in through the open windows. Celia feels it on her skin. She takes a deep breath, then dips her head and coos softly to Aria still drinking from the bottle.

～

Shane shoulders open the front door. His arms are wrapped around several bags, which he carries straight to the kitchen. Celia's there, barefoot in her robe. Her auburn hair is down and a little damp from a shower. And she's rinsing a baby bottle at the sink.

"Hey, Celia." Arms still loaded, he gives her a kiss, then turns to Aria in her infant seat on the table. "You, too, little one," he says, managing to shake her tiny hand. "Brought some breakfast."

"I can't *wait*." Celia grabs orange juice from the fridge. Butter, too. She sets out dishes and silverware. Napkins and cream cheese. "In case you've got bagels in there?" she asks, nodding to the bags. "To go with some fresh fruit, maybe?" As she says it, she tries to peek into a bag.

"Nope," Shane says, pulling away. He can see though, by the food and plates she set out, she's waiting for some native Maine cuisine. After setting down the bags, he first lifts out a tray of fresh-brewed coffee in large, cardboard mugs.

"Oh, that *aroma*," Celia murmurs, sinking into a seat. She leans on the table, props her chin in her hand and watches his every move. "Wait." She tips her head and sniffs the air. "What else am I smelling? Something sweet, and—"

Her words stop when Shane starts setting boxes of doughnuts on the table. He opens each one to give Celia a good visual. There's an array of honey dipped and chocolate coconut. Lemon filled and maple frosted. There are raspberry-thumbprint doughnuts oozing sweet raspberry juices and drizzled iced glazing. Cinnamon-roll icing is laced with sprinkles of brown sugar. A berry-filled muffin is covered with partially melted chocolate chips.

"Oh my God, *Shane*!" Celia says, half standing to get a better look at the spread. "Gimme, gimme!"

"Okay," he says with a laugh. "And *this* is just for you, special." He reaches into the bag and sets a Maine miracle on her plate. "That's a blueberry doughnut sliced in two—with a mountain of lemon filling between the two halves."

Celia drops back into her chair and pulls it in close. It's

obvious he's won her over. Especially when she tenderly lifts that doughnut just about exploding with blueberries. "*It's still warm,*" she whispers.

Shane nods. Well, he also sits and watches her sink her teeth into that pastry. Even Aria's watching from her infant seat on the table. The baby's gurgling and pumping her fists as Celia digs in. "Breakfast is served," Shane says, peeling the lids off their steaming coffees before cutting up several doughnuts to sample.

"This is just *sinful,* Shane," Celia says while eyeing the frosted and sprinkled doughy pieces. Creams and custards ooze from some. Glazing and powdered sugar coat others.

"Don't worry." He lifts a sugar-sprinkled, strawberry-filled doughnut and bites right in. "There's plenty of fruit here, so it's good for you," he adds with a wink, all while showing the fruity inside of that jelly-oozing doughnut. "And this is only part one."

"Part one?" Celia dips a pinkie into a melted chocolate chip. Lightly, she touches her fingertip to Aria's mouth to give her a sweet taste. "What's part two?"

"A trail hike. Afterward. We'll walk all this off."

"Sounds like a plan." She picks up Aria then and holds her to her shoulder. "But I'd love to first give the baby a bath."

Shane glances toward his kitchen sink. "I think we could finagle something here."

"Okay, but before we do? Break me off a hunk of *that* doughnut," she says, nodding to one in the box. "What the heck *is* it?"

"Mocha crunch. Dark chocolate with coffee glaze and toffee sprinkles." Shane rips off a piece, dips it in her coffee and gently puts it in her mouth.

"*Mmm.*" Still sitting and holding the baby, Celia's eyes briefly drop closed. "Oh, Elsa would just *love* these," she says around the food. "She'd be over the *moon.*"

"*Elsa?*"

Celia nods, rubbing Aria's back at the same time. "Elsa's such a closet junk-food junkie. Her and Jason, especially. They have epic breakfast feasts. Decadent egg sandwiches. Crullers."

"I had no idea." Shane sits back and watches Celia reach around Aria for the rest of that mocha crunch—and take another large bite. "While you're going at that doughnut," he says, "I want to show you something, too."

"Okay, in a sec?" Celia stands with Aria—and sneaks one more bite of that chocolaty doughnut. "I'm going to put her in the crib and see if she'll sleep even for fifteen minutes. Before we start up her bath."

When Celia returns, Shane's waiting for her. He'd cleared some of the table and is stirring his coffee. A leather photo album is in front of him. Celia sits, too, and lifts her coffee for a sip. "Aria drifted right off," she quietly says with a glance in the direction of the bedroom. "So we can talk a little bit."

"Good. Wanted you to see this." Shane opens that photo album, flips through a few pages and pulls out an old picture. He slides it across the table.

"What is it?" Celia asks.

"What's it look like?"

Celia pulls the photograph closer. "A picture of you?"

"That's me all right."

She looks up at Shane, then back at the photo. In it, Shane sits in a small kitchenette booth. He's young here— in his early twenties, maybe late teens. There's a baseball cap on his head and a close-shorn beard on his face. He's wearing a white, sleeveless undershirt and gives a wincing grin beneath the brim of that hat. Oh, and he's twisted around because his left arm is extended *behind* him on the booth's tabletop—which is kind of a mess. It's covered with inkpots, and a bottle of liquid antiseptic, and a well-worn pamphlet of tattoo styles. Gauze and napkins are scattered around. Another man sits in that booth seat, too. Bent over Shane's arm, he's wearing blue disposable gloves and holding some sort of pen. A wad of cotton is balled in his other hand as he focuses only on Shane's skin.

"You're getting a tattoo?" Celia asks, looking up at him now.

"I am." He nods at the picture. "Notice any other tattoos on me there?"

"No …"

"Right. Because that's my first one. Can you make it out at all?"

Celia pulls the picture even closer and squints at it. "Is that … *6h 12m?*"

"It is." He pauses until she looks at him again. "And do I look passed-out drunk?"

There's a beat of silence before she answers. "Not at all." Her voice drops, then. "Shane."

"What?"

"You had this picture all along?"

He nods.

"Why didn't you just show me this yesterday?" Celia asks, swatting his arm as she does. "Then I would've known Mandy was flat-out lying."

"Because I had to see."

"See what?"

He sits back, watching only her. "If you had any faith in me."

Celia's eyes drop to the picture again. The table in it is in really tight quarters. It's obvious Shane's below deck on some lobster boat or another. In his sleeveless undershirt, his arms are jacked from his work. And his crewmate holds that tattoo pen just over the finished tat.

"Listen, Celia." Shane leans close now. His low voice in the quiet house makes the words more serious. "Remember this past Friday night?" he asks. "After the vow renewal? When we sat at the kitchen table in my cottage? It was late?"

Celia, still holding the picture, only nods.

"You asked me about *that* very tattoo." He extends his left arm and points out the *6h 12m* there.

"And you told me it signified when the tides change. Every six hours and twelve minutes."

"Which spoke to me as a novice lobsterman. But if I'd been seventeen years old and passed out drunk for six hours and twelve minutes, and my crewmates gave me that as a reminder?" he goes on, nodding at the picture. "I'd have *told* you. It wouldn't have been a big deal—one wild night from my past. I got nothing to hide. And maybe you'd have laughed and chalked it off as crazy kid shit."

"Which it wasn't."

"No."

"Shane, I'm really sorry about doubting you. Yesterday."

"No apology necessary," he says, reaching for the picture and tucking it into the photo album. "Just know."

"Know what?" Celia reaches for his left arm and strokes that tattoo. "That you're pretty straight up with me?"

His eyes lock onto hers. "What you see is what you get."

Celia nods, then lifts a sweet glazed doughnut and bites in. "So … you were actually testing me yesterday?" she asks around the food.

"I *had* to."

"To see if I trusted you?"

"And trusted yourself." Shane tips his chair back and puts the photo album on the countertop. "You passed the test," he says with a wink.

Celia, well, she can't help it then. She half stands, takes Shane's face in her sugary hands and gives him a doughnut-glaze kiss.

"Come on," he says into that kiss—staying with it before dotting some powdered sugar on Celia's nose. "Let's get Aria that bath. She'll be ready for a nice walk afterward." He stands and points to the sunny deck. "It's a great day for it."

"Okay. But I don't have her little tub here." Celia tightens her robe and glances down the hallway. "Maybe I can get her cleaned up in the bathroom?"

"I've got a better idea." Shane heads to the sink, opens a lower cabinet and pulls out a good-sized dishpan. It's rectangular, about a foot and a half long and six inches deep. He turns to Celia and holds up the dishpan with a sticker still on it. "Brand new, never used."

twenty-four

OH, THE NOISE.

Maris counted on the construction racket happening on her property Tuesday morning. She knew there'd be *some*—with the chaos of workers arriving. Parking pickup trucks. Yelling. It's why she kept her outfit casual as can be—black V-neck tank over shredded denim shorts with an utterly frayed hem. Long threads hang from it. Between the noise and the dust, no sense in dressing up.

But what she didn't count on was the dog's agitation. Before the workers arrived, Maris brought her manuscript notes, coffee and tin-can flowers out to Neil's old writing shack. Maddy followed behind her. Knowing it would be a crazy day, Maris also packed a few chew toys and dog biscuits. *And* it's another hot morning, so she left the shack door open. Any sea air lifting off Long Island Sound helps cool the shingled shack. She filled Maddy's bowl with fresh water, too.

Anything to keep the German shepherd calm and out of the crew's way.

To no avail.

It starts early. Maris settles in her seat. She moves the tin-can bouquet Jason gave her to right beside her laptop computer. The black-eyed Susans and purple coneflowers and tiny white blossom sprigs remind her to come back to the novel's cut flowers in the scene she's working on. Then she flips her pewter hourglass, raises her hands to the keyboard—and the dog rushes out to the driveway when Cody's truck pulls in. Of course, Maddy knows Cody from being on job sites with Jason, so she's happy to see the foreman here now.

Maris goes out, too. She talks a little to Cody, then returns to the shack with the dog. And barricades the doorway with the sand chairs from her and Jason's beach day. And tries to write again.

It works. For a few minutes.

But Maddy's interruptions mount. The guys' work boots thumping up and down the deck stairs, and the noise of kitchen cabinets being ripped out and tossed off the deck down into the dumpster, and men's voices, and whirring power saws—all of it elicits a response from the dog. She whines. And paces. Noses Maris' arm. Barks. Presses against the sand-chair barricade. Pants.

So Maris reciprocates. She talks quietly to the dog. Pets her. Gives her a biscuit. Scolds her when she tries to get past the chairs. Maris also manages to answer Eva when her sister texts her that it's Taylor's first day of school. *Coffee later this week?* Maris texts back.

Can't, Eva answers. *Work conference.*

With the dog still antsy then, Maris takes her outside to cool off in her plastic kiddie pool. "*Ooh*, you rascal!" she calls while chasing after Maddy when she lopes up the deck stairs, instead. Catching the dog, Maris leashes her and leads her back to the shack. Types a paragraph here, a few lines there—all between stopping the dog from squeezing through that sand-chair barricade and digging a hole beside a nearby hydrangea bush. Maris even soaks a towel with cool water from the hose and lays the towel across Maddy's belly—right there in the writing shack. That trick *always* works to calm her down.

Except not this time. Maddy gets up and shakes off the towel, right away.

"*Maddy!* You're being *so* bad," Maris tells the dog. "Which means it's time to track down Jason and *he* can deal with you." The dog tips her head, watching Maris pick up her cell phone. "If we have shared custody," she says, pressing Jason's number, "then today's *his* turn."

～

Day two of Cliff's early-morning workouts with Matt happened right on schedule—at the crack of dawn. After his run and lunge-walk and boardwalk stretches, Cliff hurries through a shower and breakfast back at the trailer. Anything to squeeze an extra half hour of free time into his day.

Which shouldn't be too hard. Reviewing the guard schedule with Nick, posting notice of the Hammer Law expiration on the community bulletin board, then stacking the extra Labor Day speed barriers back in the Stony Point

Beach Association storage shed only eats up a couple of hours. Still, this is an epic week for Cliff—asking Elsa to marry him—and he has to look sharp. Knows just the way to do that, too.

By midmorning, he's ready to grab that extra half hour for himself. So he locks up the storage shed, returns to the trailer, grabs his car keys and does one more thing. On his way out, he snags the lucky domino off his desk and gives the talisman a twirling flip—catching it one-handed and pocketing it as he walks down the four metal trailer steps to his car.

⁓

Ten minutes later, Cliff's walking across the checkerboard floor of *Coastal Cuts*. Marty whips open a black cape and motions him to his chair.

"What do you want today, Cliff?" the barber asks him. "Your regular cut?"

Cliff settles in the chair and looks at his reflection in the mirror. Miniature tall ship replicas line a shelf over the mirrors. But Cliff notices something else, too—Marty's father, Max. He's the other barber working a few chairs over with another customer. And of all people, it's that Mitch Fenwick! Mitch is sitting in a black-padded seat and getting his graying blond locks trimmed.

"Maybe skip a full cut, Marty," Cliff says then. "What do you think, just clean it up?" As he asks, he's listening to the *other* barber, Max, talk to Mitch. They're going at it about *Castaway Cottage* filming that's supposed to start up after lunch.

"What do *I* think?" Marty asks. "More like, what does

your *lady* think. Didn't Elsa send you here? She liked that cut I gave Kyle a few weeks back."

"She did."

"Well, how about this?" Marty turns Cliff's chair to demonstrate in front of the mirror. "What if I texture it today?"

"Texture it?"

"Absolutely." Marty lifts a comb through Cliff's hair. "Highlight that salt-and-pepper thing you've got going on. I won't take too much off. But a choppy texture will give it a distinguished look—with a youthful bent."

"Okay." Cliff turns his head and considers his reflection. "I *like* the sound of that."

When Marty lifts the scissors from his neatly aligned combs and clippers, Cliff watches. Keeps tabs on Mitch, too, as Max lathers up his face.

"Don't shave it, Max," Mitch tells him. "Just get it closer, down to some stubble."

"Bit of a change, Mitchell?"

"Yeah. It's for the camera." When he glances over and sees Cliff there, Mitch manages a nod. "Not to mention, teaching resumes this week, at the college."

Funny, though. Both men quiet once they're aware of each other's presence in the barbershop. Oh, Max and Marty make small talk to keep the dialogue going. As Marty lifts a spray bottle to wet down the top of Cliff's head, he asks Cliff what's new at Stony Point. And as Max pats down Mitch's face with a hot towel, he asks him what classes he'll be helming.

Finally, Cliff's glad to see Max lift off Mitch's black cape and straighten his chair.

"You get nervous being in front of the camera?" Max asks while they walk to the register.

"I had been," Mitch says, swinging an arm around Max's shoulder. "But someone's been helping me with that. And the stage fright's damn near gone."

"How about that," Max says.

Yeah, how about it, Cliff thinks from his chair. He's almost done now, too. Marty works a dollop of gel into his newly shorn hair.

"Nice work," Cliff remarks, watching his reflection—and Mitch at the register behind him. By the time Marty brushes off Cliff's neck and lifts his cape, Mitch is finishing up and leaving.

Unfortunately, their timing is just right. Cliff walks to the register at the same exact moment that Mitch turns and passes him on the way out.

"Clifton! Good to see you, man," Mitch says with an easy wave.

"Mitchell," Cliff adds with a nod. "Thought that was you." He says no more, though, as he pulls his wallet from his back pocket and takes care of his tab.

twenty-five

EARLY THAT AFTERNOON, MARIS STANDS with Maddy near Jason's SUV. It's parked on Champion Road behind the Fenwick cottage. When Jason opens the liftgate, Maddy jumps right in, circles around, then jumps out. The dog's tail doesn't stop swinging as she now stands at Jason's feet.

Maris pulls a bandana out of the bag of dog things in Jason's arms. "The charger for her collar is in there," she tells Jason. "Some new treats she likes, too."

"I was surprised to get your call," Jason admits while setting the bag, along with Maddy's leash, in the back of his SUV. "Especially after you *took* Maddy from me last week."

"Yeah, well." Maris motions for Maddy to jump back in the SUV cargo area. "Like I said, I have lots of research to do for the book," Maris lies—not letting on about how her kitchen demo has the dog a wreck. "So ... I'll be in and out, and need you to watch her," she adds while tying the bandana around Maddy's neck.

"What's that for?" Jason asks, right as a cameraman claps his shoulder when passing by.

"Jason!" Maris adjusts the dog's bandana before looking over her shoulder at him. "Maddy has to look pretty in case she's on camera!"

When the dog jumps to the ground, Jason closes up the SUV and walks with Maris and the German shepherd toward the cottage. There's a flurry of activity there: CT-TV production assistants buzzing around with clipboards in hand; a water station set up beneath a white canopy; Mitch talking to Trent.

"Oh, *Maris*!" Mitch calls when he spots her. "Getting a lot of writing done?" His tan tee is loose over cuffed jeans; his fading blond hair is wavy beneath that safari hat he wears. "Coming down the homestretch with that novel?" he asks, heading to Maris and Jason—right as a production assistant stops Trent.

"I am. Shouldn't be too much longer," Maris tells Mitch.

"Listen." Mitch stops her and Jason there on the sand beside his big old cottage. "If I can be of *any* help with that book, you let me know. If you need details about the cottage," he says, hitching his head to it. "Or any storm facts from when the hurricane hit."

Maris thanks him. "I really appreciate that, Mitch. And will keep it in mind."

As Trent motions for Jason then, Mitch extends an elbow to Maris. She takes it, and he walks her away from the crowd. When they stop near a stand of dune grasses, Mitch lowers his voice. "You know, I also wanted to talk to you about something else."

"Okay." Maris turns to him. "What is it, Mitch?"

Mitch shakes his head. "No, not now." He motions to the crew. "Too mobbed here. But are you free later this week? Something's been on my mind lately. And I'd love to hear your thoughts on it."

"Mitch?" Maris tips her head. The sun beats down hot at midday and in her pause, she hears the waves breaking on the beach. "Is everything okay?"

"Sure, sure." He takes her arm again and they head around toward the cottage's main deck. "How about Friday? You busy then, after dinner?"

"Well, I don't think so."

"Maris!" a voice calls from above. It's Carol. She's leaning on the deck railing and surveying the filming commotion. "Want a lemonade? I've got a pitcher for the crew."

"Yes, Maris!" another voice calls out. "Hold up."

Maris waves to Carol, then turns to see Trent flagging her down. He and Jason are standing on a sandy embankment by the cottage.

"Maris, glad you're here!" Trent says, motioning her over. "This is perfect, actually."

"Um, Maris," Mitch interrupts as she heads toward Trent. "So we're good for Friday?" he quietly asks.

"What?" She turns to Mitch and puts a hand on his arm. "Oh, *yes*. I'll be here. Around six."

At this point, Jason and Trent are both approaching her, too.

"Finally!" Trent is saying. "Maris, how about we grab some promo footage of you and Jason together. *Really* need it for the show's title sequence."

Maris touches her slack ponytail. "Now?" she asks. First she looks at Jason, utterly at ease in a denim shirt over a gray tee and dark shorts rolled at the cuffs. His denim shirtsleeves are folded back; his worn leather shoes, loosely tied. Then she glances at her own slub-knit V-neck tank top half-tucked into shorts—shredded *denim* shorts with *lots* of long threads hanging from the frayed hem. "Oh, boy," she goes on. "Trent. I'm just not ready for that," she says, motioning to her really casual cutoffs.

"That's life, sweetheart," Jason tells her while crossing his arms and taking in the sight of her panic. "Things come our way that we're not ready for."

"But—" She looks quickly from Jason to Trent, also standing there. "But my outfit ... Let me go home and change. It's not far."

"Nonsense." Trent takes her hands in his. "Keeping it real here. Your husband," he says, hitching his head to Jason, "has a five-*day* shadow of whiskers on his face. And, well ... you look just right for the show—straight out of a laid-back summer beach day with that getup."

When she looks to Jason—and turns up her hands with a silent expression *pleading* for him to get her out of this— he gives her a wink! Oh, there's some grin beneath those whiskers, too.

"And hey," Jason tells her, "with your hair pulled back like that, it shows those beautiful earrings."

Maris' hand instantly reaches for a blue topaz stud. She touches it, then looks to Trent. And to Mitch watching. And to Carol still surveying from up on the deck.

So Maris knows. She's trapped. But she still insists to Trent that she has to go inside the Fenwick cottage and freshen up, at the very least.

And feels all eyes on her as she climbs those deck stairs.

⌒‿

Everything's pretty much a blur inside. Maris sidesteps the film crew and asks for scissors from Carol—who finds a pair in a kitchen drawer. Rushing into the half bathroom off a hallway then, Maris shuts the door and doesn't stop. She pulls a brush from her tote, takes out her pathetic ponytail, flips her head and gives her brown hair a good brushing. After flipping her hair back, she leans close to the mirror, dabs on lip gloss and straightens her slub-knit tank top. Adjusts her gold star pendant, too. And takes a long breath.

All the while, noises come to her from outside the closed door. The dog's collar is jangling. The crew is setting up lights and mics—some in the kitchen, some out on the deck. Voices give orders. Jason's voice is in the mix, too.

Quick, quick! Maris thinks. She grabs those scissors off the small bathroom vanity and begins hacking long threads hanging off her shorts hem. The threads dangle randomly right over her legs. So she lifts the various threads, here and there, and snips. Snips some more. Gets some off the sides of the shorts, too, before putting down the scissors and turning to the door.

"*Shit!*" she says when giving one last look in the wall mirror. More of those pesky threads hang down the *back* of her legs. So she twists around and maneuvers the sharp scissors there now. Gets one thread here, then another. Tries to look over her shoulder for more. Turns in front of the mirror and works on the other leg. With one hand, she feels another really long thread grazing the back of her thigh. And though she can *lift* the thread with her fingers, she can't *see* it—no matter how much she twists her torso.

A sharp knock sounds at the closed door, mid-twist. "You almost ready, Maris?" Jason calls out. "We're on soon."

"Hang on a sec," Maris answers while blindly clipping that last, long thread. Her hair falls in front of her face as she's half-bent and twisted while scissoring. "*Ooh, ooh, ow!*" she calls out then—right as those damn scissors slice her left ring finger. Blood spurts from the cut, so she quickly hits the toilet paper roll, grabs a wad and presses the clump of tissue to her bloody finger. Turns to the sink, too, tosses aside the reddened tissue and runs warm water over the sliced-open skin. When the water hits her cut, the stinging gets her hissing and spewing groans again.

And still her finger bleeds. There's enough blood for her to flush that first wad of soiled toilet paper and grab more from the roll—her uninjured hand desperately slapping at it.

〜

The way that bathroom door flies open, Jason jumps back. Just in time, too, as Maris runs out into the kitchen.

"Jason! I cut myself," she says, holding up her injured hand. "I'm bleeding! And it won't stop!"

"What?" But Jason can't miss it, that bloody toilet paper wrapped around her finger. So he grabs a couple of paper towels from the kitchen counter. "Here, use these instead. Put some pressure on it."

Maris gives him the bloody toilet paper and presses those paper towels to her cut. "It just won't *stop*," she says, stamping her foot at the same time.

"What happened?" Jason asks, stepping closer and eyeing the injury.

"I didn't know I was going to be filmed today," Maris says, nodding to crew members clustered in the doorway. "So I was trying to cut some long threads off my shorts so I wouldn't look sloppy on camera."

"Cutting *threads*?" Jason tosses the soiled toilet tissue in a trash can, then turns back to her. "What are you doing picking up scissors when you're this tense?"

"Well I wasn't tense until I *cut* myself—which I didn't *mean* to do. I was just reaching around behind my leg and couldn't really see. That's when I sliced my finger."

As she's explaining, and holding up the wrapped, blood-pulsing cut to show Jason, he notices something else. Some of the construction crew is in the room now. And Trent moseys into the kitchen, too. As does Maddy—Maris' distress gets her trotting over.

"Carol? Mitch?" Zach calls while the camera is lifted to his shoulder. "Could you get the dog out on the deck?"

Maris looks from the dog—prancing away when someone whistles—to her paper-towel-wrapped finger. "I can feel it *throbbing*."

"It'll stop." Jason walks right up to her and takes her hand. "Here, let me see."

She unpeels the paper towel to reveal a nice gash in her fingertip. In a second, more blood bubbles up, so Jason gives her another wad of paper towels. Looks over his shoulder, too. "Mitch!" Jason calls out. "Do you have any bandages?"

Mitch rushes in from the deck. "Everything all right?" he asks, hurrying closer.

"Yeah," Jason explains while motioning to Maris. "Just a little cut going on."

"Jason!" Maris is wrapping her slashed finger with those fresh paper towels. "*Little* cut? I don't even know if I can go on camera now!"

Mitch works his way past the crew, and Trent, and filming equipment in the kitchen. "Well," Mitch says, running a hand down his goatee as he takes in the sight of Maris' wound. "There's a first aid kit in a wicker basket on the bathroom shelf."

Jason moves Maris aside and hurries to that half bath. "Okay, found it," he calls out, returning to the kitchen. "Come on," he tells Maris. He's got a few bandages in one hand, and touches her arm with the other. "Let's sit at the patio table outside, on the deck." Her head is bent as she intently studies her wrapped-and-gashed finger, so Jason tips up her chin. "You look a little pale," he quietly admits.

"I *do*? Oh my God, Jason!" she says, following after him. "From loss of blood? Maybe I need an aspirin."

"No." Jason stops at the slider and motions for her to go out ahead of him. "Aspirin *thins* the blood. You want it to *clot* now, Maris," he adds.

"Are you sure?" Maris stops outside and waits for him. "*I'm so embarrassed, Jason,*" she whispers.

"Just get some air," he tells her, nodding to the nearby patio table.

As he leads Maris there, and pulls out a chair for her in the shade of the table's umbrella, Carol asks what happened. The gaffer asks if Maris is okay. Other crew members move aside and act like they're not watching this all go down.

But Jason just sets the bandages on the table and turns to Maris. He sits in a chair right beside her, beneath that patio umbrella. The shade feels good. A slight breeze lifts off the water here. "All right," he says to Maris. "Take a breath. And let's *slowly* lift off the paper towels."

"I don't want to." Maris covers her injured finger with her other hand. "I'm really afraid." As she says it, Jason's carefully lifting first her hand, then the newly bloodied paper towels. When he does, Maris gasps. "*It looks so bad!*" she harshly whispers.

Jason pulls her hand closer, leans low and dabs a clean paper towel on it.

"Do you think I need stitches?" Maris asks. "Should I go to the walk-in clinic?"

"No, sweetheart." Jason tucks a lock of her hair behind an ear. "Let's just get you bandaged up and see how it holds." He shoves up his cuffed denim shirtsleeves, carefully rips open a bandage and wraps it around the sliced finger. "Feel okay?" he asks, looking at her so close beside him.

Maris nods. "But it's still throbbing."

So Jason opens a second bandage, and this one he very tenderly wraps over the first. When he's done, he gently, *gently* presses the bandage's adhesive, too. "Good?" he quietly asks.

Maris takes a sharp breath as she still leans as close as possible to Jason's tending. "Yeah, I'm all right." But she doesn't sit back. Doesn't pull her hand away. She practically leans into his shoulder as he brushes the bandage.

Jason looks at her sitting right there in her black V-neck tank top and those frayed denim shorts. And he just watches her dark eyes for a long moment. Then he lifts her injured hand and presses the lightest kiss on the back of it. The whole time, his eyes never leave hers.

"*Awesome*, Jason. Nice touch," Trent announces into the silence that follows.

Which gets Jason to spin around. "What the hell?" he asks when he notices the film crew—*and* Mitch, *and* Carol—all silently riveted to him and Maris.

"Got it all," Zach tells Trent while lowering the camera.

"*Phew!*" Mitch says then, getting Jason to look *his* way now. When he does, Mitch steps closer, lifts off his safari hat and fans Jason at the table. "Things were heatin' up a bit, no?"

"What's going on?" Maris asks.

"Camera's always rolling once on-site and set up, Maris," Trent says, motioning to Zach putting down his camera.

"*Always?*" she asks back.

Trent nods. "Can always cut what we *don't* need. But we can *never* grab footage we missed—so we try not to miss any. And we got a good one just now."

"Of *us?*" Jason asks, sitting back in his chair and feeling, well, a little bit *used*.

"Definitely. Couldn't have planned that better if we tried," Trent explains. "Real *life*, with your wife, Jason. Great stuff. Sexy, too. We'll weave it right into the show's opener."

twenty-six

THEY HAVE TO DO IT. Celia knows they have no choice.

Even though the September morning is beautiful. The skies are blue; the clouds, few.

Even though it would be so easy to lounge out on Shane's big old deck facing the distant harbor. Recline in a chair; breathe that sweet salt air; listen to the gulls calling out as they swoop over a departing lobster boat. Hear the bell buoy clang. Hold Aria. Feel the late-summer warmth. Maybe even write a little song there.

But they don't do any of that.

No, instead—after Aria's dishpan bath—they walk off those doughnuts.

Walk them off in pure Shane style, too.

"Thought you'd like this place," he tells Celia as they wheel Aria's stroller along a twelve-foot-wide boardwalk. "It's the Rockland Harbor Trail."

"Shane. Everywhere I turn here? There's a new version of paradise." Celia takes in the blue waters before them. She lifts Aria out of her stroller and points out the harbor seals sunning themselves on the rocky banks.

Shane nods and motions for her to sit on a wooden bench there.

Which becomes a problem—albeit a good one. Because it's just too beautiful a spot to leave. With Aria on her lap, Celia leans into Shane beside her and watches the soaring seagulls. A windjammer cruises past, too— its sails pure white beneath the sunshine. Before they know it, a few minutes sitting there become half an hour.

When they do walk again, Shane pushes Aria's stroller this time. He points out ocean stars to the baby. They veer off the trail and onto a small beach, where Shane carries the stroller across the sand and sets it near the lapping waves. Aria bounces and gurgles at the sight of the close water. As she does, Shane first slips off his shoes and cuffs his jeans. He scoops up a few flat stones from the shallows, too. Standing at the water's edge, he skims those stones, one by one, over the calm inlet. Points them out to Aria as the stones skip and jump, leaving a spray of the sea behind them.

Celia stands back and watches. She hooks her sunglasses on the belt loop of her black denim shorts. Straightens her sleeveless chambray top, too. After a moment, she comes up behind Shane as he's skimming and wraps her arms around him. Presses her face to his shoulder and watches the water beyond him now.

Shane stops skimming, then. He pockets the one stone left in his hand and gently leans back into Celia's embrace.

His arms hold hers around his waist. Aria's in her stroller beside them. When Celia stretches up on tiptoe to leave a kiss on Shane's whiskered face, he turns his head and bends a little to take that kiss.

As she does it, as her lips brush his face, Shane says something to her. It happens as he's leaning down and she's stretching up and leaving that kiss on his jaw. They're not facing each other—it's more of a side kiss. They're not even really *looking* at each other. But Celia hears the words as much as she feels him say them. Right in the middle of her kiss.

"I love you, Celia," Shane says, his voice low.

Celia smiles, and leaves a second kiss there on his jaw. As if, well, as if this moment was just part of their summer day. His serious words as natural as the sea breeze lifting off the water.

But then Celia realizes *precisely* what he just said. She pulls back and gives him a questioning look. But Shane says nothing more. He just lifts an arm around her shoulders, pulls her close and kisses the top of her head.

The thing is, as she loops an arm around his waist and leans into him there, and as she later lifts Aria out of her stroller and dips her toes into the water, and as they leave the sandy beach and head home, Celia occasionally sneaks a look at Shane. Brushes her fingers over the rolled sleeves of his white Henley tee. Toys with his braided leather cuff. In her mind, hears again those private words *almost* lost in the sea breeze.

~

When they're back at Shane's shingled house, and she gives Aria her bottle, changes her, and settles her in for a nap, Celia still steals those looks. As Shane stands at his kitchen counter and makes their lunch—leftovers from the Red Boat Tavern—she watches him.

"I always order extra. Tastes even better the next day," he says, setting down the plates and sitting with her at the table.

Celia nods and digs in. "After we eat ... I really want to sit out on your deck. Bring my guitar. Maybe write some music out there."

"That's decent," Shane says. "Do you write much?"

She gives a little shrug. "Here and there. And I'd like to, today. Unless you wanted to wash the car. It's salty from driving around."

"Nah. Too hot to clean cars. I've got a better idea."

"You do?"

"Yeah." Shane wipes his mouth with a napkin and leans back, eyeing her. "But you go ahead. Finish your lunch outside and work out that music while the baby's sleeping. I'll catch up with you in a bit."

⁓

It's a summer that won't let go, in more ways than one. First, there's Celia having a sweet hold on him. And his brother's in his life again, too. Then there's just Stony Point—casting its spell *every* time he drives beneath the stone trestle.

The heat won't let go, either, Shane thinks. Standing there in his loose white tee and cuffed jeans, he hooks his garden hose to an oscillating sprinkler on the side lawn. He sees Celia sitting over on the built-in deck bench. Her auburn hair is down, one side tucked behind an ear. She's barefoot, and wears her sleeveless chambray button-down over frayed black denim shorts. Her wide silver thumb ring flashes as she strums her guitar, stops and picks up a notepad to jot the music she's feeling. Then there's more strumming, pausing, moving her fingers to a different chord on the fret, and humming. It's clear she's in the zone.

So Shane turns on the spigot, and sixteen streams of water reach skyward from the sprinkler. The water glistens in the sun as the droplets fall on the lawn.

"Hey, Celia," Shane says when she crosses the side lawn. "Sounding good."

"You like?" she asks, glancing back to where she'd left her guitar on the deck.

"Definitely. Can't wait to hear the whole song."

Celia turns up her hands as she nears him. "Won't be today. Too hot to write much more," she says. "But I had such an itch to work out a new tune."

"You ready for a break, then?"

"And do what?"

He hitches his head to the sprinkler. "Cool off some." Shane takes her hands, pauses, then does a slow spin with her beneath the hot sun and sprinkling water drops. It gets Celia to tip her head back and smile—just like that. They do a little waltz right there on the green grass—holding each other as if on a dance floor as he twirls her again beneath his raised arm, and they sway in the spray of water.

"Shane!" she calls out when the streams of water pass across them. But she says no more as he pulls her close—

so near the sprinkler that those gentle streams work right up over their bodies. Their clothes drip—his jeans and tee, her top and shorts. The fabric is clammy against their skin. Their faces get wet; their hair, damp. He tips his forehead to hers. The sun shines down. Water droplets fall around them. And they just stand there—his hands on her waist; hers on his shoulders; faces, so close.

But only for a few seconds.

Only until Shane surprises her. He scoops her up, reaching beneath her legs and around her back and hoisting her—barefoot and laughing—high up in his arms. She loops *her* arms around his neck as he lightly jostles her up higher, then she leans her head against his shoulder.

And he goes for it. Holding her close in his arms, he runs right through the spraying water, takes a leap over the sprinkler, turns and does it again—so that they're drenched through and through—laughing beneath the silver droplets falling around them.

twenty-seven

MY, OH MY," ELSA MURMURS late Tuesday afternoon at Sea Spray Beach. She leans forward and squints out the windshield when she spots Ted Sullivan's cottage. Jason Barlow's hand in the design is clear. Those honey-colored cedar shingles, the wide white trim, the brass wall lanterns glimmering in the low sunlight—all of it's classic New England coastal. When Elsa parks and gets out of her car, she also notices a striking stained-glass window on the second level. The intricate glass pieces form an image of a great white egret standing in the reeds. That window has her slow her step on the way to the front stoop. There, she shifts her black straw tote and a bag she carries before trying the door. "Jason!" she calls out while opening it.

"In the kitchen," his voice calls back.

Elsa steps into the foyer, greets Maddy rushing to see her, then hurries down a hallway, passes the living room and stops, speechless, in the kitchen doorway. The dog is at her feet, nudging her, prancing around.

But that kitchen! The cream-colored cabinets—some with glass fronts. The gray-swirled marble island. The stainless-steel farmhouse sink. And the *ceiling*—its planked hardwood takes her breath away. She slowly enters the room and sets her bags on the island. Jason's at a counter near the slider.

"Wasn't sure you'd show up," he says.

"Five o'clock—right on time. Though I certainly didn't appreciate being *ordered* here." With the dog sitting at her feet and watching her, Elsa lifts a container from a bag. "And I can't *believe* I brought dinner just to be scolded."

"Not scolded," Jason tells her over his shoulder. He's dressed in a gray tee and dark shorts rolled at the cuff. He's also closing the flaps of a box at that counter. A messy pile of newspapers and a burlap-wrapped happiness jar are beside the box. "I just want to talk," he says, picking up a black marker.

"With no agenda?" Elsa asks, walking closer.

"I didn't say *that*." Marker in hand, Jason turns and gives her a quick hug.

"This cottage—" Elsa sweeps a hand to the rooms. "There are just no words for it. You've outdone yourself."

"Well, after everything, Ted deserved the best. So make yourself comfortable," Jason tells her, then gets back to that box and writes something on it.

Elsa moves to the counter, too. "And would you look at that happiness jar," she says, touching the burlap strip around the glass. The jar's filled with sand, sea pebbles, driftwood sticks and shells. "Did you make this here?"

"No," Jason says. "Maris made it for Neil. On the day of his Memorial Mass."

"Bless her heart. It's *beautiful*." Elsa nudges it closer, spotting a note tucked in it, too. She's quiet for a moment, before turning to that gorgeous kitchen again. "Well, whatever you want to talk about—it's *not* what you're thinking."

"And what am I thinking?"

"That you walked in on something private between me and Mitch this morning," Elsa explains while opening one cabinet, then another, before finding plates. She sets two on a white kitchen table tucked into the most charming windowed nook. "That I wasn't just having banana pudding with Mitch, but that I'd spent the *night* there," she says, stealing a look at Jason. He's moving that closed box beside the happiness jar.

"What am I supposed to think, when you're having *breakfast* with the guy?" he asks.

Elsa lifts an insulated container out of her bag and sets it on the island. "Can't two neighbors have breakfast together?"

"Breakfast." Now Jason crosses his arms and leans against the counter. "In that silky robe you were wearing?"

"*Please*, Jason. You *know* I'd never be caught outside in my pajamas. That wasn't a *robe*. It's a casual beach dress. And … and … You started all this!"

Still just watching her, Jason says, "So something *did* start up between you and Mitch."

"You're twisting up my words." Elsa finds a pot now and sets it on the gourmet stovetop.

"And you're not denying them." Jason snaps his fingers at the dog following Elsa. "Maddy. Go lie down," he orders, hitching his head to the dog bed near the slider.

"Regardless," Elsa says, spooning food from the insulated container into the pot, then starting the flame beneath it. "It really *is* all your fault."

"Mine?" Jason pats the dog in her bed, then walks to the table, lifts a denim shirt off it and drapes it over the chairback.

"Yes. You gave Mitch Fenwick my phone number to get in touch for filming tips."

They go back and forth about this as Elsa lifts a sack of tomatoes from her bag. She pulls out some green tomatoes and lines them on the windowsill.

"Tomatoes, Elsa?"

"Oh, I've got a *glut* of them in my Sea Garden now that there are no inn guests to cook for. All those tomatoes will go to waste if I don't give them away. So let the green ones ripen, here," she adds, nudging one more on the sill. "And do you have a dish? For the red ones?"

Jason finds a platter in a cabinet, gives it to her, then checks out the simmering pot on the stove. "Looks like meatballs?"

"Turkey meatballs. With mozzarella in the center." Elsa arranges more red tomatoes on the platter. "That's what I did today," she says, nodding to the stove. "Made all those meatballs … and wanted to *throw* some at you!"

"But instead we'll make a nice grinder, huh?" Jason grabs a bag of potato chips and pours them into a bowl on the island.

"Those look good." Elsa steps closer and tastes a chip.

"They're the rosemary-and-olive-oil chips I told you about. From Eva."

"She was here?"

215

"Yesterday."

"Why?" Elsa asks, grabbing another chip.

"For one thing, to fill me in on the kitchen reno at my place," he tells her while bringing the bowl of chips to the table.

"*Oh!* Jason!" Elsa spins around to him. "That was a *secret.*"

Jason waves her off. "I already knew about it," he says, sitting again and eating a chip. "Cody was being evasive, wasn't at job sites—and he's my best contractor. So I figured something was up and got it out of him."

Elsa puts her hands on her hips and squints over at Jason. "Eva did *not* come all this way to tell you her sister's secret. Nice bluff, Jason."

"You're right. She brought me chicken cutlets, too." He gets a plate of them out of the refrigerator. "Want some?"

"Eva's cutlets? Sure. But listen," Elsa continues, opening drawers and looking for flatware. "I'm not going to talk about personal things while we eat." She finally lifts out forks and knives, and sets them on the kitchen table. "We're *just* going to enjoy the food."

"Fine." Jason fills Maddy's bowl with kibble. Then he sets napkins and glasses on that table in the nook. Opens some windows there, too. "And how's Cliff these days?" he asks.

Elsa's back at the stove now. "*Uh-uh-uh,*" she says while stirring the warming meatballs. "*Mangia.* Let's eat."

⌒⌄

And eat, they do.

Turkey meatball grinders. Eva's chicken cutlets covered

with melted cheese and drizzled tomato sauce. Potato chips. Salad. They sit in the kitchen nook; a sea breeze wafts in the open windows around them; they talk easily.

Elsa does something else, too. She notices things. Notices Jason's papers and keys on the counter. Notices mail and envelopes. His checkbook. A half-filled box of powdered doughnuts. His work tablet and blueprint tubes off to the side.

"I don't like seeing you here like this," she says, pushing away her dish now. Her voice drops, too. "Don't like visiting my nephew-in-law where he clearly doesn't belong."

"I know, Elsa. I know. You're not the first person to tell me that." Jason takes a long breath and sits back in his chair. "Listen. Why don't you go in the living room while I clean up here? Go sit on the couch. And we'll talk there."

~

"Okay. The doctor is in," Jason says, walking into the living room awhile later.

Elsa's watching him from the driftwood-gray sofa. She's got on a white tank top over paint-spattered jeans. Her white crochet sweater is tossed over the sofa back. Her thick brown hair is down; a gold bangle is on her wrist. Classic Elsa, except for one thing—her drawn face.

"Lay it on me," Jason continues, sitting in an upholstered chair across from her. "Tell me about this love triangle I'm catching wind of."

Elsa takes a quick breath. Reaches down and pats Maddy sitting there, too. "I wouldn't call it a *love* triangle."

"What is it, then?"

Elsa stands and goes to an open window. At this dusky hour, the sky outside is violet blue. The sound of the waves breaking on the beach reaches in. "It's just that … Oh, I'm in *un mare di guai*."

"English, please."

Elsa takes another quick breath and turns to him. "I'm in a sea of troubles. Okay?"

"That's better." Jason motions for her to sit on the couch again. "At least you admit it. First step in facing a problem."

"And a problem it is," Elsa groans, sitting on the sofa and rubbing a hand on the fabric. "I'll tell you something else, too."

"Go on."

"Yes," she begins, nodding to Jason. As she does, Maddy rests her muzzle on the sofa cushion. "Yes, there *is* something between me and Mitch. I'm not sure what it is yet. But you're a smart man, Jason. You can fill in the blanks … Things have happened."

"Jesus Christ." Now it's Jason's turn to take a breath, sit back and eye Elsa. "*Things?*"

"*Merda, merda, merda,*" Elsa says.

"Ah, no translation necessary."

"That's right, Jason—*shit*."

"I *knew* it." He stands, retrieves Maddy's squeaky fetch stick from the floor—and sternly points that fetch stick at Elsa. "I just knew it."

"And I *don't* know what to do. Mitch," she says, raising one hand now. "And Cliff," she goes on, raising the other. "Cool everything? With everybody? The inn included?"

"What?" Jason slides the dog toy Maddy's way. She grabs it up and settles on the floor, all while gnawing the stick held between her paws. "Cool the Ocean Star Inn?"

"Yes, the inn, too. Because I even made a mess of things with Celia. So lately?" Elsa asks. "*Every* move I make seems wrong."

"I hear you."

"And I can't keep living some kind of double life. But please believe me—all this with Mitch just ... *happened.*" She leans forward on the sofa. "I certainly didn't plan it."

"I didn't think you did, Elsa." Jason runs his knuckles over the scar on his jaw. "But what about Cliff? He's been by your side through *everything* this past year. And to me—and everyone else—it looked like he's your guy."

"Well. I mean ..." Elsa sits back and brushes a hand over those paint-spattered jeans. "I know, but—"

"But ... what?"

"That's the problem," Elsa admits. "*But* then there's Mitch."

"Elsa, come on. You've only known him—what? A week?"

"*Hey*," she warns. "You're headed into scolding territory, mister. Keep it up and I'm out of here."

"Okay, okay." Jason holds up his hands. "I just thought you and Cliff were the real deal, Elsa."

Elsa stands then. Stands and paces the living room. She circles around the coffee table, passes the fireplace, slows near the open windows looking out to the evening.

Jason watches her. It's apparent this isn't some light issue. It's actually way more serious than he'd thought. She's really conflicted. "Listen, I can't tell you what to do,

Elsa. But I find it helps if you stay busy. You process your thoughts that way."

"Maybe." Elsa still walks the room.

"Aren't you working on that inn issue, with the zoning office?"

"No."

"*No?* What do you mean, no?"

"I mean, I'm taking a break." She spins around from where she's standing at the mantel. "It's been nonstop with that inn—buying it, the reno, the business plan, filming for your show. And then I hit a brick *wall* last week with zoning!"

"Let me handle some of it."

Elsa sweeps her hand to Ted's cottage. "You've got *enough* to handle, Jason Barlow. And I *don't* mean about your work."

"Well, if you're putting the brakes on the inn, what will you do instead?" Jason presses her. "What's your plan? Your *life* plan."

"Not much. I garden in the morning. Do some housework." She begins pacing again while vaguely talking. "Catch up on emails with old friends in Italy. Deliver tomatoes. Visit neighbors."

"Yeah. One in particular, apparently. A very available widower who happens to be king of the beach with his cottage."

Elsa waves him off. "*Anyway.* Celia's in Addison and taking a few days to herself. So I am, too."

"And look what you've gotten yourself into."

"Oh, you once did the same thing, Mr. Barlow."

"What?"

"Yes, you did. Before Maris rolled back into Stony Point, she was *engaged* to a perfectly nice fellow in Chicago."

Jason nods. "Scott."

"That's right. She even had his ring on her finger." Elsa marches back to the sofa and sits again. She leans her elbows on her knees and looks directly at Jason. "But you thought *you* were the one for Maris. You, *yourself*, turned the situation into a triangle and went after her. *And* took her away from that man."

Jason gets up and heads to the kitchen. "Totally different scenario," he calls over his shoulder. When he returns with two bottled waters, giving one to Elsa, he continues. "And I *knew* Maris from when we were kids."

"Doesn't matter. Maris was committed to someone." Elsa opens her water and takes a swig, then sort of points the bottle at Jason. "Which, by the way, I'm *not*."

Jason blows out a breath. And drags a hand through his hair. "Don't appreciate it when you use my own life against me, Elsa."

She gets up—to leave, apparently. Scooping up her light sweater, she heads to the kitchen for her tote. "Do as I say, not as I do?" she calls out on the way.

"Hang on, hang on. Before you storm out of here, I've got ice cream. Want dessert? Coffee?"

"No, not tonight," her muffled voice comes from the kitchen. When she returns, her topper is on and she's slinging that straw tote onto her shoulder. "One more thing," she says. "You are not to tell Maris *any* of this about Mitch and Cliff." When Jason starts to resist, Elsa cuts him off. "I can't have Maris know until *I* know what to do."

"But Elsa," Jason argues. "That's really hard because

I'm trying to be very open with her."

Elsa quickly shakes her head, then digs her keys out of her tote. "I don't ask you a lot. But I *don't* need any more cooks in the kitchen." She heads out of the living room toward the front door. "And may I remind you," Elsa says, turning to Jason—and now the dog—following behind her. "Maris has *enough* on her plate. Like, her book. Her kitchen. And … her marriage?"

"You're deflecting," Jason says, then gives Elsa a hug at the front door. "But I won't tell anyone," he assures her as she turns and hurries down the front steps. "You just be careful, all right?" he calls into the evening shadows—all while holding Maddy's collar to keep her from running out, too.

⁓

Closing the door once Elsa's driven off, Jason returns to the kitchen and heads straight to the large pantry. He lifts another empty carton from a stack there. Setting the box on the kitchen counter then, he lifts that burlap-wrapped happiness jar and carefully puts it in the box. Lifts a few sections of newspaper, too, and lightly crumples them before tucking them around the jar. That done, he reaches for his black marker and writes *Happiness Jar – Fragile* on the carton and slides it beside the other carton—the one marked *Shoes*.

twenty-eight

IT'S A LITTLE LIKE BEING out at sea.

Shane can almost feel the subtle sway of the boat. There's a light sea breeze, too, lifting off the water. Hell, if he closes his eyes right now, he could be somewhere on the Atlantic—with land nowhere to be seen. There's just water. Everywhere. And that swaying sensation.

He doesn't *always* feel the sway on the boat—particularly if he's busy hauling up pots, banding lobsters, working with the boys to get the job done. Doesn't feel that sway, either, if the boat's motoring along at full throttle. But there are times, like when the captain shuts off the engine on calm days, with no wind, when the seas are peaceful. That's when the boat just floats … and drifts. Rises and falls. There's only the sound of the sea lapping at the hull. And that gentle motion. The sway.

He's *not* out at sea, though. He's as close to home as he can get. All because of a sign Celia came upon earlier, one posted at the dock entrance.

"Look, Shane," she'd said, glancing back at him while reading the announcement. "End of summer concert on the docks. Tuesday," she went on. "That's *tonight*. Seven o'clock, after dinner." Again she looked at him. "Want to go?"

So they made it a date—and here they are.

The night's perfect for an outdoor concert, too, the way the heat of the day holds on. With the lavender sky over the harbor, and gulls perched on roped dock posts as though listening to the music, Shane stands with Celia here on the lawn of the harbor park.

Well, he sways with her.

Aria's in her stroller beside them; townsfolk are scattered around on the sloping grounds; the band is set up on the adjoining dock; Penobscot Bay is blue beyond.

And the music plays. The vocalist's voice carries in that sea breeze as she sings about how her world has suddenly changed. About believing in the things we see.

Standing behind Celia, Shane loops his arms loosely around her neck, her shoulders—and he knows. Oh, how *his* world has suddenly changed. He presses his face close to the side of her head, and to the relaxed beat of the music, they sway.

Side to side.

Easy.

Gentle.

Celia wears a blue ombré tank-top dress. The light fabric is crinkly, and fitted on top. But its high-low hem has it looser at the hips and legs. That swingy fabric moves with her now. Shane feels it. Feels her soft hair against his cheek, his jaw. Sees her silent smile as she listens to the song and simply leans back into him.

They move as one to the slow tune—just swaying in the summer twilight.

twenty-nine

THE QUICKER ELSA GETS HOME, the better she'll feel.

Oh, her dinner with Jason wasn't easy. But the comfort of her own kitchen, and living room, will settle her thoughts. So once off the highway and on Shore Road, she guns it—driving past a bait-and-tackle shop. She also briefly tailgates a slower car ahead of her, then backs off. Does something else, too. Looks in the rearview mirror when a police car's flashing light comes up behind her.

Another delay, Elsa thinks, pulling over to let the cruiser pass.

But it doesn't.

Slightly panicked, she watches again in her rearview mirror—this time as the police car *parks* behind her. With its light still flashing, a young officer gets out and approaches.

"Is there a problem?" Elsa calls to him through her open window.

"Little bit. See that stop sign back there?" he asks, motioning to an intersection down the road.

Elsa twists around and squints through the shadows. "Yes, of *course* I see it," she says to the officer—who must be fresh out of the police academy, he's so young.

"You went through it."

"What? No, I stopped." Elsa glances back a block to that stop sign in question. "I *know* I did."

"That's not what I saw. And a *tap-and-go* is not a stop, ma'am. I'll need your license and registration, please."

With a long breath, she digs her license from her tote and her car registration from the glove box. "Let me just say that stop sign *is* somewhat obstructed by beach grass. It really ought to be cut back," she goes on. When the officer only nods and takes her papers to his cruiser, Elsa flops back in her seat. The night's steamy, now that the sun's setting. A mist rises over the distant salt marsh—but it doesn't cool things down. Crickets slowly chirp. A lone robin holds onto its song in the shadows of a roadside tree. Traffic is light here on Shore Road.

"*Wait a minute*," Elsa whispers when a vehicle slowly drives past—a *safari*-style vehicle with its top off. A very *familiar* vehicle. One in which she's actually been a passenger. Her hair blew in the breeze that evening last week—with Mitch Fenwick at the wheel.

So, okay. Now tonight, Mitch is witnessing her traffic indiscretion.

"*Oh, no*," she still whispers, watching that vehicle of his make a careful U-turn and head back in her direction. "This can't be," she says while sinking lower in her seat. Because now Mitch is parking right in front of her car.

"Elsa?" he asks, quickly walking over. He's wearing the same tan tee and faded jeans from their sunrise breakfast all those hours ago. His usual two-strap leather sandals, too. "Everything okay?"

"Mitch, yes," she answers, leaning out her open window. "I'm all set here, no need to trouble yourself."

"Nonsense, it's no trouble. What's going on?"

She briefly relays how the officer said that her *stop* was more a *tap-and-go*, or some such thing, and now she's no doubt being issued a ticket.

Mitch squints over at the young officer just getting out of his patrol car. "You wait here," he tells Elsa, giving her arm a squeeze. "Be right back."

As if she's going anywhere, anytime soon. Instead, she sits there and watches Mitch in her side-view mirror. When he nears the young officer, the cop looks up—and *smiles!* Broadly! And extends his hand for a very hearty shake. So she leans further out her window just in time to hear the officer's words.

"*Professor Fenwick!* Good to see you again!"

⁓

Of all nights to get pulled over, Mitch just had to drive by. And now he's befriending this cop?

Sitting in her car, Elsa curses herself for going to dinner at Jason's. He cut right through to the truth. And every bit of worry and angst wrung out of that dinner manifested itself in her foot—heavy on the gas, light on the brakes. Now all she wants to do is get home.

The minutes tick past while she waits. And waits. Mitch

and the young officer chat, and lean against that patrol car, and chat some more. Finally—*finally*—the cop approaches and hands back her license and registration.

"Okay, Mrs. DeLuca," he says through her open window. "Just a verbal warning today."

"What? Am I hearing you right?" Elsa asks while clutching her papers.

The officer nods. "I made note of the obstructing beach grass. But please be respectful of those stop signs in the future."

"Of course." She tucks her license in her tote, then turns quickly to the window. "And thank you!" she calls as he returns to his parked cruiser.

A moment later, more footsteps outside. She looks over to see Mitch approaching.

"You all set now, Elsa?" he asks through her window.

Elsa looks up at him in the evening shadows. His blond hair is brushed back as he draws a hand over his goatee. "You talked my ticket down to a warning, didn't you?" she asks, squinting at him. "Because that cop was all young and full of himself—and seriously ready to write me up."

Mitch waves at the police cruiser as it pulls out to the street again. "Lucky for you, the officer was one of my students," he says to Elsa then. "Always late handing in his essays. But we turned that habit around by end of semester," Mitch muses, watching the cop's car depart. "And that nice officer believed that *you* can turn your *tap-and-go* around, too."

"*Ach! Tap-and-go*," Elsa gripes as she leans over the front seat and returns her registration to the glove box.

Mitch leans low to Elsa's open car window. "You're a

little shaken up by the incident, Elsa," he says. "So I'll just follow you home to be sure you make it okay."

The whole way back to Stony Point, those headlights shine steady behind her. Mitch's headlights. And Elsa's careful to obey every traffic rule, but honestly? She can't get back to her inn soon enough. A nice cup of hot tea is just what she needs to simmer down. Because first there was that uncomfortable dinner with Jason, and now *this*—Mitch Fenwick witnessing her criminal activity. And bailing her out, no less.

Turning beneath the stone trestle, Elsa stops—*fully*—to chat briefly with Nick at the guard station. After he waves her in, Nick turns to Mitch's safari-style vehicle behind hers. She notices, too, how Nick tips back his guard cap and looks quickly from Mitch, to Elsa, then back to Mitch before waving him through. But … Nick *also* steps into the quiet beach road—Elsa can't miss that, either. He stands there and watches them both drive off—in the *same* direction.

By the time Elsa turns into the crushed-stone driveway at the inn, her nerves are pretty well frazzled. The last thing she needs is Nick putting two and two together about her and Mitch—who's also pulling into her driveway now.

Elsa grabs her straw tote and gets out, saying to herself, "What a day. *Gesù, Santa Maria.*"

"Beg your pardon?" Mitch asks from his open-air driver's seat.

"Oh, Mitch," she says, waving him off. "Just been a crazy day, that's all. So thanks for seeing me home and ... good night."

"Now wait a minute, would you?" Mitch shuts off his vehicle and hops out. Looks at her, too, then off in the direction of the distant boat basin. Again he draws a hand over his goatee. "Don't you have a rowboat of some sort?" he asks.

"A rowboat?" Elsa hoists her tote up on her shoulder. "Yes. Yes, I do." She glances up at the evening sky. Tiny stars are starting to press through the darkness. "Why?"

"Well," Mitch begins, stepping closer. "Seems like, to calm everything down for you, the night calls for a little paddle." He extends a hand to her. "Shall we?"

⌒⌒

Well. Here she goes again.

Fifteen minutes later, Elsa's in a sea of troubles once more—floating on the sea itself with Mitch Fenwick.

Mitch rows that old wooden boat into the marsh. He's languid with the paddling. Pulling back on the oars and lifting them out, he often lets those oars hover ... and the boat just floats. It's a mellow feeling, Elsa thinks, the salt water keeping her body *and* mind buoyant in the darkening night. Sitting in that boat, she pulls her crochet topper close and slips off her sandals. Flutters her fingers in the water. Breathes the salt air. Sighs.

Dip ... dip, as the paddles drop into the salt water.

Drip … drip, as the paddles rise back over the water.

Taking a cue from Mitch, Elsa simply pauses her life and is mindful—of the sweet salt air, and the swaying marsh grasses, and the swish of a school of minnows. Mitch's voice is low and steady as he rows. The rising crescent moon drops a swath of pale gold light on the marsh. A slight mist skims the water.

Well now, Elsa thinks. If this is what a sea of troubles feels like with Mitch Fenwick, paddle on.

thirty

THE HOUSE IS QUIET. AFTER the dock concert, Shane sits alone at his kitchen table. The room is shadowy—the only illumination coming from the light over the sink. The back door is open to the deck, open to the night. Sea air drifts into the kitchen as he sips some wine.

After checking on Aria in her crib, Celia sees this all. No detail escapes her as she walks down the dark hallway to the kitchen. "Sad to say," she admits when she pulls out a chair at the table, "but I really have to get back to Addison."

"Oh, man. Much as I don't want you to leave, I get it. Tomorrow?" Shane asks.

She nods, then sips from her own wineglass. "Aria and I will spend a day with my father first, then hit the road to Stony Point."

"It's probably a good idea, heading out. Captain will be in touch one of these days, too. I really have to be ready to roll when that happens."

"And with me here, you won't be."

"No, got to get you home first."

"The question for me is … home to what?" Celia asks while standing up. She walks to the screen door to the deck, crosses her arms and just looks out toward the harbor.

Shane turns in his chair. "What do you mean?"

"The inn's closed—so I'm out of work. And I'm not sure what to do, moving forward. Elsa hasn't been much help, either." Celia looks over her shoulder at Shane. "She's so vague about when she'll actually open the inn now."

"And you need a job."

"Sure do. I've got the baby to think of, and I *don't* like this uncertainty."

Shane takes a swallow of his wine, then joins Celia at the door. "Any ideas?"

"Oh, some. Getting back to house staging, at least temporarily." Still wearing her blue ombré dress, Celia leans against the doorjamb and looks out at the night. Misty sea air comes through the screen and touches her bare arms. "Just so you know," she says, turning to Shane behind her, "your invitation here was really appreciated."

"How so?"

"It gave me a break. From thinking. From *everything*. The inn. Elsa's plans. My own life plan." She reaches out and strokes his whiskered jaw. "This time here's been a *much* needed breather."

Shane takes her hand and pulls her closer. "I'm glad, Celia."

Celia looks at him. She brushes her fingers across his tee, over his shoulder. "Hopefully, I can put some work ideas together over the next few days. I'll have to talk more to Elsa, too."

Shane nods. And gives her a light kiss. "Can I do anything?"

"You already have." Celia kisses him back. "More than you know."

"Come on, then," he says, hitching his head to the table. "Relax on this last night here. Finish your wine."

When they sit, though, Celia notices a change. It's because this is ending. This Maine escape. This privacy. This secret visit to Shane's shingled harbor house. This, and the freedom that comes with it. The change is obvious by the new silence in the room. By Shane putting away dry plates from the dish rack. By his wiping off the countertop. By his not saying much, only asking her if she wants anything to eat, a snack.

When Celia doesn't answer, he turns. She only shakes her head, then. And takes a long breath. "We should get some rest," she reluctantly tells him. "It'll be a long drive tomorrow. Five hours to Addison. And for you, five hours back here." She sips her wine. "That's too much driving in one day. Unless you'd like to stay in Addison overnight?"

"No."

"No?"

"I've got a place nearby where I can crash."

"Where?"

Shane crosses his arms and leans against the countertop. "I rented that little beach bungalow through the end of October."

"*You did?*" Celia whispers.

He nods.

"At Stony Point?"

Shane's voice is low in the room, in the night. "Thought

it was a good idea," he says. "In my time off—at least for now—I need to be near the people who are close to me." He turns up his hands. "People who mean something to me. My old beach friends. My brother, Kyle."

Celia looks at him from her seat at the table. "Me, too?"

"Eh. You're okay, I guess."

After he says it, he crosses the room. And stops at her seat. Tips up her chin, bends and kisses her. Celia does all she can to fight some God damn sob that wants to bubble up. She doesn't succeed, though, as she kisses him. Still, her gasp doesn't stop her. Doesn't stop Shane, either. Nothing can, apparently. Because without pausing that kiss, Shane kicks out the chair next to her and slowly sits—still kissing. In the kitchen, his hands cradle her face; their kiss deepens. He leans close as they sit knee-to-knee.

But he's not close enough.

So—still kissing—Celia manages to scoot right onto Shane's lap. She sits there in her dress, as close to him as she can get, and wraps her arms around him. Manages to stop kissing him, too, just for a few seconds. Just long enough to sadly tell him, "You're not so bad yourself, sailor."

◦﹏◦

Shane knows how good things *could* be.

But they can't be. Not with three hundred miles looming between them.

Under different circumstances, things could be as good as they've been the past few days.

But this is it—Celia's last night here.

He wants more, though. Wants Celia in his life tomorrow, and the next day. And the next.

Instead, this last night stands like a wall between what *is* possible—and what can't happen. Not with the lives they lead.

So he makes this last night count. In the bedroom minutes later, he tries to slow it down. Sailor-knotted ropes hold back the long curtains. The windows are open to a crescent moon casting faint light. Misty salt air drifts in. The air is warm. The night, quiet. It's late. No noises come from the nearby harbor. The bell buoy is silent. The fog horn, too.

Sitting on the bed with Celia, she turns so that he can unzip her tank-top dress. The fabric is light and crinkled, the color changing from palest sky to deep ocean blue at the hem. With her legs curled beneath her, Celia tips her head down, lifts her hair from her neck and waits.

He does, too, before gradually pulling the dress zipper. He stops halfway, though, and kisses the skin on her back, her neck. Slow. Slow. A little more gentle unzipping, a pause, and kisses moving lower on her back. Her skin is smooth. Her back lifts with her breathing—which gets deeper now. She's into this. When she starts to turn, whispering his name, he stops her. Puts his hands on her upper arms and holds her in place—her back to him as they sit on the turned-down bed. He leaves a trail of kisses from one shoulder to the other now, before tugging that zipper a little more. As he does, the top of her dress loosens and slips down her shoulders, too. But the dress is fitted on top, and flares on the bottom, so only those straps fall.

And Shane knows. He's no fool. The night can't pull

anything on him. This is it. Each minute is ticking past, getting ready for tomorrow to separate him and Celia again. And it frustrates him. He doesn't know *how* to change things. Stopping time right here isn't the answer. It'll only kick him harder afterward.

So still sitting behind Celia on the bed, Shane slides his hands along her bare skin. In the darkness, he feels the shape of her body. His fingers, reaching around her sides, touch upon the swell of her breasts. She arches her back, and half twists toward him. They kiss over her shoulder. And when Shane's hands lock her in place again—not letting her fully turn—he senses Celia's desire. She struggles to face him. To quicken the moment.

But he doesn't let her. He just presses close behind her, holding her—all while his frustration grows. Because when will he get to be with her again? Wake up with her? Love her. Well, he's not going to let this last night win. Not going to let it stop them. So his hands? They reach around and do turn Celia then. Turn her and press her down on the mattress. That soft, crinkled fabric of her dress is twisted around her as Shane bends and kisses her. Deeply. As he does, his hands get the dress untwisted. She lifts her hips to help, then reaches for his belt—which she swiftly unbuckles.

He does the rest, though. He gets out of his jeans, his boxers. While still in his tee, he leans over Celia and reaches beneath her dress for her panties. Slides those off quickly.

Because the *night* is passing quickly. There's no slowing it. There's not enough time to even get Celia's dress off, so he grasps a handful of the soft fabric and pushes it up. The night feels like some sort of an ending now, and has him grab at whatever he can. Has him take something from it. As his body covers the length of hers in the darkness, Celia whispers his name. Kisses his face. His mouth. He takes her arms and briefly pins them down. She raises her legs around his hips. Slips her arms out of his hold and pulls him even closer. Frantically, she lifts off his tee, then clutches his back with her hands. Everything's tangled around them. The sheets; her dress; the darkness; their situation. It's all there. The sex comes fast and hard. There's noise now, too, in the quiet night. Celia's gasps. Shane's murmurs. The bed creaking. Their bodies moving, intent.

Afterward, Shane lies atop her and they just breathe. He finally pushes up, looks at Celia and brushes a strand of hair from her face. It's damp with perspiration. Her chest rises and falls. A moment later, he helps take off her twisted dress, then lies on his back and holds her in his arms. He kisses her forehead. Squeezes his eyes shut. Feels her kiss on his shoulder, his throat.

Well, the night fooled him, didn't it? The minutes he thought he'd slow down and linger with? Gone in a heated, passionate flash.

Done. Just like that.

"*Shane?*" Celia eventually asks in the darkness.

He says nothing. Just holds her close beneath the cool sheet now, and kisses her head.

"Remember at the car wash, when you invited me here?" she quietly goes on. "And I said I was afraid of something?"

Shane nods.

"Do you remember *what* I was afraid of?"

"I do."

Celia takes a breath. Traces a finger over his chest. Touches his damp hair, brushes a bead of sweat from his brow. Kisses his mouth. When she does, Shane turns and cradles her face. Kisses her back. Hears her words between the kisses that grow longer as she moves over him this time. "*Guess we got in deep*," she says.

thirty-one

EARLY WEDNESDAY MORNING, JASON PULLS out all the stops in Sullivan's cottage. He's about had it with not being home—and is going to do whatever it takes to get back there.

So he begins.

After showering and putting on his prosthetic leg, he gets his shaving gear out from the bathroom vanity. *All* of it, this time. No quick shave with just his razor and shaving cream. No, today it's the shaving brush, shaving soap. New razor blade. The works—neatly set out on the countertop.

And … he shaves. *Really* shaves. Lathers up that bristled brush and dabs it over his face, on his neck and throat. Not a hair is missed. That razor then gets pulled up, to the side, angled, rinsed and repeated until *every* facial hair is gone. He's about as clean-shaven as can be.

After hanging the shaving brush and razor in their stand, he lets the gear dry on the counter. Gets dressed, answers a few emails. Feeds the dog. Reviews the week's Fenwick itinerary. Packs up his work stuff.

Then he packs up his now-dry shaving things. Carefully, he sets them in his leather-trimmed canvas shaving bag. Everything goes in—just so. The brush, razor, stand. All of it. Extra blades. Shaving soap. Some here, some in compartments. After zipping the case, he brings it downstairs to the kitchen. Looks around for a moment, too, before setting the packed shaving bag on the counter near the door. He makes room between the two boxes already there—one with some summer shoes in it, the other with Neil's happiness jar securely wrapped and packed.

Jason gives a whistle for Maddy, getting her to scramble out of her dog bed. Grabbing his keys and work duffel then, they head out just as the sun's rising.

⌒

"*Oh, I'm a hot mess,*" Elsa whispers as she types the words.

Right after showering and dressing this morning, she'd opened her laptop on her marble kitchen island, poured a cup of fresh-brewed coffee and decided to answer an email from her dear neighbor in Milan. And Elsa knows the words she *could've* typed in response to Concetta's question: *How are you?* It would've been simple enough and a lot less aggravation to type, *Sto bene.* But saying that, saying only, *I'm fine*, would be the easy way out. And there *is* no easy way out of her predicament. Anyway, she and Concetta go way back, and Elsa counts her as one of her closest friends.

So she keeps typing.

Next, she reads a bit more of Concetta's email. *What've you been doing?* her friend asks.

Hmm. *Got myself into a sea of troubles*, Elsa types. Did she ever—when she *should* be decorating the inn, maybe. Or working with zoning. Gardening, even. And spending time with her family.

The inn's closed, Elsa types instead. *And I nearly got a traffic ticket! Then I took a rowboat ride through the marsh with a certain someone last night. And oh, signora, it wasn't Cliff.*

Elsa grabs a sip of coffee, but right away her hands get back to the keyboard. She just can't stop them now.

A boat ride that paused in the inlet, beside whispering grasses. In the misty sea air, we got to talking there. And, well, there may have been a kiss beneath the moonlight.

"*May* have been a kiss?" Elsa asks herself, fingers hovering over the keyboard. She remembers that crescent moon, the water lapping softly at the boat's hull. The one kiss that most certainly *did* happen. And Mitch asking right into it, *When can I see you again?*

With a wave of her hand, she brushes off the memory and ends Concetta's email.

Now I'm off to deliver bags of tomatoes.

Ciao,
Elsa

⌒〜

In this blessed September heat, Elsa knows just the vehicle with which to deliver those tomatoes, too.

Wearing a black tank top with a mesh neckline, faded denim Bermuda shorts and flat leather sandals, she puts on her big cat-eye sunglasses. Grabs up several bags of tomatoes from the kitchen counter, too. Heading out the inn's side door then, she makes a beeline straight for Celia's gingerbread cottage.

And to the bicycle leaning on the back porch there. Celia doesn't pedal it much anymore, now that she has the baby. With that thought, Elsa dashes off a quick text.

Taking this out for a spin this morning, she types to Celia— then sends along a photo of herself beside the bike. *Wishing you and Aria a beautiful day. Love you!*

"*Perfect,*" Elsa whispers after wheeling that bicycle off the porch. The bike's an old-fashioned cruiser with fenders over the wheels. Mounted on the handlebars is a wicker cargo basket, too—one big enough to drop in a few tomato sacks and her cell phone beside them. That done, she climbs on, gives a few wobbly pumps to the bike pedals— and takes off!

"*Woo-hoo!*" she calls out while turning onto the sandy beach road. She gives the bell a *ting-a-ling* and pedals along. Her hair blows in the breeze; she waves to a neighbor watering flowers. After making her first tomato delivery at Lauren's, Elsa pedals the beach roads again and rings the bike bell outside the Stony Point Beach Association trailer. By the time she dismounts the bike, Cliff's at a window in the white, flat-roofed modular trailer. He's holding a walkie-talkie while watching Elsa approach.

Elsa gives a wave, walks up the four metal stairs, and straightens the dune-grass wreath she had Cliff hang there. Finally, she opens the steel entry door and steps inside.

"They're filming today?" Cliff is asking into that walkie-talkie. He's back at his tanker desk and looking at his computer screen, too. "On the boardwalk this morning? Put sawhorses on the sand, Nicholas. Don't need spectators interfering."

A walkie-talkie squawk, then Nick's voice, "Ten-four, boss."

"Keep folks back for Jason," Cliff adds before signing off and glancing to Elsa. "Be right with you, Mrs. DeLuca. Let me just finalize this Hurricane Emergency Plan. Already updated the Stony Point Handbook with safety protocol." He scrolls a document on his computer. "This is a reminder flyer for the bulletin boards," he vaguely adds when the printer starts up in a nearby small office. "Has key safety points. I also convinced the Board to issue every family a wind-up radio with built-in flashlight and phone charger. For emergency use."

Elsa half listens while looking around the old trailer. The accordion-style door closes off the rear section, where she's sure Cliff's got the a/c blasting. She lifts her sunglasses to the top of her head and turns now to Cliff working at his desk. It's obvious he's busy, so she simply drops her sack of tomatoes on the utilitarian desktop. That gets him to finally look up at her.

"I came by earlier to drop these off," she mentions. "But you weren't here?"

"I was out jogging," Cliff says offhandedly.

"Jogging?"

"With Matt."

"But ... *jogging?*" Elsa sits in a desk-side chair. "You once said your old bones weren't meant for jogging."

He shrugs. "Maybe they're not that old. Something wrong with staying in shape?" He nods to the trailer's open door. "There *you* are toodling around on a bicycle."

"That's because it's good, that exercise. For my … *anxiety*." Which gets Cliff to raise an eyebrow. "You know," Elsa quickly adds. "From the inn's zoning issue."

"Sure, sure." Cliff hurries then to the small printer office and grabs his flyers. "Lovely seeing you this morning, but I have to run."

"As do I." Elsa stands and lowers her big sunglasses to her face. "To the next cottage on my tomato list. Having no inn guests now means no one to cook spaghetti sauce for. No one to add sliced tomato to salads for. So I'm *overloaded* with fresh tomatoes." When Cliff lifts his uniform cap off his desk, Elsa stops him. "Wait. Did you get a haircut?"

Cliff nods and runs a hand through his freshly shorn locks. "Marty gave me a trim yesterday. Added some texture to change things up."

"Well hello, handsome! That Marty does such good work. He cuts Kyle's hair, too."

"That he does." Cliff scoops his keys off the desk then. "On my way to Barlow's now."

"What for?" Elsa asks, following Cliff out of his trailer-apartment and eyeing his *Commissioner*-inscribed polo shirt, shorts and … work boots?

"To mow. Jason said his grass is getting high—him not being here and all. And he's worried he'll get slapped with a blight violation." Cliff stops to lock the trailer door. "So I offered to give the yard a quick mow," he says over his shoulder.

"That's really nice of you to help him out." Elsa stops in the potholed parking area and waits for Cliff. "I'm sure Jason appreciates it," she says, brushing a thread off Cliff's shoulder, then leaning in and giving him a little kiss. A kiss that goes on longer than her intended peck, so she steps back and quickly turns toward her bicycle.

Cliff points at her while walking to his car. "Save the rest of that kiss for Saturday night."

Elsa raises the bike's kickstand and gets on. "What's Saturday night?"

"Concert at the bandshell in Niantic. Outdoor gig." Cliff gets in his car and calls out through the open driver's door, "Those old standards we like."

"I'd *love* that. And have never been there," she says, watching Cliff from behind her dark sunglasses. "Is it formal?"

"We can *make* it formal."

"Oh, I have just the dress."

"And I can't wait to see it. I'll pick you up." He closes his car door, but quickly rolls down the window. "Text you the time later in the week!" his voice carries—right before he guns it onto the sandy beach road.

$\sim$

By midmorning, Jason, Trent and Zach are set up on the Stony Point boardwalk. The sun's beating hot already and they're anxious to get started. Filming is finally about to begin when a noise gets them all to turn. A *thump-thump-thump-thump*, followed by a double *ting-a-ling!* Jason has to look twice, because it's Elsa, for crying out loud. Her hair's flying behind her as she's quickly pedaling a bicycle straight at them.

"*Ahem.* No bikes on the boardwalk, Elsa," Jason tells her when she gets off the bike and puts the kickstand down.

Elsa, wearing some black mesh tank top and faded denim shorts, turns to him. Lifts her big sunglasses on top of her head, too. "Oh, it's a one-time thing," she says, right as Maddy bounds up off the sand and onto the boardwalk.

"Lucky for you Cliff's not around. He'd fine you for that bike violation," Jason reminds her while grabbing the dog's collar and holding her close.

Nick looks over from where he's standing beneath the shade pavilion with Trent and Zach. "Cliff?" Nick asks, whipping a ticket pad out of his cargo shorts uniform pocket. "What about me?"

"Hey, hey now, Nick," Elsa warns—smiling at him, too. "Would a bag of tomatoes change that?" She lifts a sack from the bike basket.

"That's *guard* bribery, Elsa. You know that. *Another* violation." Nick starts filling in the first ticket. "*Elsa DeLuca,*" he whispers as his pen jots.

"Well, just know … *If* you rip up that ticket?" Elsa goes on while pressing the back of her fingers to her perspiring forehead. "You've got a *week's* worth of delicious BLTs in this bag."

"Seriously?" Nick looks over while tearing the ticket off the pad. "BLTs, you say?"

Elsa nods just as her cell phone starts dinging in her bike basket. "Ripping up that ticket would also help *me* out by being my second ticket *evasion* of the week," she says— ignoring the phone.

"*What?*" Jason asks. "What are you—in trouble with the law now?"

Elsa looks over and waves him off with a *tsk*.

Instead of pressing the ticket issue, Jason turns to Elsa's still-dinging cell phone and grabs it out of the bike basket. "Well, at least it's not the Feds," he says while glancing at the phone in one hand and still holding Maddy with the other. "It's someone named Concetta—"

"Give me that." Elsa snaps her fingers for the phone.

But Jason's fast and silently scans Concetta's text message: *A sexy rowboat kiss? Details, amica! Who, pray tell, is your new mystery man???*

"You give me that phone right now," Elsa orders through her teeth.

"And *you* just remember what I told you about having too much idle time," Jason says while handing over her phone. He also lets go of Maddy, leaving her to run back in the sand, bow down playfully and give a small bark.

Amidst the chaos, Elsa reads the text, promptly glares at Jason, then drops her phone in the bike basket.

"Okay, okay," Nick pipes in, oblivious. "Guess I'm happy to oblige a ticket evasion for you." Nick balls up the half-written ticket. "Even exchange," he says, holding it out to Elsa. "Crumpled ticket for a bag of reds."

She agrees, of course. Right as Trent moseys over, too.

"Did someone say something about BLTs?" he asks, sidling up to Elsa's bicycle basket.

"I did." Elsa puts those big cat-eye sunglasses back on. "And it would certainly lighten my ride back to the inn if you'd take that last bag of tomatoes."

"*Oh, my God,*" Jason says under his breath when Elsa

249

dumps her last bag on Trent. These guys have no shame. Jason salutes Elsa when she hops on her bike and continues her *thump-thumping* ride across the sandy boardwalk planks. And when she gives that shiny silver bell another *ting-a-ling*, he turns to get back to work with Zach and Trent.

Trent—who already lifted one of those fat, red tomatoes from the bag and is biting into it at that very moment. Red juice dribbles down his chin.

"Now," Jason says, taking his filming position then. "Where the hell were we?"

~

"Hang on," Trent says once he's downed that tomato. Pressing the back of his hand to his chin, he squints at Jason. "What'd you do to yourself?"

"What do you mean?" Jason asks back. He tosses up his hands and sits on the boardwalk bench. The sun is getting hotter every minute. Even Maddy's joined him in the shade. She's dripping wet from a romp in the water, and now lies panting on the boardwalk planks. Meanwhile, a bead of perspiration is sliding down Jason's face. He's too warm already in his short-sleeved chambray shirt over dark cargo shorts.

Trent steps closer. "Did you *shave* today?"

Zach lowers his camera for a better look, too.

"Yeah." Jason draws a hand down his smooth face. "Got a problem with it?"

"Kind of." Now Trent tips his head and studies Jason from a side angle. "I mean, yesterday you practically had a beard. A light one, anyway. But your face was definitely shadowed when we filmed at the cottage."

"So?" Jason asks.

"Well, you're really clean cut today. More ... formal? I don't know. You look like a *totally* different person—which can be jarring to the viewers. You know what I'm saying?"

"Not really."

"Eh. Just wish you ran this by me." Trent turns to join Zach just as he's lifting that camera again. "Don't do anything else drastic," Trent tosses Jason's way.

"Hey, man," Jason says, standing and taking his position on the boardwalk again. "Told you from the get-go, remember? When you chased me down at that architect awards ceremony? What you see is what you get. And I felt like a shave, okay?"

"All right, all right," Trent tells him, holding up a defensive hand. "Let's just get the cameras rolling. If I don't film daily, it's easy for CT-TV to slash a project from the budget. And I don't want *this* segment on the chopping block."

"Got it. Keeping it short, though. I told you, I have to stop at another job this morning. Beach Box. Need the owner to approve some design changes there."

"Short. Will do," Trent agrees. "But just remember my motto. A-B-F."

"What's that?"

"Like yesterday, with Maris. Always. Be. Filming."

Jason nods, clears his throat, waits for some direction and goes into his speech.

"My brother, Neil, fully believed that a house never lies," Jason tells the camera from where he stands on the sunny boardwalk. "Look closely and *any* house will hint at the truth of the lives inside it. But a house can damn well hold its secrets, too. Like *this* castaway cottage does," he says, stepping aside and motioning to the last-standing cottage further down the beach. It rises tall, and alone, on the sand. Ocean stars sparkle on the water beyond it. "For decades now, that cottage has kept one sad story very private. Ever since its hurricane shutters were buttoned up tight, back in the sixties. And the doors were planked over against a storm. But a storm was brewing *inside* its walls, too. One that tragically cost a man his life. And since then, this big old cottage has held that forgotten secret close."

"Cut!" Trent calls, stepping toward Jason. "Great angles of the cottage in the distance, especially against that blue sky. So a good stopping point right there, Barlow. That clip'll make a nice teaser for the viewers—everyone loves a good secret."

Jason wasn't sure how much longer he could've filmed without wilting, anyway—it's so ridiculously hot out. Perspiration beads on his face now. And he's sweating in his shirt. So he walks further down the boardwalk and grabs a water bottle from a CT-TV tote there. After unscrewing the bottle cap, Jason takes a swig. But then he looks at the bottle, steps onto the sand, tips his head up to the sky and pours the whole damn thing over his face, his hair, his neck. The cold water feels good, cooling down his skin beneath the blazing sun. When the bottle's empty, he runs a hand through his wet hair and turns back to Trent and Zach on the boardwalk.

Zach—who's just lowering his camera.

"Oh, come *on*!" Jason says.

"Remember, Barlow," Trent reminds him. "A-B-F."

"No, that's *B-S*, Trent." Horsing around, Jason tosses that empty water bottle at him. "You edit out that last minute, guy."

"Not a chance," Trent tells him with an easy laugh. "Leaving that one in for the ladies."

thirty-two

CELIA CAN'T BELIEVE IT'S WEDNESDAY morning already. That she's been in Maine for days. Her bags are packed and stacked on the bed now. But instead of carrying them out to the door, she goes to the dresser mirror. Straightens her bandana-print tank top there. Adds a turquoise buckled belt to her cuffed denim shorts. And does one more thing—quickly, though, because Shane thinks she's just getting dressed. Celia scans the room again and spots a spiral notepad and pen on a simple painted shelf. She'll jot him a note for whenever he's back here. It's kind of their thing.

Her message is brief and she doesn't overthink it. Folding the paper, she writes Shane's name on the front, then discreetly tucks it beneath the tarnished brass crab on his nightstand. After putting back the pen and notepad just so on the shelf, she leaves his bedroom and takes the long way to the kitchen.

In the living room, Celia pauses. There's the cozy sofa, the brick fireplace, Shane's red sailboat on the mantel. The boat's sails lean against a stolen framed seascape painting there. In the hallway to the kitchen, more paintings—some in heavy gold frames—hang on the walls. All the paintings look museum-quality. Her eyes linger on the sight.

She turns into the kitchen, then.

To Shane. He's sitting in a chair at the table and giving Aria her bottle. The baby's comfortable with him. Her little fingers grip the fabric of his tee while she drinks. Celia stands in the doorway to watch. Finally, she walks to Shane, touches his shoulder, then pours them both a cup of coffee.

～

Later that morning, they're taking one last ride here—this time to a boutique gift shop in town. They walk up and down the aisles. The wooden floor creaks beneath their shoes. The aisles are filled with display cabinets and wood shelves. Local artisans' wares—carved pine trees, honey jars, seashell art, knitted blankets, woven dream catchers—are everywhere. Aria's strapped to Celia in her sling; Shane keeps adding items to the shopping basket he holds.

"I want to bring a few gifts back to Stony Point," he tells her.

"A *few?*" Celia asks, glancing at his brimming basket.

But there's something she's feeling, too. She's happy. Happy for Shane as he buys gifts for people who matter to him. Happy that he has that now, after so many years when he didn't.

～

How many things in life go *just* as you'd hoped? Shane Bradford doesn't need anyone giving him the answer to that question. He damn well knows it by heart. And that answer is—not many. He can probably count the times on one hand.

So when things *do* go the way you want, there's no mistaking it. This is one of those times. He knows it as he and Celia stop for a final coffee at the shed on the docks. Just a little seaside break before their five-hour drive to Addison.

Just a few minutes of sipping coffee and feeling the warm sea breeze touch their skin. That salty air lifts a wisp of Aria's hair beneath the sunbonnet she wears.

A few minutes of the baby watching a prickly seagull perched atop a dock post.

A few minutes of Celia leaning into Shane. Of her leaving a light kiss on his face.

A few minutes of watching a lobster boat chugging out to sea.

Afterward, Shane doesn't mind loading up Celia's car. Doesn't mind filling the trunk, and turning duffels and boxes this way and that to get everything to fit. Doesn't mind walking through the house one last time with Celia and Aria—checking to be sure they got everything.

Maybe he doesn't mind because of this: Because they leave behind the baby gear he'd bought before coming here together. The portable crib, and nightlight, and mini mobile, and music box—all picked up with some scrap of hope in a big-box department store. It all stays behind. He insisted.

Celia's leaning into the back of the car now, settling Aria in her seat. "You *sure* you want to leave those nursery things here?" she asks him one last time. "I can take them off your hands. Leave them at my father's, even."

"I'm sure. Just in case," Shane tells her as he closes the trunk.

"In case of what?" Celia asks while strapping Aria into the car seat.

When he's quiet, she backs out of the car and turns to him standing there. He looks at her, tucks her auburn hair behind an ear and quietly says, "*In case you ever come back.*"

thirty-three

FINALLY, MARIS CAN GET SOME work done. She settles in at her laptop out in Neil's old shingled shack. The day is hot, more like a dog day of August than an early September Wednesday. But she's comfortable, wearing a scalloped camisole over her cropped skinnies tie-dyed at the frayed hem. Her hair is in a twist. The shack door is open to any sea breeze that might lift off the water over the bluff. A sip of coffee first, before raising her hands over the keyboard—

"*Knock-knock,*" a man's voice says behind her at the same time he raps on the open shack door.

Maris spins around in her seat. "Cody!"

"Sorry to bother you, Maris, but we've got a problem. I opened up a box of floorboards for your kitchen and unfortunately? Wrong color."

"Oh, no." Maris wheels her chair back. "What color came?"

258

"Sand. Instead of that barnwood brown you wanted. There's enough of the sand color there, though. So you can either use it or I reorder the correct color."

"Which will take—"

"Another week."

"You were installing it today?"

"No, no. Just checking materials. We're also short two cabinets."

Maris sinks back into her chair and shakes her head. Seems her *quick* kitchen reno has flown the coop. "Can you just order the right floorboards, Cody? It all coordinated with everything else."

"Sure thing," Cody tells her, giving a wave and heading back to the house.

So Maris takes a breath, collects her thoughts and gets back to writing. It's a little tricky with her bandaged finger. But she types a paragraph or two, when suddenly—another knock at the door.

"Please don't tell me more bad news," she says, spinning her chair around to see *Cliff* in the shack doorway. He's wearing his gold-stitched *Commissioner* polo shirt over shorts and work boots.

"No bad news," he says. "Just here to cut your lawn."

"What?"

He nods. "It's currently at seven inches; I just measured it. Close to breaking the blight ordinance, and your husband asked if I could give it a quick mow."

"*Jason* asked you?"

"Sunday, at The Clam Shack. Reminded me again at lunch Monday—after ring shopping."

"Oh, Cliff," Maris says, rushing to him and clasping his

arm. "Jason showed me a picture of the diamond ring you bought. My gosh, it's a stunner!"

"Hope Elsa will think so, too." Cliff pulls a pair of work gloves out of his back pocket. "In the meantime, got to get this grass mowed. Jason gave me the keys to the tractor."

"Okay. Okay, it's in the garage. But you don't have to do that."

"I know, but I want to. And hey, before I begin," Cliff says, looking over his shoulder at the dumpster in the backyard. "What the heck is that for?"

Maris steps just outside the shack with Cliff. Construction workers are up and down her deck stairs. The slider is open to the kitchen. A sledgehammer smashes something inside the house. And the dumpster is filling up with debris. As the commotion goes on, she explains her kitchen reno.

"Listen, Cliff," she says, watching as one of the men tosses a slab of old countertop into the dumpster. "Since I'm keeping your proposal a secret, you'll *have* to keep my secret kitchen renovation under wraps, too."

Cliff holds up his now-gloved hands. "You've got my word," he says, then heads out toward the garage. "I won't be long mowing, maybe an hour."

"Oh! Cliff!" Maris calls, catching up to him. "One more thing."

"Name it."

"Do you have *any* idea when you're proposing to my aunt?"

"Figured that was coming," Cliff says with a jangle of the tractor keys.

To which Maris gives a little shrug.

"Well, I'm prepping first," he explains. "Eating healthy,

jogging. Keeping fit, you know. Psyching myself up for the big moment."

"That all sounds good. But you don't want to overthink it, Cliff."

"I know, I know. On top of that, there's lots of end-of-season commissioner duties to attend to. A BOG summer wrap-up meeting. A newsletter to write."

"Let me help you, then."

"With the newsletter?"

"No! With the proposal! How about if I help you pick out a new outfit for the occasion."

Cliff's eyes drop to his lawn-mowing threads. "Something wrong with my clothes?"

"What? No. But … I helped Kyle with his vow renewal suit. Didn't you like how that looked?"

When Cliff says he did, and starts backing toward the garage, Maris tells him they can shop later today.

"That's probably good," Cliff calls out over the sound of a whirring saw now. "Could be I'll need an outfit for Saturday."

"Saturday?"

"There's a bandshell concert. Already asked Elsa to be my date, and seems it might be the right place to—"

"*Propose?*"

Cliff gives an easy wink, his blue eyes twinkling. "That *is* a distinct possibility."

"Okay," Maris says with a firm nod. "We should stop at Clinton Crossing, the outlet stores. Today. Let me get some writing done, and we'll go after dinner."

If Maris could only *get* some writing done. But between her old cabinets crashing down into the dumpster, and hammers swinging, and her bandaged typing finger, and now Jason's lawn tractor engine blasting outside her writing shack, she's at her wit's end. No words come out of her hands. No more paragraphs are crafted.

Well. There's only one way to handle all this noise. And distraction.

So she picks up her cell phone and makes a call.

"Oh, Aunt Elsa! Please help me! Is my writing nook still set up at the inn?"

～

At first glance, Beach Box could look more like a shed than a cottage. But with Stony Point's Hammer Law lifted, Jason's finally able to work his magic. Demo's begun, and the tiny little cottage on Ridgewood Road is about to be transformed. The foreman's giving orders to the crew; plaster is being scraped off walls; dust is rising. The chaos has Jason presenting his adjusted kitchen design to the owners out on the back deck. After they approve it, *and* approve the hit to their budget, Jason's ready for lunch— but not in the construction zone. Instead, he grabs his mega lunch cooler from his SUV and heads to a picnic table in the cottage's side yard. It's a nice shady spot out on the lawn, and for once, he's got some alone time in his day. Because another small miracle? Though sawhorses and lumber are set up nearby, that table is empty.

So he settles in with his food. Unwraps tinfoil from a hefty sandwich and flattens the foil like a plate. Dumps a bag of chips on it. Sets a peach off to the side. A roll of string cheese, too. Opens a bottle of water. Relishes the quiet and digs in. The sun shines warm; the green lawn spreads out around him. Maddy's dozing in the cool shade of a leafy tree. The dog's all tuckered out from her morning beach romps during filming.

"Yo, Barlow!" a familiar voice suddenly calls out.

Jason turns to see Kyle crossing the lawn. "Kyle, what's shakin'?"

"Well, I just finished emptying the very last moving box."

"Seriously, Bradford?" Jason lifts a half of his chicken-cutlet sandwich dripping in lettuce, tomato and dressings—mayo, olive oil, some mustard. "You moved into your house in June, and it's September now. It took three months to unpack?"

"Hey, you try moving and tell me how long it takes—but after *ten* years of marriage and with two kids in tow." Kyle sits backward beside Jason, rests his elbows on the picnic table and stretches his legs out in front of him. "Anyway, then Lauren told me I should get rid of the empty boxes while I still have my old clunker," he goes on while Jason's eating. "So I just loaded them all into my truck and was on my way to the dump. Noticed your SUV out front here," Kyle says, motioning to the street, "and pulled over."

"You're not working today?" Jason asks around a mouthful of sandwich.

"Later. Afternoon shift. Jerry opened the diner for me this morning." Kind of reclining there on the picnic table bench, Kyle tips his face up to the sun. "What about you? No work at the Fenwick place today?"

"Did some filming on the boardwalk earlier. Now I'm overseeing things here for a couple of hours. Taking a lunch break, first."

Kyle sits up and checks out the tiny, shingled Beach Box, then turns to Jason. "Sheesh, look at *you*, baby face," he says, giving Jason's jaw a slap. "Clean as a whistle. Trent on your case to polish up for the cameras?"

"Nah, man." Jason drags a potato chip through mayonnaise drippings on his tinfoil. "More like it's the last shave I'll have till I'm living at home again."

"Whoa! You finally moving back?"

Jason shakes his head, then takes a swig from his water bottle. "That's still up to Maris," he explains. "But remember how she came out to Sullivan's Friday night?"

"Sure." Kyle sits forward, elbows on his knees now. "Used and abused you, then hit the road."

"Yep, that's about right," Jason says, taking another bite of his sandwich. "Anyway, when she was there, it bothered her seeing my shit all spread out in Ted's cottage. Clothes, mail, work gear. Like I was permanently settled in, you know? So I decided to change that. Starting to pack up."

"That right?" Kyle asks, then gives a wave to someone approaching.

"You bet." Jason glances over at Nick crossing the yard now. "And whatever gets packed," Jason goes on to Kyle, "I won't use again until I'm home. Including my razor."

"What about filming?" Kyle asks.

"Doesn't matter." Jason rubs the back of his fingers along his clean-shaven jaw. "No more shaving," he says as Nick sits across from him. "The station can take it or leave it."

"All *right*, guy," Kyle tells him, cuffing his shoulder. "So you kind of have a shaving strike going on."

"What?" Nick asks as he opens his bagged lunch, too. "Why'd you quit shaving?"

"You missed the story, punk," Jason tells him.

"Seems like kind of a rebellion, dude," Kyle muses.

"What are we rebelling?" a new voice asks.

They all turn to see Matt. He's out for a jog and veers through the yard to the guys' lunch table.

"Jason's on a shaving strike," Nick says, opening a sandwich and container of cold pasta salad.

"No shit, man." Matt slaps Jason's back before sitting on the other side of the table with Nick.

"Hey, Officer. What're you doing here?" Jason asks. "Change shifts this week?"

"Vacation," Matt answers. "Got the week off while Eva's headed to that real estate conference. Doing some home projects. Driving Tay to school stuff, that sort of thing."

"Well, that's good." Jason presses the rest of his cutlet sandwich into his mouth. "You're off the streets for a week."

"Sure am." Matt leans an elbow on the picnic table. "So ... what's this about a shaving strike?"

"I'll tell you what. Barlow gave himself a nice shave this morning," Kyle says, turning and sitting sideways on the picnic table bench. "And that's it. Now he *quit* shaving until he's home with his old lady again."

"Jesus, Barlow. Think that'll happen in this century?" Matt tosses out there.

"Thanks for the vote of confidence," Jason says, giving a wave to Cliff now.

"Jason!" Cliff calls out. He's sweaty, and his work boots look to have fresh grass stains on them. "Just finished up at your place. Lowered the blade on the tractor, so your lawn's nicely trimmed."

Jason picks up his peach and bites in. "You're all right, Commish."

"Wait." Nick scoops up a spoonful of pasta salad. "You're doing landscaping now, boss? What the hell?"

Matt reaches for Nick's plastic knife and divvies up his chicken-salad pita. Takes a slice for himself, too. "Put me on your list," Matt tells Cliff.

Cliff waves them off. "No time, fellas. Calendar's booked with work. Just did Jason a favor today."

"Making time on that calendar for wooing, guy?" Jason asks.

"Matter of fact," Cliff tells him, "I'm taking Elsa to an outdoor concert Saturday. A big band's covering all the old standards over at the Niantic bandshell."

"Saturday?" Jason wipes a dribble of peach juice off his chin, then takes another bite of the fruit.

"Yes, sir," Cliff says. Standing there, he adjusts the cap on his head. "Got a big night planned."

Jason does a slow nod. Slightly raises his water bottle, too. Because he knows. Cliff's letting him in on the proposal plan. So Jason gives him a silent toast—right as Cliff twists open a water bottle he'd brought, and Kyle stretches across the table for a slice of Nick's pita, and Matt pulls over a plastic chair for Cliff.

thirty-four

THE DAY, LIKE EVERY DAY spent with Shane, flies by.

The five-hour drive beneath a warm summer sun; the stop at a scenic rest area to stretch their legs, tend to Aria and have the lunch Celia packed; the cruise through Addison's winding country roads; pulling into the driveway of her old yellow bungalow; Celia getting out of the car to greet her father there; Shane moving a few of his bags to his pickup; all of them having something cool to drink on the porch.

"How was the trip?" Gavin asks Celia then.

"Really good, Dad," she says. She's settled on a slatted-wood chair on that porch; her arm's looped around Aria sitting on her lap; Shane leans against the railing beside them. "Really good," Celia says again, reaching for Shane's hand and giving a squeeze.

⌒

When Shane remembers that the bag of gifts he'd bought is in Celia's backseat, he heads to her car to get it.

Gavin follows after him. "Shane!" he calls out.

Shane looks over his shoulder and stops there on the lawn. They're just far enough for Celia not to overhear the talk. Not to hear her father.

Gavin toys with a blade of grass in his mouth. "Got to tell you, Shane. Today's the first time in a long time that I haven't seen some sadness in Celia's eyes."

Shane only nods.

"So, thank you," Gavin says while clapping Shane's shoulder. "And hope to see more of you around."

Shane looks from Celia, back to Gavin. "Me, too."

～

After Shane's moved his gift bag into his pickup, Gavin gives a wave and heads inside. "Safe travels, Shane," he calls.

Celia watches from her porch chair. She knows it's been a long day already, and Shane still has another hour drive to Stony Point. So while holding Aria, she walks to the driveway. She and Shane talk some there. At the truck, he leaves the lightest kiss on Aria's head.

"Bye-bye, little one," he says, then turns to Celia. "And *you* …"

"Shane. I had a beautiful time," she tells him.

"Likewise, Celia," he says, bending and kissing her. "I'll call you later, when I'm at the cottage?"

Celia nods and steps back as he gets in his pickup, starts it and drives away. Squinting through the midday sunlight, she sees his hand wave out the window, too. The thing is? The week turned out better than she'd hoped. It *was* beautiful. So with Aria still in her arms, Celia walks to the road. She watches Shane's truck pass the farmhouses and bungalows, pass the crumbling rock walls. The whole time, she remembers the words Shane said yesterday. They were walking that strip of ragged beach in Maine. Skimming stones, hanging out.

Now, she answers him back. Standing roadside as his truck rounds a bend, she barely whispers, "*I love you, too.*"

⌒‿

Shane never tires of the sight. Never has, never will. Even now—after the forty-five minute drive here.

"*The trestle giveth,*" he quietly says as he takes the turnoff to Stony Point. "*And the trestle taketh away.*" Driving beneath the stone tunnel, he sees Nick at the other end. He stands there at the guard station and waves when he recognizes Shane's pickup.

"Yo, man. What are you doing here?" Nick walks up to the truck's open passenger window. He leans inside and gives Shane a handshake. "Shouldn't you be out to sea right about now?"

"That was the plan," Shane explains, tipping up his newsboy cap. "But the boat's fuel pump gave out. So I'm grounded until the captain gets in touch. Few more days, maybe."

Nick lifts his clipboard from the roadside guard post. "Well, it's good to have you back in these parts."

"Appreciate that, Nick. Getting to feel like a second home here."

"Just let me grab some deets for the log." Nick clicks open his pen. "Where you staying this time around? Your brother's place?"

"Nah. Rented that same cottage awhile longer. Over on Sea View."

"Got it," Nick says while jotting the info. "You're good." He waves Shane through—just as a car pulls in behind him.

But before taking off, Shane reaches into that gift bag on his front passenger seat. "Hey," he says, tossing Nick a smaller bag through the open window. "Catch!"

"What's this?"

"Brought a little something for folks here. You, included."

"No shit." Nick opens the bag and pulls out a leather keychain. He runs a finger over an embossed fish.

Shane leans across the seat toward the passenger window. "That's Maine's state fish. Landlocked salmon. And I know you like to fish, Friday nights."

"Sure do."

Shane tips his newsboy cap, puts the truck in gear and pulls away.

"Thanks, man," Nick calls out. "Join us on the rocks again sometime!"

Driving the winding beach roads then, Shane heads to his rented bungalow. The streets are quiet. It's late Wednesday afternoon, and the kids are back to school. Most of the vacationers are gone. The sun shines low when he turns onto Sea View Road. Off to the east, Long Island Sound glimmers. The water is calm; the salt air, heavy.

At the cottage, he parks and gives the old place a good

look. Wild dune grasses sweep along the planked walkway to the back porch. The cottage shingles are sea-weathered, and cream trim paint around the windows and door is peeling. He finally unloads a duffel and his bags from the truck and carries them to the front porch. Taking the stairs two at a time, he sees the driftwood sign hanging from a string of twine. The cottage name could just about sum up his whole damn life right now.

"*This Will Do*," he says with a nod, then goes inside. "Sure will."

~

But Shane's still got some of that rambling feeling—left over from being on the road all day. So after splashing water on his face, changing his shirt and opening some windows in the musty cottage, he leaves again. Grabs up that bag of gifts, heads to his truck—then does an about-face to the old shed in the yard. Might be a good time to walk off some kinks from that five-hour drive. So he goes in the shed, squints through dust and cobwebs and finds what he needs: a red wagon with rusty wheels. He grabs a rag, too, hanging from a nail in the wall, and dusts off the wagon before loading it up with his bag of goodies. This time heading out, he's *walking* the beach roads. And tipping his cap to neighbors he passes. And soaking in the late-afternoon warmth.

Minutes later, he's knocking at the door of Elsa's Ocean Star Inn.

"Shane!" Elsa says, stepping onto the porch. She's wearing a striped tee over black leggings. A chambray shirt is tied around her waist; white slip-on sneakers are on her feet. Her honey-streaked brown hair is up in a high ponytail—showing gold hoop earrings, too. "What a surprise!" Elsa cautiously squints at him, then. "Everything okay?" she asks.

"Couldn't be better, actually." After giving her an easy hug and explaining why he's back, Shane motions to his wagon's gift sack. "Just here for a quick delivery."

Yeah, right.

Because *another* minute later, Elsa's got him settled in with an iced limeade at her marble island in the kitchen. She explains she just finished watering her hydrangea bushes and was getting dinner ready.

"Then I won't keep you," Shane says, giving her a white canvas tote with hemp rope handles. A navy anchor is printed on the tote's canvas. "It's a little something from Maine, Elsa."

"Oh, I *love* it!"

"Good, good. I thought of you when I saw that anchor," Shane explains.

"Of me?"

Shane nods. "You helped me anchor myself in Stony Point again. If not for your kind hospitality when I first arrived here, I might've left before ever making things right with Kyle."

"Well, I'm happy to have been a part of that reconciliation," Elsa says while holding up her canvas tote. "You two brothers need each other."

"We do. Which is why I also extended the lease on that cottage I'm renting. This way, when I'm off the boat, I can be here."

"Wonderful!" Elsa says, sitting beside him and clasping his arm.

"There's no getting back the fifteen years Kyle and I lost," Shane goes on. "But we can sure as hell chip away at it. And with the lobster boat being laid up in the boatyard, and the captain having a headache with it all, it gives me a few more days to be here."

"Isn't that the way. Someone's bad news bodes well for someone else?"

"Roger that," Shane says, turning on his stool. "Now listen. You go ahead and *open* that tote."

Elsa looks from him, to the tote, and pulls out a box of fresh Maine doughnuts. "Shane!" she says, opening the box to assorted frostings and sprinklings and sugar coatings.

"Heard through the grapevine you've got a sweet tooth going on," he admits. "So, a little something for that, too."

"This is *really* thoughtful." Elsa inhales the doughnuts' aroma, then looks to Shane. "Want to stay a bit? Have some dinner?"

Shane looks over to her own glass of wine and dish of salad set beside a magazine holder on the island. "Only if it's no trouble."

"*Basta.* Trouble? You? I'll put a plate of spaghetti together. With turkey meatballs I made yesterday."

"Well." Shane takes off his newsboy cap. "Don't mind if I do stay, then."

As Elsa readies his dish, Shane walks around some. Checks out her mini red herb pots in the garden window. Takes a look in the dining room—where rays of late sunlight stream through the floor-to-ceiling windows. He tells Elsa, too, that maybe Celia would enjoy some of those doughnuts.

"I'll save some for her," Elsa says while spooning those meatballs onto his plate. "She's away for a few days."

"That right?" Shane asks, sitting again at the island.

Elsa nods, pours Shane a glass of Chianti now and joins him for dinner. "She called me a little while ago. Celia's been staying with Aria at her father's house. You know, taking some time to get her thoughts together about the inn … and where things are headed."

Shane nods, twirls a forkful of spaghetti and raises it to his mouth. "But my God, she's missing a great dinner," he says around the food. "Hope she's feeling all right?"

"I think so. She's resting up and coming back in the morning. *And,*" Elsa adds while spearing a hunk of meatball, "I *called it* that tomorrow night is *Nonna* night. Aria's sleeping over here with me. She's only been gone a few days, but oh how I miss my little love!"

Shane gets it—hell, does he get it. Doesn't say it, though. Instead he just eats, dragging a turkey meatball through the tomato sauce. Scraping his fork over what bits of spaghetti are left on his plate. Sipping the Chianti. All while missing Celia and Aria, too—and it's only been *hours* since he's seen them. Not days.

"Well," he says when he pushes away his dish and sets down his fork. "I'm heading to my brother's next. Bought Lauren a tote, too. And something for Kyle and their kids," he tells Elsa. "Here, check it out." He begins showing her all the gifts he'd brought.

First, the blanket with the state of Maine's outline imprinted on it. "That's Evan's. For when he's camping, maybe. Or to use on the end of his bed."

And a necklace, including a sterling-silver state charm

with a tiny heart cutout in it. "For my niece. Hailey. You know. Girls, and jewelry, and hearts."

Finally, there's a green-tinged, cast bronze lobster bottle opener. "Special for Kyle. Nice to be able to crack open a beer with my brother again."

Before the sun goes down then, Shane collects his gifts and thanks Elsa for everything. "Remember, if you're *ever* in Maine, you let me repay the favor," he says on his way out the inn's front door.

"Listen, Shane. You're busy working a very taxing job and certainly don't owe me *any* favors," Elsa tells him as he leaves her porch and drops his bag of gifts in that wagon. "A dinner payback is *not* necessary."

"Is, too. And dinner's on *me* next time," he tells her with a finger-point and a wink. Then he starts pulling the wagon behind him. "You have my number."

Elsa nods and waves him off.

So Shane walks to the sandy road—wagon in tow. Its wheels turn gritty on the pavement. There, he pulls his newsboy cap from his pocket and puts it on, glancing back as he does. Funny, but Elsa's still standing, arms crossed, as she leans in her inn's doorway. She watches him and gives another little wave, too.

⌒‿

Shane takes the long way to his brother's—and with good reason. He pulls his wagon across the boardwalk; the wagon wheels *thump-thump* over the planks. Eventually, he stops and sits on the boardwalk bench facing the stretch of sand. Because there's something about a September beach.

Some sadness in it, the way the yellow sunlight pales. And the dune grasses turn golden. Late-day shadows grow longer. Small waves lap lazily onshore—almost as though they're tired at summer's end.

Shane tips up his cap and takes it all in. Finally, he pulls his cell phone from his pocket and calls Celia.

"Where are you?" she asks.

"On the beach. It's nice. Just me and a few seagulls hanging out." He stands and looks toward the lone Fenwick cottage on the sand. "Sun's going down. But there's some golden light over on the rocks still. And the water's really quiet. And calm."

"Oh, I miss it," Celia tells him, her voice soft. "Aria likes a stroller ride across the boardwalk. I can't wait to be back."

"Me, too. And listen," he says, sitting again. This time, he leans forward, elbows on his knees. "I hear tomorrow night is *Nonna* night? Aria's staying with Elsa?"

"Shane! How do you know these things?"

He smiles. Leans back. Breathes in that September salt air. "I have my ways. And I also know the weather's supposed to be gorgeous tomorrow. So how about dinner at my cottage?" He pauses, looking out at the pink horizon over the water. "Just you and me."

thirty-five

LATE WEDNESDAY, JASON WAITS ON the stoop
with Maddy. The way she's slunk down, he can tell the dog
knows she's been fresh—chewing slippers, jumping on the
couch again, misbehaving for Maris. But the final straw?
Maddy getting crazy dirty in the sand this morning during
Castaway Cottage filming. The dog's sand frolic was followed
by a dousing in the salt water, and another roll in the sand
afterward.

So Jason looks down the straightaway here at Sea Spray
Beach. And there it is—PetPlace's mobile grooming van
rolling down the road. He snagged the day's last
appointment.

And so it begins. Once Maddy's whisked inside the van,
Jason heads to the deck to finish a frozen dinner. While
forking off hunks of Salisbury steak and spooning green
beans from the heated tray, he hears whining and random
barks from that van. And by the time he's chowing that

fudgy brownie, a transformed Maddy is back on the deck. Happy now, too, as she devours a complimentary PetPlace biscuit.

"Whoa, Maddy. Is that you?" Jason asks, patting her shoulder. After thanking the groomer for working a miracle, he pays the bill, too. It was totally worth it, getting Maddy bathed in the big metal tub, followed by a blow-dry and hefty brushing, *and* having her nails filed and clipped. The dog is as fluffed and soft as Jason's ever seen.

Now Maddy follows him into Ted Sullivan's cottage—from the kitchen, to the living room. She even shadows him going up the stairs, nearly getting him to trip on her. She nudges his hand every chance she gets. In the guest bedroom, Jason ignores her while packing a box with short-sleeve button-downs from the closet. Next he drops in a few very light tees. Adds a handful of bandanas from the top dresser drawer, too, before tucking in the carton flaps and bringing the box downstairs.

Which must be Maddy's cue. The German shepherd races past him on the stairs and bolts for the kitchen. By the time Jason gets there, she's standing at the closed slider. Her body is still—except for that wagging tail—as she waits to go for a nighttime walk.

"Oh, no," Jason tells her while carrying that full box of clothes. "You are *not* having a beach walk tonight. You're all gussied up—and *done*."

He walks right past her and sets his clothes box on the counter near the happiness-jar box and box of shoes. Picking up the black marker there, he writes *Summer Shirts* on the latest carton. That done, he grabs an empty box from the stack in the pantry and sets it on the kitchen table.

He'd brought a few things from home—coffee mugs, plastic containers of food—plus there are dishes here from Eva and Elsa, too. As he packs it all up, Maddy sinks to the floor at the slider. She sets her muzzle on her front paws and watches him.

Jason glances over at the dog. "Don't look at me like that. *Argh*, fine. You win," he says. "We'll walk later. But *on*-leash, tonight."

~

"Cliff!" Maris says as he stops in front of a large three-way mirror outside the men's dressing rooms. "That's it. We're done. Stop looking!"

Cliff turns and tugs down his jacket sleeves. He and Maris have been shopping at the outlet stores for a good hour. Now he's trying on a beige linen blazer over a cream button-down and straight white jeans. The blazer has three brown leather buttons at each sleeve cuff; a thin strip of the same brown leather tops each pocket.

"You look so dapper. Wait till Elsa sees," Maris says from her bench seat in the waiting area. "But you're quiet. What do *you* think?"

"I'm not sure." Cliff shoves up the jacket sleeves. "It's got a good vibe, though," he notes, looking at his reflection. "Yeah. I think I'm liking this."

"Me, too. The look suits you." Maris stands and steps closer. "Pull up the shirt collar. And … and mess the new layers in that haircut of yours." After he does, she bends and rolls the thinnest cuff on his jeans, takes her phone and snaps a picture. Steps back, too, while scrutinizing the image. "On Saturday? You wear the outfit *just* like this. I'm texting it to you right now," she adds, her thumbs flying over her phone keyboard. "And to go with it? We'll pick up a pair of those mesh oxfords we passed in the shoe department."

Cliff adjusts his collar and looks over his shoulder in the mirror. "This is hitting home now," he says. "Making it all real."

"It definitely *is* real." Maris is squinting at him. "But the outfit still needs something. Something special for when you pop the question." She looks out into the men's department. "Go get dressed," she tells Cliff then. "And meet me out there. I'll look around for just the right finishing touch."

～

As Maris heads to the men's accessories, she passes shelves of blue jeans. Some are stonewashed. Some hand-sanded. Some whiskered. A feeling comes over her, then. It's almost a longing that gets her to stop and run her hands over the jeans. This was her whole world for many, many years as a denim designer. *Damn*, she thinks. *How do you know if you're making the right decisions?* Patting the fabric, she moves on. When Cliff catches up to her, she's adding pocket crewneck tees to his cart.

"You wore something like these camping, Cliff. And you should keep it up, it's another good look for you."

"All right. And what about a necktie?" Cliff asks. "For Saturday. Should we pick one out?"

"Oh, no. Keep the look loose. More casual than

formal …" Maris' voice fades as she looks around at belts and sunglasses and wallets. "But try *this*," she finally says, lifting a navy silk pocket square. "For the chest pocket on your jacket."

"Very classy," Cliff remarks. He takes the pocket square and drops it in the shopping cart. After trying on the mesh oxfords—light gray with brown trim—they head to the checkout.

"I had fun here," Maris tells Cliff on the way. "But wow," she says, motioning to those shelves of blue jeans, "sometimes I forget how much I miss working with denim."

"I can see why," Cliff admits. "You're quite the expert in the fashion department."

"Thanks. It's just that … huh." Maris glances back at the denim. "I guess I'm actually missing a *lot* these days."

"Well, looks like we'll be here awhile," Cliff says as they take their place in the long checkout line. Several customers stand ahead of them. "So while we wait, why don't you tell me just what it is you're missing?"

～

And Maris does.

She tells Cliff how she's been missing her day-to-day life with Jason. And that she misses her fashion career sometimes. Misses Neil, too, when she's working on his book.

The thing is? It's easy to talk to Cliff. He listens with no bias, no preconceived notions. That openness must come from his years of being a judge in family court. Years of listening to one side's argument, then the other's. Years of monitoring accusations and reasonings tossed across the courtroom. Years of hearing difficult stories and details and emotions—then deciphering some truth in it all.

That's how he listens now—carefully—as Maris tells him that her life seems stalled, too. Nothing's significantly moving forward. Not the book. Not her marriage.

"I even had a surprise *kitchen* setback today. The wrong flooring arrived, and it'll push the reno schedule out a week, at least." Maris waves off her thoughts. "But heck, I'm not here to unload on you, Cliff."

"Well," he says. "That's what families do. They unload."

"Family?"

"Maybe. Come Saturday." Cliff shrugs. "If my final wooing works."

Maris smiles, then. A genuine smile—she can feel it. She nods to Cliff, too, as the cashier motions that they're next. "I'll wait outside while you pay," Maris tells Cliff. "Do some window-shopping."

~⁓~

Walking past the outlet shops, Maris slows up at the window of a home goods store. White wooden picture frames are displayed for sale inside. They lean against a blue wall and are set at varying angles.

"See something you like?" Cliff asks minutes later, joining her at the window.

"Yeah. For my new kitchen. I've got something in mind to fill those frames," she says.

"Those ones?" Cliff points to two shabby-chic frames

leaning off to the side. They're large, and the white paint is elegantly distressed—showing some wood grain beneath.

Maris looks from Cliff, back to the window display, and only nods.

"You wait right here." Cliff gives her the shopping bags holding his Saturday outfit. "For all your help today? Those frames are my treat," he says, then hurries inside the store.

thirty-six

AT DAWN THURSDAY MORNING, SHANE'S on the docks and heading straight to an old fisherman's shack. Its white shingles are weathered gray. The eaves and window trim, a faded red. Fishing net is draped over one side of the building. A red tin lobster is mounted over a large paned window. Salt water laps at the dock posts.

Shane slows and just inhales the briny air. Hell, every sense lies to him right now—each one telling him that he could be in Maine. There's the touch of sea damp on his skin. And he hears the low moan of a foghorn, not to mention the dock planks creaking beneath his step. He sees the vessels moored in the mist; the seagulls swooping past. Tastes the salt of the air with a good, deep breath. All his senses have him think he's walking the docks in Rockport Harbor.

He's not, though. He's in Connecticut and approaching his old friend's eatery—Lobsterland. Though the restaurant's closed at this hour, any fisherman worth his salt is up and at 'em with the rising sun.

Noah Conti is no exception.

Shane looks through the door's window into the shadowy seafood joint. His old captain stands at a counter there. Decades of a life at sea show on Noah's leathery skin; in the red bandana holding back his silver hair as unruly as that sea; in the grit and strength on his face beneath a trim silver beard. Noah looks over when Shane gives a quick one-two knock before opening the door.

"Well, I'll be. It's Shane from Maine. What the hell you still doing around here, kid?" Noah asks into a back-slapping hug. "Thought you'd be up north by now, out on the wild seas."

"Should be, Noah," Shane says, grabbing a seat on a stool at the little restaurant's counter. "But life had other plans."

They catch up on the two weeks since they'd last seen each other. The talk is all business and weather and busted boats and captain troubles. Shane mentions changes happening in the lobster industry, too—warming waters, specifically. He's worried about what that could mean for his livelihood, as well as Maine's.

But the whole time, it's like Noah's just *waiting* to ask some other question.

"And Celia," he finally says, looking past Shane's shoulder. "She stick around, tough guy?"

"What do you think, Noah?" Shane pulls out his cell phone and points to a photo on the screen.

Noah reaches for the phone. He studies the picture taken just days ago back in Maine. It's of Shane, Celia and the baby. The three of them are huddled close beside Shane's shingled house.

"Not sure I ever saw you happier, kid," Noah mentions. "Hey—speaking of which. You got a kid of your own now?" he asks, pointing to Aria in the photo.

"Nah, that's Celia's daughter. The father actually died pretty suddenly last year."

Noah gives a sad *tsk-tsk* and hands back the phone.

"Yeah, it's a helluva story. And Celia's why I'm here, my friend," Shane assures him. Then he stands, pockets his phone, and heads over to the saltwater lobster tank in back. Fresh lobsters line the tank's floor. "Give me four of your best, would you?"

"Absolutely." Noah grabs a big pair of tongs and turns to Shane. "Planning a special dinner with her?"

"Something like that," Shane says while surveying the tank of lobsters.

Noah looks at the lobsters, too. "I get it," he says then.

"Get what?"

"You've got it bad, my boy." Noah reaches those tongs into the tank and lifts out a dripping lobster. "And *every* dinner is special with your lady, no?"

Shane waits till Noah looks over his shoulder at him. Even then, he only turns up his hands and says no more.

⁓

This is one cottage door Jason *never* thought he'd be knocking on. But here he is, midmorning, driving down Sea View Road and headed there. Shane's rented beach bungalow is only a stone's throw from Long Island

Sound—and looks it. The old cottage wears the sea well, with its weathered shingles and peeling trim paint. Jason's architectural eye appreciates the bungalow's sparse structure, especially that back porch. Its simple olive-painted steps; that sloped roof extending from the rear of the cottage; the open-air space where windows and screens *should* be. But that open window space is the bungalow's structural feat—offering expansive views of the sweeping Sound beyond. The porch *has* to be unassuming to allow for the grandeur of the sea. Shane's lucky to have snagged the place this summer.

Parking his SUV now, Jason heads to the front porch, not the back. The interior door is open, so no doubt Shane's around. While holding a heavy bag, Jason pauses, reads the cottage sign—*This Will Do*—then gives a few sharp raps on the screen door.

"It's open," Shane's voice calls out from somewhere inside.

"Yo, Shane," Jason calls back as the creaking screen door slams behind him.

"That you, Barlow?" Silence, then, "I'm in the kitchen."

Jason walks through a musty living room. Thin checked curtains frame the windows; paneled walls are painted white; blue and green fishing floats hang in the corner; wood beams cross the ceiling.

"Have something for you," Jason says when he gets to the kitchen. Shane is just pulling a huge white enamel pot from a lower cabinet. The pot is dull and dinged and has obviously seen years of use. "A tomato delivery."

"Hey, is that right?" Shane asks, setting the pot on the counter, then clapping some dust off his hands.

Jason nods and lifts the tomato bag. "Me and the TV crew cooled off in Elsa's central air, it was so damn hot filming earlier. She came down that secret path of hers and called us into the inn for something cold to drink—impossible to do in Mitch's cottage, mid-demo."

"Leave it to Elsa to take care of things like that."

"Definitely. She mentioned you were back, and meant to pawn off a bag of tomatoes on you. Guess she's trying to unload her crop, what with the inn not opening."

Shane pulls a few plump tomatoes from the bag and sets them on the kitchen windowsill. Gives a low whistle at them, too.

"Elsa knew I was off to another job," Jason explains while pulling out a chair at the table. "So she asked me to get those to you on the way." Sitting now, he tips back his chair and glances to the porch. "What the hell you doing back, anyway?"

"Captain's boat gave up the ghost. Fuel pump busted, so my week opened up—till the repair's done."

"No shit. But I thought your rent was up here. On Labor Day."

"It was." As he says it, Shane's lifting handfuls of wet seaweed from the sink. Opens the refrigerator next and leans inside. "After I got word from the captain, I actually called the cottage owner. Arranged to rent this salty joint for the fall," he explains while opening and closing drawers in the fridge. "Need a place to crash here when I have a few days off. Like right now," he adds, closing the refrigerator and washing his hands at the sink. "You know, I want to be around to keep the connection going with my brother. The gang here."

288

"That's decent, man," Jason says as he gets up and opens that refrigerator—thinking he'll grab a bottle of water *and* see what's up with all that seaweed. Not thinking he'll see four fresh lobsters tucked in the clear crisper drawers—two lobsters in each. Cool, damp seaweed is spread on top of them.

"Whoa," Jason says, stepping back and eyeing those lobsters. "Got some crustaceans going on here." He looks to Shane drying his hands with a dishtowel now. "Having Kyle and Lauren over for dinner? You know," he adds with another glance at those full crisper drawers. "Keeping the connection going?"

Shane gives a short laugh. "Not exactly."

"Well, now. I guess not," Jason says when he notices something through the back screen door. He steps onto the porch and squints out past the open-air windows to the yard. What looks like old wooden boat oars stand upright, propped in the ground. Paper lanterns dangle from wire looped between those tall oars. Wild beach grasses edge it all. Beyond, sunlight glints off Long Island Sound. Jason turns to Shane—he's standing in the doorway with his arms crossed. "Damn," Jason says. "Doesn't look like a dinner planned for a brother and sister-in-law. Looks ..." He throws another glance at those paper lanterns. "Looks pretty intimate, actually."

"Yep." Shane walks onto the porch now and leans his hands on the half-wall. Takes in that sight and turns back to Jason. "You got me there, Barlow. You got me there."

Hell, the last thing Shane counted on happening today was his and Celia's secret getting out. But the gig's definitely up with Jason scoping out the backyard décor. Now Shane walks the length of the porch's half-wall. "*Shit, shit, shit,*" he barely whispers before hoisting himself up on that ledge and leaning back against a porch post. "Guess it's obvious I'm expecting a dinner guest?" he asks.

Jason grins and leans against that same half-wall. "So you *are* seeing someone."

"I am."

"I *knew* that was a line of bull at the campground when you said otherwise. That you were … *married to the sea,*" Jason air-quotes.

"Yeah. Just didn't need everybody up in my business."

"Must be pretty *serious* business, based on that," Jason says, motioning to the paper lanterns.

"It is, actually." Shane lifts the fabric of the now-damp tee sticking to his skin. Hops off the half-wall, too, and paces the olive-painted floor of the porch. Walks past old lanterns sitting on weathered crates, and a rusted milk can filled with dried beach grasses. All the while, his mind is racing.

Because he knows. Jason won't let up. Those Barlow brothers never do. Jason's questions will keep coming. He'll casually tell other people, too. Meaning there's no way out of this.

So Shane's trapped.

Unless.

Unless he muzzles Jason.

Quickly, Shane turns toward him. Walks to that half-wall, leans his hands on it again, then looks at Jason still stationed there. "You and Maris busy tonight?" Shane asks.

"*Tonight?*"

"Yep."

"Well, I'm free. But I'll have to check with Maris."

"Come on. You two are still separated?"

"Shit, almost three weeks now." Jason looks out at Long Island Sound, blows out a breath, then turns back to Shane. "It fucking sucks, to be honest."

"Hey, man. Jesus, I didn't mean—"

"Don't sweat it," Jason says, waving him off. "Anyway, we're working on things. Me and Maris. Kind of dating, you know?"

"Heard something about that." Shane squints over at him. "So how about this?"

"What?"

Shane nods to those paper lanterns he'd found in the shed and carefully strung earlier. "Let's make it a double date. You and Maris, with me and my date." He holds up a hand when Jason starts to interrupt. "No, listen. Help me move a table and chairs—out there beneath the lanterns—and we'll turn that table into a dinner date for four."

"Seriously?"

"Yeah. I bought extra lobsters. They're yours, now. This way, you can meet my girl."

"I can't *believe* you're seeing someone, you sly bastard. And she's down with having dinner with two strangers?"

"Think so."

"You *sure?*"

"Yeah. Yeah, I am." Shane hitches his head toward an old wooden table on the porch. "Give me a hand moving that, guy."

"Right now?" Jason asks, checking his watch first, then scrutinizing the shabby table behind Shane.

"Yeah, now." Shane walks to that table and pulls out its paint-faded and chipped chairs—a ladder back, a cross back, a classic farmhouse and a slatted folding chair.

"Okay, but make it fast. Got to run, client's waiting at another job site." Jason crosses the porch and lifts the slatted chair. "Preliminary consult scheduled."

"All right, we'll do this quick. Then come back later with your wife," Shane tells him while carrying that ladder-back chair down the seven painted steps. "For dinner," he says over his shoulder. "Seaside."

∼

Either it's the hot September weather, or it's the way he and Barlow finagled that heavy wooden table off the porch and set it up in the yard—but something's got Shane worked up. His damn tee is soaked through. So as soon as Jason's gone, Shane heads inside to his bedroom. He peels off that sweaty tee there, balls it up, pats it against his damp skin and finally puts on a fresh shirt.

Then he gets his cell phone off the kitchen counter.

So okay, maybe *this* is what's got him sweating. He brings his phone out onto the back porch. Sits on the half-wall again and takes in the sight of tonight's dinner table. Looks pretty nice, actually, the way the four mismatched chairs are set casually around it. Wild beach grasses rise beyond it.

"*Enough stalling already,*" Shane tells himself then, right before making the one call there's just no escaping. "Celia?"

he begins when she answers. "Please don't be mad."

"Huh. Never good words to hear, Shane," she softly says.

He takes a long breath of that salt air. Let's see if it cures this. "I really had no choice," he explains into the phone. "But you'll never believe who's joining us for dinner."

.

thirty-seven

THIS IS IT.

The moment is imminent. Shit, Shane feels more like he's tying the knot than introducing his girl to these two. Only hours ago, Jason helped him move tonight's table outside. Now, he and Maris are killing time in Shane's cottage—pacing, looking out the windows, asking questions—all while waiting for the big arrival. Pots steam on the stovetop. Food warms in the oven. Maris must be picking up on Shane's anxiety, too. She stops Jason in the kitchen and straightens the tie he's wearing for the occasion—which he obviously dressed for. Along with dark khaki pants, Jason's got on a short-sleeve olive utility shirt. It's all formalized with that black tie. A skinny tie Maris still fusses with.

Maris, who also dressed up. Leave it to the fashion designer to elevate her black halter top and black denim bell-bottoms with a crochet inset in the bell. All it took was her short beige-and-white blazer and long necklace of beads and white stones to class it up. Her hair's down, with an accent braid along the side. Wide silver hoops hang from her ears.

Standing in his kitchen, Shane glances at his own pocket tee, cuffed jeans and leather boat shoes—all while fielding curious questions from these two. Questions about the mystery woman due to arrive. *Known her long? What's she do for work? She's making the trip all the way here?* A light jab in the arm from Jason, then, *You serious about her?*

Shane evades each question.

"I think I heard a car! She might be here," Maris says now, rushing to the living room windows to check. "Shoot, I don't see anyone," her muffled voice carries back.

"Let me give her a call," Shane lies, grabbing his cell phone off the counter and hurrying down the hall to his bedroom. The lie's a good cover anyway—better than admitting he's got to punch up the tired clothes he's got going on. He heads straight for the closet and brushes through his few things here in this rented cottage. A button-down's always good, so he puts on the pale gray stripe, then slips into that formal black vest he wore for the vow renewal—but leaves the vest open.

"Casual," he tells himself. "*Casual.*"

Folding back his shirtsleeves, Shane moves in front of the dresser mirror and tugs everything straight then. Puts on a watch and his braided leather cuff, too. Before turning away, there's one last thing. He picks up a tube of styling gel at his dresser. After dragging a dab up through his hair, he spikes it some, then leans closer to the mirror for a better look.

"Okay," he whispers. *"Showtime."*

━───

Back in the kitchen, of course Maris notices his updated outfit.

"Shane! That looks *great*," she says, brushing her fingers across his vest lapel. "Nice touch. She'll like that."

"Eh, you know," Shane tells her. When Jason comes in from the back porch then, Shane motions him over. "Listen, there's an old blue blanket in the linen closet down the hall. Get that for me?"

"Sure thing." Jason flicks his fingers on Shane's shoulder. "And rad threads," he says before heading down the hallway.

"So … Shane." Maris crosses her arms and leans against the counter. "You've got to tell me *something* about this mystery lady. Come on … *something*? I mean, what's she even look like?"

Shane grabs a couple of lemons from the fridge. "She's very beautiful," he says.

"But I need *details*! Is she tall? Petite? A blonde, maybe?"

"You'll have to wait and see."

"Okay, fine." Maris toys with her beaded necklace. "But did you talk to her, just now? Is she almost here?"

Shane slices the lemons into wedges, then arranges each wedge in a shallow frosted-glass bowl. "It's early yet," he tells Maris right as she picks up a loose bouquet of hydrangea blossoms from the counter.

"Well …" She looks around the kitchen. "How about if I find a vase for these flowers I brought?"

Shane directs her to the aqua-painted cupboard off to the side. "Check in there," he says. "Got a hodgepodge of things on the shelves."

"*Ooh*, perfect." Maris pulls out a white ceramic pitcher and quickly arranges her hydrangeas. "I'll bring these outside to the table," she says. "They'll look pretty beneath the paper lanterns."

Shane turns and glances out the screen door. "Yeah. Was lucky to find some of this stuff in the shed earlier. The lanterns. Wooden oars."

"You never know what'll turn up in these old cottages, huh? Give me some matches, and I'll get those paper lanterns lit for you, too."

Shane sets down his lemon-slicing knife and picks up a small remote from the kitchen counter. "This'll do the trick," he says, handing it to Maris.

"A remote?"

He nods. "No candles in the lanterns. LED lights."

"Okay, I'm on it," Maris tells him as she heads out with the flowers and remote.

"Here's that blanket," Jason says, walking back into the kitchen just then.

"Oh, great." Shane sets aside the lemon wedges and motions for Jason to follow him to the porch. "Bring it out here. I've got just the spot for it."

As soon as they're through the screen door, Shane takes a long breath of salt air. "*Jesus, breathe*," he quietly tells himself. Beyond the yard, the sun is nearly setting. Twilight approaches, with the sky just turning lavender over the blue waters of the Sound. Shane takes the blanket from Jason and gives it a shake-out.

"Your girlfriend running late?" Jason asks, watching Shane while leaning against the porch's half-wall. "She driving down from Maine?"

"All I'll say is she's on her way." Shane gives another good snap to the blanket. Beyond Jason, he sees Maris lighting those dangling paper lanterns. One by one, each glows in the evening dusk. "And no more questions, guy," Shane tells Jason while heading down the painted steps to the yard now. "Give me a hand with this instead, would you?"

Jason follows him to a long white bench set out beside the dinner table. Years of salt air have done a number on the backless bench. Wood grains show beneath its faded paint. Together, he and Jason first fold the blue blanket in half before draping it over this serving bench—using the blanket like a table runner.

Which is when everything suddenly shifts into overdrive.

The round table Shane and Jason carried out earlier gets set with blue-and-lavender striped placemats, white dishes, crystal wineglasses and white linen napkins.

Shane lights two black vintage hurricane lanterns on the tabletop. There are more lanterns, tall white ones clustered together on the white bench, and even more—a few silver lanterns—set on the green lawn. The wicks catch his match flames, and the lanterns glimmer around them.

Jason pours the wine.

Maris brings out salad tongs and flatware. She then folds

a white linen dishtowel imprinted with blue lobsters and places it on that serving bench.

Finally, the food. Jason sets out a tomato-and-cucumber salad. Maris manages a warm plate of roasted fingerling potatoes drizzled with olive oil. And Shane carries out the big white enamel lobster pot. He puts the pot and bowl of lemon wedges on that blue blanket on the serving bench.

And it is done.

The food, the rigged-up piecemeal décor from a dusty shed, the chipped cottage dishware, the mismatched rickety chairs—it's all spread before him.

There's nothing more to arrange.

Shane stands on the evening lawn with Maris and Jason and takes in the sight.

The shabby round table is set.

Lantern light flickers.

Alongside the arched beach grasses, those wooden boat oars are randomly propped in the ground.

The faded paper lanterns strung between the old oars softly glow now.

And the lavender of twilight makes it almost unreal.

Beyond, the dark water of Long Island Sound spreads to the horizon.

There is only the splash of distant waves. The whisper of those beach grasses.

All else is still.

But just for a moment.

Just until Shane motions for his friends to sit at the table. As they take their seats, he steals a look over his shoulder for Celia—but she's still not here. *Come on*, he thinks. *Don't do it. Don't bail on me.* Grabbing his cell phone from his back pocket, he checks for any messages from her.

Nothing.

Just show up, he silently pleads while checking his watch, too. Celia's late. She should be here by now.

But she's not.

Another quick look. And nothing.

So he wipes his palms on his jeans, pulls out a chair at the table, and sits.

All that's left now is the wait.

The beach friends' journey continues in

THE
GOODBYE

The next novel in The Seaside Saga from

New York Times Bestselling Author

JOANNE DEMAIO

Also by Joanne DeMaio

About the Author

JOANNE DEMAIO is a *New York Times* and *USA Today* bestselling author of contemporary fiction. The novels of her ongoing and groundbreaking Seaside Saga journey with a group of beach friends, much the way a TV series does, continuing with the same cast of characters from book-to-book. In addition, she writes winter novels set in a quaint New England town. Joanne lives with her family in Connecticut.

For a complete list of books and for news on upcoming releases, visit Joanne's website. She also enjoys hearing from readers on Facebook.

Author Website:
Joannedemaio.com

Facebook:
Facebook.com/JoanneDeMaioAuthor

Made in the USA
Middletown, DE
28 June 2022

67947322R00187